WHEN THE HERO COMES HOME

EDITED BY

GABRIELLE HARBOWY AND ED GREENWOOD

When the Hero Comes Home

To Maggy,
Enjoy the journey...
one of these days, we'll
take a quest together!
Gabrielle
7/2013

WHEN THE HERO COMES HOME

EDITED BY

GABRIELLE HARBOWY AND ED GREENWOOD

DRAGON MOON PRESS

CONTENTS

DEDICATION

Though a hero may lose companions along
the journey, they are never forgotten.

This book is dedicated to

Jennifer Rardin,
who should have lived long enough to
participate in this adventure

and Adrienne (Dinny) Blicher, Gabrielle's mother,
who should have lived long enough to read it.

ACKNOWLEDGMENTS

There are many people responsible—directly and indirectly, deliberately and serendipitously—for the existence of this book, and not enough space to mention them all. Thanks to Alana Otis and the Ad Astra Programming Team, and Cameron Swift, without whom I would not have been in a too-cold room in Toronto in March, 2009 meeting Ed Greenwood for the first time. Thanks to Jennifer Brozek and Marty Halpern, who taught me everything I needed to know about anthologies, and to Kristen Nyberg for design inspiration. Thanks to Gwen Gades and Laurie McLean for believing in this vision and helping to make it happen. Thanks to all our authors for making this such a fun, rewarding process, for the wonderful work you've done and the friendships we've forged in the process, and to Ed for being the best possible companion on this journey. Thanks to my dad for believing in me, and to my husband Matt, who brings the stars within my reach.

-Gabrielle

Thanks to Homer and to Harold Lamb, for breaking the trail. And to Gabrielle, for so happily walking it with me.

-Ed

INTRODUCTION

Susan J. Morris

HEROES DON'T DREAM OF a hero's welcome. Those who dream of being heroes might—but heroes are rarely those. It's antithetical to their nature. Besides, every hero knows they can never come home again.

Heroes. They could as easily be called dreamers, idealists, or idiots. No mother wishes heroism for her child. Driven by demons of their past, heroes fight for abstract concepts like truth, love, and honor, and would risk life and limb for people they've never met. It's not a very sane approach to a long life or happiness.

"I'm doing it for you," a hero might say to his lover on the eve of battle, and he might even believe it. But she knows that's not true, and deep in his heart, he knows it too. That's just a fairytale told to justify the tears, the distance, and the blood.

"I'll wait for you forever," the lover might answer, and she may even believe that, too. Though he knows it to be false. Oh, she'll cry when he leaves, and there will be talk of a hero's welcome. Of feasting, dancing, drinking, and finally settling down with a couple of pigs and kids and a patch of beans. Staring up at the night sky, drunk with the stars and the innocence of youth, it's easy to believe that Romeo's night will outlast the dawn.

But make no mistake—when you become a hero, there is no turning back.

The moment you leave, your home is frozen in time. You may treasure the unchanging faces of your family and friends in letters and photographs. But you will not be there when your son says his first word, or your daughter falls in love for the first time. You will not be there when your mother is dying, or your loved ones are in need. You will not be there for their joys and sorrows, to comfort them, to celebrate with them, and to protect and serve them as you protect and serve everyone else.

That sacrifice will make you stronger. No one appreciates love more than those who have lost it. Those who fight, fight with some hope of regaining it—when all the fighting is finally done, when the threat is banished and the demons who drive you to heroism are banished along with it.

But some things, once seen, can never be unseen—and they mark the eyes of those who bore them witness.

When you return, unheralded, your face will have been forgotten or rendered unrecognizable, and your deeds will have been reduced with distance, time, and the absence of threat. People will flinch when you walk by, because every scar is a reminder that the world contains more than white picket fences. And at night, when you are forced to relive what you have seen, no one will hear you scream, because every nightmare is proof that you belong to another world now. An uncomfortable world filled with pain and sacrifice, where good does not always triumph and every victory comes with a price.

You will not be able to dismiss your world so easily, but if you continue to insist it exists, you will be held to blame for the disruption it causes. The problem is that you are part of the problem. Murderer, victim, and hero—all exist in the same world, bound by ties of blood far stronger than those of birth. Like consumption, it's a problem of containment. If they can contain the problem, their world is most likely to go back to normal the fastest.

Eventually, you will find you have more in common with those you save than those you come home to. So when the day comes that someone else is in trouble, and they look at you with need in their eyes, with no one but you to hear them scream, you will find that you cannot turn a blind eye the way the rest of the world does.

So you will pick up your blade again, and it will be as though it never left your hand. You will scrape off the rust, buckle on your armor, and start back down that road again. The only road left to you.

But you won't be leaving home, because that town wasn't your home anymore. Not since the day you left and became a hero. A hero's home is in their heart.

This book is not an easy book to read. We want to believe that a hero's sacrifice is worth it. That if we were a hero, we would be appreciated, loved, and welcomed back to a life that is just like it used to be, only better. But we are never told that a hero doesn't just risk their life when they battle their dragon—they also risk losing the life they led before they became a hero.

Whether the heroes in these stories succeed or fail in their quests, their lives are irrevocably changed by them. None of them expect the form their homecoming takes, and very few eventually find the welcome they wished for—or have the faculties to appreciate it.

Savor these stories. Whether you're reading about the only surviving soldier of a war struggling to return to a home that doesn't exist anymore, a rebel leader who has lost everything she fought for and must start from scratch, or a hero who has fought for her village her whole life only to retire into without ever being known for her deeds, every one of these stories touches on the humanity of the hero. Each story reveals a different kind of battle the hero must fight, and the different demons that drive them on. We learn what they love so much that they will abandon it in order to save it—and to save themselves. We learn what compels them to sacrifice everything to fight for what they believe in. And we learn whether it was worth it.

∾

A Place To Come Home To

Jay Lake & Shannon Page

BABA O'RILEY HAD MADE her way home, back from the dead. That's what the other kids had told her, anyway. It might even have been true. She still didn't remember much. The past was a gray curtain like the fog on Divisadero early in the morning. Shapes, movement, even flashes of color. But no definition, no detail.

The future was…Well, the future was whatever she made of it. The problem was, she didn't know how to make anything. Some mornings her hands surprised her simply by still being attached to the ends of her arms.

Being dead had significantly interfered with her prospects, it seemed.

The cop who'd handled her exit interview from SFPD's bod squad shop down in the Mission District had been more than kind about things. A middle-aged woman who could just as easily have been Baba's mother. How the hell would she know?

"Really, honey," Detective Sergeant Carole Candelaria had told her. "You did very, very well. You've got to remember that."

What kind of name was that, anyway? Sounded like a porn star, Baba had thought, then wondered how she knew that. Of course, the other kids had been making fun of *her* name for days, down in the tanks.

"I'm sure I did, ma'am," Baba replied. "But I still don't remember much." For that value of 'much' that equaled 'diddly squat.'

Candelaria sighed. It was a weird sigh, sucking air in through her teeth with her lower lip scrunched under. Like she wanted to bite somebody. Her silvered-blonde bob waved slightly as she tapped her chin. "Look…We're not supposed to tell you much."

Confidentiality. Trauma. All kinds of reasons. The social workers were always down in the tanks talking about that stuff. "That's easy for you to say." O'Riley knew her voice was sullen, and found she didn't care. "You know who you are. What you did. Do. Whatever. You know what you had for breakfast last week."

"Rice Chex, probably," Candelaria said absently. She focused on O'Riley once more, from wherever her attention had briefly wandered. "It's the Scrags. We *have* to keep the public calm about them."

The bod squad had been getting busier, she'd been told down in the tanks. Ten years ago, no PD in the country had such a detail. Now it was one of the biggest units within SFPD. "You can't keep a secret forever. Not when you're discharging a couple dozen of us a week."

"No one listens to street people." A strange, pained expression crossed Candelaria's square, not-too-pretty face. "That's where most of you wind up. Shouting at lamp posts."

"I'm no shouter." O'Riley sank further into her fatigue jacket. Had she ever really owned such a thing? *Before?*

Candelaria whistled another of those sucked-in sighs, then jotted something down on a torn bit of paper and passed it to O'Riley. "I know you don't know what you did. Odds are you never will." She closed the girl's fingers into a fist around the scrap, crushing it amid skin and a sheen of sweat. "But you're the reason my daughter's still walking around. You're a hero, Baba. You deserve more than this. And I haven't told you a thing."

Finally O'Riley woke up to the fact that the detective sergeant hadn't been distracted. She'd been weeping. It was like seeing a teacher cry in class.

Baba stumbled out of the anonymous police building, not even remembering to pick up her starter pack or the fifty-dollar food voucher in its neat little fake credit card.

That night she crashed with some krusties in a sheltered nook that harbored a grease trap and a pair of dumpsters behind a row of restaurants on Valencia Street. The kids hadn't even bothered to rough her up. Just a bit of name calling.

"Yo, Gray, you good luck or bad?" one had said—a girl with shoe-polish black hair and an antique house key driven through the little bit of skin between her nostrils. Like a Victorian cannibal or something. Her striped tights were dirty, maybe bloody even, and her leather skirt and top looked like vinyl to O'Riley.

Still, sleeping in a group was safer than sleeping alone. She wondered how she knew that, too. "I ain't no luck at all," she replied.

"No good, no bad, none," said another one. A dark, grubby boy wrapped in sports jerseys.

"None. No one." She had nothing to offer. No skunk, no food, no cash.

They'd let her into the crowd, even given her a pity slug off the bottle of Crown Royal one of the kids had boosted from the bodega up the street. She didn't eat, though, not until 2 am when the scraps started coming out and the kids had needed to scramble away for a little while. Not too long, not too far, or they'd lose their place.

Even in the summer, San Francisco was stupid-cold. The krewe of krusties had moved off shortly after dawn, leaving her behind. The kindness of the night before—such as it had been— evaporated with the morning dew. Baba O'Riley was hungry, hard-pitted hungry in her gut like she hadn't been since…since…

Since before.

Before.

A dangerous concept. The social workers had warned them about spending too much time thinking about 'before.' "You're back, accept it. Enjoy it. Every one of you is a success just by being here breathing, with color in your cheeks."

"Then whu-whu-why they call us Grays?" someone else had asked, voice dull and lifeless.

The answer hadn't mattered. She'd tuned out the discussion. Most of the rest of kids in the tank were droolers and mumblers already. Baba had been one of the few who could still focus. Could think past the easy patter of the counselors and cops.

Such as that was.

She chased a mangy orange cat off a bench at a tiny neighborhood playground and dug Detective Sergeant Candelaria's scrap of paper out of her pocket. It was an address. 190 Parnassus, #1, it read in the woman's crabbed handwriting.

Parnassus. Cole Valley neighborhood, O'Riley thought. It was weird, how the things in her head that weren't so much about her seemed to be coming back. Places, streets, old movies, even books she'd read.

But her? Home, parents, school, boyfriend? Or girlfriend?

Nothing. Like she'd been eaten alive, and spit out dead to start over.

Cole Valley she figured she could find. San Francisco just wasn't that damned big. Seven miles square. Baba O'Riley started walking. It wasn't like she didn't have the time, after all.

Over in the Castro, she got shouted down and chased away for being a Gray. Even gay people had to hate someone, it seemed. O'Riley wasn't sure how they could tell, but then, she wasn't sure of much.

She climbed the impossible hill of 17th Street above Market. The yuppie moms stared at her, steering their jog-strollers away. Or maybe they were yuppie nannies. She couldn't really tell the difference, and the yuppie dads were probably screwing them all anyway. Uranus Terrace made her giggle, wondering why the Castro hadn't relocated up there.

Then it was down into Cole Valley and wandering toward Parnassus. The day had warmed up a little, enough that she didn't feel corpse-cold inside the oversized jacket. She thought maybe she should be able to see the ocean in the distance, over the flatlands of the Sunset, but the view vanished in high fog, or low clouds, or both.

O'Riley wondered why the cops and their pet social workers down in the bod squad didn't do more for the Grays. The survivors. Whatever she was. 'Revenant' was the word she'd seen on one social worker's yellow tablet, glimpsed across the table during an encounter session.

She kind of liked the sound of that.

190 Parnassus turned out to be an apartment building that looked a hundred years old. It seemed huge for something only three stories high, raised up off the sidewalk on foundations like a fussy woman sitting with her skirts billowed around her. Little decorative cornices chased themselves around the structure, while tall glass windows bowed slightly so that reflections were as untrue as dreams.

She hadn't dreamed since before, O'Riley realized.

There was a Walgreens across the street, and catty-corner over Stanyan a little grocery and flower shop. She still didn't have any money, though—stupid to have left without her voucher. Boosting a candy bar would be tough. None of her muscles worked quite right, not any more than her brain did; she didn't move as smooth or as fast as she kept expecting to.

O'Riley knew she'd just spaz out and drop the merch before she could sidle out the door. Hungry was only a state of mind, anyway.

A sudden scream of sirens startled her nearly to pissing her pants. She darted up the steps to the shelter of the apartment building entrance, glass door set back from the street, in hopes of hiding, before she realized the racket came from a fire engine.

Not a cop. Not an ambulance. Not the bod squad in their dark vans. *How did she know* that, *either?*

Then she realized someone was looking at her from the other side of the glass. A woman about Candelaria's age, brown hair cropped lesbian-close to her skull, staring from the shadows of the apartment building's shared black-and-white tiled entry hall. Crying.

O'Riley stared back, wondering what was wrong, caught by the moment, until the woman reached with a trembling hand to unlock the heavy door and tug it open.

"Lisa?" she said, in a voice like a strangled rabbit.

"My name is Baba." But O'Riley wasn't sure she believed that, even of herself.

"Li—Baba." Shuddering, the woman fought for control of herself. "W-would you like to c-come in?"

O'Riley's stomach growled. "Got any food, lady?"

"Oh, my. Yes." Her eyes lit, responding to some sense of reprieve. "Of course I do."

They sat at a rickety white enamel-topped table. She didn't think apartments usually had kitchens this big. Marian—that's how the woman had introduced herself—piled up plate after plate, bowl after bowl, until O'Riley began to wonder if she herself wasn't the craziest person in the room after all.

It was a week's worth of eating. Cold cuts, some leftover jambalaya, little broccolis, M&Ms in a bowl that someone had picked all the orange ones out of, two kinds of bread, five kinds of cheese, some cold fried chicken, fruit salad, something mysterious and Chinese in a paper box that dripped brown sauce, olives, peanuts, a banana. It went on and on until Marian looked like she would break down all over again.

O'Riley ate like she hadn't had food for a week. Really, it had only been a little more than a day. But still, the way things were going, she wasn't going to waste a chance.

"I wasn't sure what Gr— you people liked to eat," Marian finally said, apologetically.

"Food," O'Riley answered around a mouthful of whatever the heck Chinese it was. All she could taste was peppers and teriyaki.

"Right." Marian wrung her hands, fingers slipping over the other wrist back and forth. "Everybody likes something. Pistachio ice cream, for instance."

Something about the hopeful look in her eyes bothered O'Riley. "I don't eat ice cream." She'd only said it to twit the woman, to push back, but Marian looked as if she'd been slapped.

"Hey…" O'Riley said, more softly. "I didn't mean anything by that. I'll go. But thanks for the food."

"No!" Marian was scared now. Of something, not of her.

"Look, lady, I'm a revenant. A Gray. Whatever that means to you…well, no one wants me around."

Marian found her dignity. "My daughter is a revenant," she said quietly. "Gone, but not forgotten."

O'Riley reflected briefly on the fog of her own memories. "Oh, she's forgotten, I promise you."

"Why did you come here?" Curiosity warred with desperation in the older woman's voice.

"Dunno." A shrug, the universal answer. But O'Riley knew there was more to the question. She'd been *sent*, after all. "Got this address from a frien– from someone." Candelaria's words came back to her. Nothing wrong with O'Riley's memory now. Just before. "She said I was the reason her daughter's still walking around."

"Yeah. I know."

"You, uh, know any cops?"

"Just one or two." Marian visibly summoned her courage. "C-can you wait a minute? I want to get something from the other room, to show it to you."

O'Riley shrugged again. "Okay, I guess." She poked at the cheese, cutting off bits to nibble. Cheese must have been something she liked, before. That thought made her wonder about the pistachio ice cream. It would be cold, though. Seemed like she'd had enough cold.

Marian came back from rustling around in the other room. She had a newspaper, stiff with age. "This is two years old," she told O'Riley. "Two years, one month and thirteen days."

It didn't fit well in her fingers. This didn't seem like something that needed to be crumpled or torn, but the paper itself was growing brittle. O'Riley stared at the headline a while.

LOCAL TEEN KILLED SAVING SIX FROM SCHOOL SHOOTING

One of those sweet-but-posed yearbook style photos of a girl stared back at her. Grainy with the low-quality printing of the newspaper, she still seemed familiar.

"Lisa Babouska," O'Riley read aloud. "And you're Marian Babouska, huh?"

"I went back to my maiden name years ago," Marian said softly. "I'm Rogers now. But Lisa is…was…*is* my daughter."

"How did she die?" O'Riley really didn't want to read the story. Something about it was making her ill. "Shot?"

"None of them were shot," Marian said. Her voice had receded somewhere far beyond the room. "The headline is a lie. They got scragged. Lisa…stopped the Scrags. She was a hero."

"Scrags?" Candelaria had used that word. None of the social workers had, not down in the tanks.

"Zombies, maybe, but that word's too Hollywood. It's not George Romero out there. People don't talk about it much. No one asks about the cover stories. No one *wants* to know. But they keep popping up, mostly among teenagers." She paused, then added, "This can't go on, it can't last. But…" Marian glanced at her feet, biting off whatever she'd been about to say next.

"Yeah." Despite herself, O'Riley had to ask. "How'd she stop the Scrags?"

"Pepper spray from her purse, then held them off with a Bunsen burner from the chem lab, the police said." Marian sounded proud.

"But they nailed her."

"Yeah. In the end. But she held out long enough for the SWAT. The Scrags didn't get the other kids in her lab unit."

Silence opened between them.

"And then…?"

"Saved six lives, lost her own. But you know, there's that new day-after stuff." Marian's voice was even more distant. "From the Korean labs. The cops fire it in dart guns or something. They go into tanks a long time, dreaming in the dark."

"Not dreaming, lady. No dreams at all. Not…after."

Marian took O'Riley's hand, the first time they'd really touched. She crushed it tight. "There's no coming home again from some journeys."

O'Riley glanced at the newspaper. She was glad she hadn't seen a mirror since before. Real glad. "Some heroes never come home."

"No." Tears stood in the woman's eyes. "They don't. They just go on."

Zombies, thought O'Riley as she walked down Stanyan toward Golden Gate Park. No way. Crazy shit. The bod squad detoxed kids who'd gone too deep, that's all. That's what the social workers told them, down in the tanks. Scrag was just a drug, like meth to the third power or something.

Nobody died for it, she told herself. No heroes here. Just strung out kids. Detective Sergeant Candelaria was full of shit.

Because a real hero would have a place to come home to. A real hero would know what she had done.

A real hero would know who the hell she was.

Still, the food had been nice.

She wondered about the pistachio ice cream.

The Evil That Remains

Erik Buchanan

THE STRAW SCRATCHES TYLER'S back through the thick blanket wrapped around his body. The soft whickering of the horses, still not used to his presence, penetrates into his sleep. His eyes snap open and his hand claws for the knife beside his makeshift bed.

Still dark. Still raining. Still alone in the barn with his memories.

Pounding rain. Soaked powder. Men and horses fighting through the mud. Marching to the Mage's castle. Muskets gripped tight in cold fingers. The ground erupts under them and horrors crawl out, clawing at them. Lights in the sky become wraiths descending on them all. Cold iron to ward them off, cold steel to kill them. Death for those too slow.

He'd lain with his wife the first night he was home, bodies thrusting hard into each other, hands grasping to reclaim a year's absence of flesh. Afterwards they lay together, sweat-soaked and laughing, nestling tight as sleep overtook them both.

He woke when her fingernails clawed open the flesh of his forearms, found her blue and gasping, eyes wide with horror and lack of air as hands tightened around her neck.

His hands.

After he let go, after he made sure she was all right and she said she forgave him, he went out to sleep in the barn. She didn't argue.

It has been a week.

Above him, the rain rattles against the wood shingles of the roof. A soothing sound of childhood and safety. Tyler remembers when this barn was a place of laughter; a place of warmth when the rain came down; a place of stolen kisses and promises of the future.

Hiding from the storms in a cold, empty barn. Men sleeping huddled together. From the rafters, shapeless blood-sucking sacks of teeth and disease falling on them where they lie, huddled for warmth against the storm. Knives to cut them away, to cut out the teeth that will not let go afterward. Then fire to burn out the infection.

Tyler looks to the corners of the barn, to rafters that he knows are empty because he checked them already, like he always does. He checks them again, anyway.

"To destroy the source of evil in the world," the priest says to his congregation.

"To destroy the dark magic for all time," the knights say in the tavern.

"To cleanse the world of evil," the squire says, leading the applause as the men sign up to fight.

"Because it needs to be done," Tyler says to his wife, holding her tight the night before he leaves.

Tyler rolls over, sighs and closes his eyes again, hoping to find darkness and oblivion instead of dreams.

In the tavern, sitting at a table near the fire, Tyler lets the heat massage his aching leg and take the cold of the early fall evening out of his flesh. It's his first time in town since he's been back. The first time seeing the faces of people whose loved ones didn't return. Tyler buys a round with some of the money left over from his soldier's pay. The crowd takes the drinks. Some give thanks. Most just give glares and grunts.

It's Brian who starts it. "So, what happened?"

A castle wall seven hundred years old, battered down with cannon. A cry of rage and exhilaration from a thousand throats as men pour into the gaps in the wall. Screams of women and children, the Mage's last line of defence, as they attack the soldiers with pitchforks and rakes and blood-red, possessed eyes.

"Go on, tell us!" says Mark. "Tell us what happened."

"Tell us how they killed the Mage."

"Tell us how they defeated his beasts!"

Tell us how you made it back when no one else did.

The last goes unspoken, but it's what they really want to hear, Tyler knows. He doesn't want to speak, doesn't want to relive what he survived, but they are all waiting. Glasses down, gossiping lips silent, they are waiting to hear how the Mage was defeated. Waiting to hear how their friends, fathers, brothers, and sons died.

He drinks down half his beer. Then, before they can press him, he begins to talk. Of marching through the rain and the cold of the mountain kingdom. Of nights of terror and days of pain. Of fighting forward inch by inch, when even the ground itself rose up against them. He shows the scars on his arms and face, when they don't believe him about the creatures. He tells them how men died. Some of the faces grow wet, others grow angry. Tyler tells them everything, spares them nothing.

He falters hours later, when he reaches the long, bloody fight up the stairs of the tower whose walls cannon could not harm. They broke the door open with chanted prayers and cold steel.

"And the Mage?" asks Brian, whose younger brother and son Tyler had seen lying bleeding to death on the mountain road, left for the crows while the army marched past. "Is the Mage dead, then?"

Two hundred died on the stairs. Now, in ranks five deep, twenty men across, they line the throne room. A hundred muskets aim up at the fat, ugly thing on the dais. It reclines on its throne, surrounded by cushions and the bodies of its defenders. It had been a man, once, but time and contact with evil left it a corrupted, bloated thing, more animal than human.

"Aim!" someone shouts. Tyler aims his musket with the rest.

"Fire!"

Ninety-nine muskets go off. Fire and smoke and a horrible roar of black powder.

"He's dead," says Tyler. "I saw. Saw what was left of his head, when the priests cut it off and put it in a box." He takes another drink. "He's dead."

Sleep interrupted by the touch of something soft against his skin.

A body soft like the flesh of rotted vegetables, a smell thick and putrid. Screaming agony as the thing sinks its teeth into his flesh. He shoves hard against it and desperately pulls out his knife, tries to hack the thing off his body.

"Tyler, no!"

Awake, blinking in the morning sun. His wife on the ground, scrabbling backwards, eyes wide with fear. Tyler tries to drop the knife but his fingers won't let go. He stares at her, horrified by what he's nearly done, then turns away to face the wall.

"Tyler?"

Her voice is close, closer than he deserves. He desperately wants to go to her, to hold her, but he can't make himself let go of the knife. He shakes, tears streaming down his face.

She touches him. Light, tentative fingers on his shoulder. "It won't always be like this," she says. "You'll be whole, someday soon." She leaves her hand on his shoulder, and for the moments it is there Tyler feels like a man, instead of a vicious animal.

She squeezes his shoulder gently, then lets go.

"Kate!" he calls as she starts to walk out. She pauses, and he manages, "I'm sorry."

"I know," says Kate. "Now come. Breakfast is ready."

A week passes. Tyler still sleeps in the barn, still keeps the knife at his side. And every morning his wife comes to wake him, though now she stands at the door and calls until he rises. And every day she cooks for him and watches him as he works, though she does not often come near.

The distance hurts him.

He splits wood, readying the stack against the coming winter. A single stroke for each cord, like his father taught him. Each cut is a moment of peace; a moment of nothing but motion; nothing but directed force. Tyler sets another cord on the stump, raises and cuts.

"Tyler." She stays far back. Her eyes go to the axe, then back up to his face.

"Hello, Kate." Tyler puts aside the axe, and Kate's nervousness retreats from her face. He loads the split wood into the wheelbarrow. "Firewood's nearly done. Then I can get to fixing the windows in the cottage."

"The squire's here, Tyler."

"It's about fairness," says the squire to the men in the tavern. "About keeping what's ours. Why, that Mage wants our wagons to pay tribute to pass through the mountain passes. He wants to drive our men from the foothill mines." He looks solemnly at them all. "They've sent monsters. To kill the men. To attack the women. Not even men. Beasts. Demons. And what they've done to the children..."

The squire shakes his head, takes another drink. "It needs to be stopped, lads."

"He wants to talk to you, Tyler," she says.

"We'll be waiting for you, boys," calls the squire as the village men march past. "We'll be waiting to welcome you home! Three cheers for the brave lads! Three cheers for our heroes!"

The squire hasn't spoken to Tyler since he's been back. Maybe because Tyler was the only one who'd come back, of the thirty who'd gone.

"I'll go speak to him," said Tyler. "Let me get clean at the pump, first."

"I'll tell him."

Kate hesitates, then steps forward. Closer, closer, closer, until she stands before him. There's fear in her eyes, and something more. Something stronger.

Love.

She leans in, almost flinching, and kisses him. She's smiling as she steps back. "I'll let him know."

"Thank you."

She walks away. Sunlight catches in her golden hair, making it shine. Her hips roll easy and slow with the same motion that caught his eye ten years before.

Tyler still feels the kiss on his lips. He watches as she walks away, enjoying the view. For the first time since that first, awful night back, he feels something like her husband.

The squire is standing by the front door of the cottage, not going in. His white shirt and grey pants are as spotless as the silver chain of office around his neck. His boots have only the smallest specks of mud, no doubt from walking up the path to Tyler's house. His horse and two-wheeled carriage are tied to the post by the gate.

Tyler, face and hands rinsed clean at the pump, limps down the path and stands in front of the man. "Good day, squire."

The man is fat and red-faced and sweaty. Pig eyes. A soft man. A drinker. A short man who looks down at you even if you stand above him. Especially if you stand above him, like Tyler does. The squire doesn't offer Tyler his hand, doesn't speak at first. Tyler finds himself taking off his hat, twisting it in his hands.

The squire purses his fat lips, looks at Tyler from under a furrowed brow. "Is it?" he says, making each word more ponderous than it needs to be. "A good day? Is it indeed?"

The captain, pursing his lips, growling down at them. Huge moustache. Pig eyes. Pot belly even after a month of starvation rations for his men. A pompous bastard and a terrible soldier. Led them into a dozen ambushes. The night creatures bit his face off two days before they reached the tower and the whole company had to listen to him scream for three hours before he died.

"Can I do something for you, squire?"

"There's been a killing, Tyler Bain."

"A killing, squire?"

"Last night, Tyler Bain. In Certriff."

Ten miles away, another town, no bigger than Fernsriff where they are standing. A small town where every family knows every other. Twenty men from Certriff had marched with the army and not come back. "Who was it, sir?"

"I didn't say it was a person," says the squire, and for a moment Tyler sees something glinting in his eyes. A suspicion confirmed, perhaps. "Why would you say it's a person?"

Tyler feels confused; like he's stepped in something he can't shake off his shoe. "Wouldn't be important if it was an animal, squire. Was it an animal?"

"It was not," says the squire. "It was definitely not. It was a woman."

"A woman?"

"And not killed in the usual way a murderer kills," says the squire. "Not shot or stabbed, no."

Madness. Soldiers turning on one another, seeing demons instead of friends. Killing each other until the spell is broken with cold iron and prayer.

"How, sir?"

"Bitten, Tyler Bain." The squire fixes Tyler with his gaze, trying to peer into the depths of Tyler's mind and soul. "Beaten and bitten. To death." The squire's eyes narrow. "By a man, Tyler Bain. You saw worse, on your travels. Done worse, I'm sure."

Pressing the red-clad soldier's head into the thick, viscous mud until the man stops fighting. Hearing the crack of a man's jaw breaking under his boot. Stabbing again and again into the gaping maw of a many-toothed thing that had no place on God's earth.

Tyler's hands shake. He says nothing, and looks at the ground.

"There will be inquiries, Tyler," says the squire. "Men will want to know why."

He leaves, and Tyler, still standing with his hat in his hand, feels afraid.

Church. First time since he's returned. A week since the death in Certriff. The priest gives the blessing and the lesson and then begins the sermon. Tells how the great Mage, the greatest evil they have known, is gone, but how his taint still fills the land. Tells how it left none untouched who faced him, how the stink of evil has followed them back to their homes, has corrupted them all.

Tyler sits, silent, ignoring the quick glances cast his way. The accusing glares aimed at him for daring to be a survivor. The small gestures, warding off evil. Kate sits, silent, by his side, but takes his hand and squeezes it tight.

"We have been a peaceful valley," says the priest. "We were peaceful before the Mage brought his evil. He spread it over the land, spread it over us all, and even with his death he leaves it to linger. Leaves it on those who destroyed him, to spread wherever they go."

Tyler remembers passing through Certriff. Remembers that the doors were barred and the tavern was closed. He wondered why, then. Now, he wonders how long the killings had been going on.

For the first time, Kate works side by side with him. Together they go through the rows of the vegetable patch, picking the best of the crop, putting them gently in baskets so they don't bruise. Carrots, squash, beans. All perfect.

They grin at each other as they load the baskets into the cart. And Kate kisses him again. She smells of fresh earth and clean sweat. Of good work done right. "I'll be waiting," she said. "I'll bake a pie with some of the apples."

They kiss again, and Tyler smiles, happy for himself, for the vegetables and the brace of chickens for sale or trade for the best price or the right customer. He'd missed this most of all, since the beginning of the long march west. Sitting by his wagon, talking with his neighbours and haggling for the best deal.

No one comes near. The ones beside him in the square don't talk to him, only talk to each other in low voices. Tyler sits for hours, watching as men and women who were once friends keep their distance; keep their eyes on him and make holy signs with their fingers at him as he sits, alone, hoping someone will buy his produce.

He goes home with a full cart. Goes home and faces Kate, who looks sad and scared and bites her lip but doesn't say anything as she takes one of the chickens to kill for dinner. Tyler retreats to the barn, to mend the stable walls and clean the harness and do a dozen other small tasks before she calls him in to eat.

He retreats back to the barn after dinner. Curls up in the straw and wraps his blanket tight around him, his knife close to his hand. He is ready to close his eyes when the door opens and Kate, lamp in hand, looks in on him. "Will you come in, tonight?"

Tyler shakes his head.

"Soon," says Kate. "You'll come in soon."

She leaves him in the warmth, in the dark, of the stable.

The squire comes round again. The sheriffs are searching for the killer. The squire tells him that the killer will not get away, and nods knowingly. Tyler nods back and goes on with his day.

In the tavern once again. Tyler sits alone. No one will talk to him, or even go near. The drink he had to go up to the bar to get, he leaves without finishing.

Mutterings in the street, when he comes into town to run an errand. Words of bad deeds done in other towns, of men returning out of their minds and doing ill to their loved ones, or to anyone else that takes their fancy. Mutterings of evil riding the ones who returned, spreading like smoke through the valley, through the country.

Tyler stays on the farm after that day, keeps his eyes on the crops and the animals that will have to feed them through the winter, since no one will buy anything that he sells. Kate goes into town and does the shopping and the trading, using the money he brought back. They still speak to her. Pity her, that she is with him. She comes home and at table she tells him all. The rumours, the priest's words of warning to everyone, the glares and the turned backs at the mention of his name.

Every night, Kate comes to him in the barn and asks if he will sleep inside, with her. And every night, Tyler shakes his head, terrified he will try to kill her again.

Only now, she comes in and kisses him before she leaves for the night.

It is a week after that, two weeks since Tyler stopped going to town, two months that he has been home, when the blacksmith murders his wife. He chases her down the street one night, hitting her again and again with his hammer. He beats her until her bones break, then beats her head in, calling her whore and bitch and slut for sleeping with the cobbler, that bastard. She dies screaming.

The squire comes to the farm the next day, with a pair of big men Tyler knows but who don't greet him or even look at him. The squire rambles on about the murder, about the wife's indecent behaviour, about the blacksmith claiming he was bewitched. That he never would have done it, had he been in his right mind.

Tyler remembers the blacksmith as a drunk and a fool who has been beating his wife for years, and says nothing.

The complaints begin in earnest. The tavern cook's wife has taken a after him with a knife. The hosteller's horses went mad and kicked a boy in the head, leaving him an idiot. A neighbour farmer's dog broke into the hen house, killing a dozen chickens. A dozen more things gone wrong in the last month, from soured milk to a daughter dallying with a boy to a son dallying with a man. Curses in the streets, more in the chapel every day, and every time something new happens, the squire visits Tyler to tell him of it. Only now he brings the priest with him, along with the two big men. The holy man stays silent, watching Tyler as the squire speaks.

One night, Kate comes to him in the barn. She kisses him and takes off her gown and wraps her arms around him. He protests but she will hear none of it, only promises not to fall asleep beside him. Tyler aches for her, and holds her close. They lose themselves in each other's arms, each other's bodies, and for a brief while, everything seems right.

In the warmth of afterwards, Tyler takes a deep breath and tells her. "I killed him."

Kate is silent, still in the dark. Then, softly, "You?"

"My musket didn't fire. It was wet with..."

The creature falls on them on the stair. Tyler jams his musket and the bayonet on its tip into the creature's mouth, to keep it from engulfing him. A half-dozen bayonets stab into it from before and behind and the thing sprays out something vile and black, though it is not blood.

"...I don't know what it was, but it stuck to the barrel and got to the flint and when I fired there wasn't a spark."

Ninety-nine muskets go off. Fire and smoke and a horrible roar of black powder.

The sound that comes next, after the blessed bullets rip into the Mage's flesh, is louder and far, far more horrifying. It is a screaming, tearing noise, ripping into Tyler's ears as ninety-nine unholy lights swallow up the men who fired, draining life and flesh from them and leaving smoking, stinking corpses.

Tyler stands alone amidst the corpses, his useless musket in his hand. On the dais, the Mage's body is riddled with bullets, but still breathing. The porcine creature that was once a man tries to raise a hand, tries to speak, but flops back onto its ruined cushions. Tyler forces himself to walk toward the throne, his boots crunching on bone and slipping on liquid that used to be ninety-nine men.

The fat thing begins to breathe deeper. It begins to look, despite a score of gaping wounds, better. Still Tyler stumbles forward, until he stands before the grotesque thing that was a man, that oozes blood and pus, and that is healing itself before Tyler's eyes.

"Know," it says, voice rattling through a near-destroyed throat. "Know that no weapon may be turned on me, no hand may strike me, without bringing death to its bearer. What happened to them will happen to any man who raises a weapon to strike me."

Tyler stares in horror as the skin on the man's face begins to knit together. He stoops, then, and picks a bloody, torn pillow from the ground. He wraps large fingers over the holes, so no more feathers can leak out, then gently places it over the Mage's face. He pushes against it.

"A pillow?" There is horror in Kate's voice for what he has done. Horror and grief for Tyler. "You killed him with a pillow?"

The fat man-thing struggles, fights, claws at Tyler, but he holds tight, pushing with his whole body weight, climbing on top of the Mage to hold him still. He stays there long after the time it takes to kill a normal man. He stays even when another band of soldiers comes into the room and sees what he is doing. Stays until the priests begin chanting their invocations. Stays until he is pulled off and a sword is raised high to take the dead Mage's head.

"They started squabbling as soon as the man was dead," says Tyler. "I saw them in the throne room, arguing over his treasure and who would pay the troops and who got what portion of the lands. The priests brained one of the officers with a mace, the officers stabbed another priest. It was…"

He sobs, shaking, and Kate takes him in her arms.

"It was the same as they had been the entire campaign," Tyler says, through his tears. "I had hoped that killing the Mage would get rid of the evil in the world, but all it got rid of was the Mage. The rest of them didn't change."

There is noise outside. Feet moving on the road and voices shouting angrily.

Tyler rises, his knife in his hand. "It hasn't changed anyone."

They dress in silence, and Tyler fetches the packs he put in an empty stable and the muskets and pistols he put in the tack room three weeks before. He pushes the straw off the trap door and pulls out a heavy burlap bag that clinks from the space beneath. He helps Kate out the back window of the barn as the mob surrounds the house.

"Evil!" they hear the priest saying as they slip onto the dark road and walk in the other direction. "It is an evil that we will purge from our lands with cold steel and fire! And tonight is only the beginning!"

〜

FULL CIRCLE

Steve Bornstein

IT WAS THE LOOK in your father's eyes that finally convinced me.

Too often, people come to me with petty grievances, problems better handled on their own. Those petitions, I turn down. My bones are old and it takes a little longer to regain my strength every time I venture out to fight the good fight. I can't take on every poor schlub that comes to me with an injustice, anymore. Sometimes I simply sleep through them. As I said, I'm old. But I was awake and feeling rather spry when the farmer came to me. It was plainly a situation beyond his abilities, and it had been too long since I'd seen the clouds. I remember, it was the way he was wringing his hands that cinched the deal.

"My lord, my sheep and cattle are yours, just please return my daughter to me! She is all I have left of her mother!" And then, the wringing. He looked fit to twist those hands right off his wrists. The "only thing I have left!" plea is cliché, there's no denying it, but in this case I knew it was the truth. I remembered the winter his dame fell ill and passed away, leaving him with a fresh headstone in the field and a giggling, rosy-cheeked bundle of trouble that occupied every bit of the little free time his farm afforded him. He loved you very much, and to lose you forever would have broken him irrevocably. His farm was small, but it was a vital supply of food for the nearby village. I wasn't going to let some over-privileged jackass ruin the prosperity of the valley I'd guarded for decades.

"Keep your stock, Brennan," I rumbled, lifting my head. I waited for the cavern's echo to fade before I continued. "You will put them to far better use than I. I will take my payment from that so-called king, and gladly so. I've some business with him and his kin I'd like to see through." The grizzled farmer cowered and backed away as I slowly got to my feet to give my ancient oath, a speech so old and repeated so many times it had written itself into my very soul. It sprang from my lips as if it was as eager for the coming fight as I.

"You call to me and I answer. I am your sword, going forth to protect the innocent and punish the wicked. Great is my challenge and I rise to meet it. May my wit be sharp, my body strong, my eye quick, my aim true, and my heart pure. I am the cleansing fire of justice."

I looked down at the old man and the tears streaming down his cheeks. "Go home, Brennan," I said in a tone as soft as my pledge had been booming. "I will bring your daughter home." The farmer nodded quickly. He flipped the hood of his cloak over his head with shaking hands and scurried back out the wide passage that led to my home.

By the time I'd gathered myself and followed him out into the windy chill of the mountainside, he'd already disappeared down the path that wound its way to the road. I lifted my head, scenting the clean sharpness of pine and a small group of deer upwind of me. Hunger tapped at my shoulder but I ignored it. I concentrated and the northern horizon leaped into focus. My quarry was that way. I'd eat soon enough.

It was just as well. The deer scattered when I took off. I could only catch them at such a range if I had room to gather speed, and avoiding the trees was always tricky business. It felt good to stretch my wings after so long, and I allowed myself the luxury of a slow soaring circuit of the mountain's peak before finally aiming myself to the north, towards King Renald's keep.

There is an eerie beauty to flying that is unlike anything else—suspended high in the sky, gazing down upon the land with naught for company but my thoughts and the sounds of the wind whistling over my body. Even so high, my shadow was large enough to scatter livestock. I like to wheel this way and that; it amuses me to herd cattle into a corner of their field. People, of course, are oblivious. That suits me just fine. It makes my job easier.

The Renaldi were acting up yet again; that they were to be the final act in my very long play, satisfied me. It was a fitting end, and the idea of it all coming full circle had me grinning wider with every beat of my leathery wings.

Castle Renald was built on a high plateau, with several outlier buildings arrayed around it and the entire affair surrounded by good walls. Defensible from a ground standpoint, perhaps, but the open skirt of rocky meadow surrounding the keep made a lovely landing field. I came down with a deliberate heavy thud. Nothing works better to spark dread in the pits of their bellies than feeling my arrival through the soles of their boots. The cries to arms floated through the thin air as I furled my wings and ambled my way to the castle walls.

I was impressed. They'd actually rebuilt them high enough that I had to crane my neck to get my head even with the battlements. Beyond them, I could see the high towers of the castle itself. I figured that you were in one of them. That was usually how it played out.

There was plenty of banging and clanging about going on behind the walls, but nothing to be seen. I waited a moment, then another. Still no greeting, not even a disparaging remark shouted over the parapet at me. I drummed my claws loudly against an outcropping of rock for effect, to no avail. I cleared my throat. "You do know why I'm here, yes?" I boomed, making the words sound impatient.

That finally got a reaction. Someone in scale mail stumbled from a corner guardhouse as if pushed into view, followed by none other than the king's heir in full plate: Prince Henden. I stifled the urge to sigh and roll my eyes. Of course Henden, who else should I have expected? At least his fool of a father knew enough to keep this nonsense at home, but the prince was a greedy oaf of a man, strong enough to replace a pair of oxen in the field and smart enough to replace a pair of oxen in the schoolhouse.

The man with Henden looked like he'd rather fling himself over the parapet to his death than stand next to the prince. I can't say I blamed him. At least he was smart enough to know what was coming. Still, I had to admire his dedication to his duty. I watched while he mostly gathered himself.

"You are trespassing on Renaldi land!" he squeaked. I lifted a bony eye-ridge and glanced at the smug Henden, his arms crossed as if daring me to argue. His mouthpiece continued. "We—we know you're here to steal away the Princess Hannah, and…" His speech stumbled to a stop and he turned to his prince, but before he could get two furtively whispered words out the prince smacked the back of his head with a gauntleted hand. I'd have laughed if the stakes weren't so high. "…And you are hereby informed that we will repel this affront to our sovereignty with all possible force." His voice cracked once, at the end.

I waited a moment before replying. The silence always unnerves them, you see. Sometimes I play a game with myself where I see how long it takes one of them to cough nervously, or utter another silly threat just to fill the quiet. I could tell, this time, that Henden was too sure of himself to think it necessary. His was courage born of stupidity.

"Are you truly serious?" I addressed the prince rather than the man standing next to him—he was busy wetting himself. "That was your plan, to marry her before I got here? Do you think that matters to me, or at all?"

That got a rise out of him. "She is my wife by law. You cannot have her!" He had a barrel chest and I suppose he was used to using the bass in his voice to cow other humans, but it only amused me. "Now remove yourself from our lands!" he added, jabbing a finger back the way I'd came.

I laughed. "By the law within these walls, perhaps, but certainly not any law that I recognize. Shall we see how sturdy these walls and laws of yours are?" I enjoyed verbal sparring, but Henden was woefully unequipped for it. At this point, we were just wasting time. I took a couple of steps back to give myself room.

Henden recognized the cue, at least, and turned to wave frantically at his forces. Archers and several war machines lifted into view. I took a deep breath and held it. Ballistae? Where had the Renaldi gotten ballistae from? Suddenly this was shaping up to be much more than just an afternoon of stretching my legs.

"I'm ready for you this time, beast!" Henden crowed, then turned to his troops on the battlement. "Make ready!" He raised his arm.

I, of course, was already ready. One step behind—that was the prince. I let loose with a long gout of flame, splattering it onto one end of the battlement and playing it along the troops towards the other side. The well-trained ones tried to fire before they got set alight. The smart ones just dove for cover. A few arrows came down on me like rain pattering across cobblestones, but a ballista managed to let loose a flaming bolt that ricocheted off my bronze scales, thankfully coming in at too shallow an angle to penetrate but leaving a trail of wood smoke to show its path. Still, it was too close for comfort. I saw Henden dive for the safety of the guardhouse before my breath could reach him. I had to press the attack now, while they were regrouping. There was no telling what other surprises awaited me inside.

With the wall in chaos and nobody alive atop it to fire down on me, I gathered myself into a crouch and then sprang into a run, thundering across the broken field and leaping onto the wall. Bashing through it with my head would have been more impressive, but I'd seen the reinforcements they'd built and didn't want the embarrassment of having to back up for a second attempt. I do have a reputation to keep, you know. Instead I leaped onto the wall like a cat on a tree, letting my full weight crash into it at speed. The sharp smell of fresh mortar caught my attention as I landed. "New masonry," I thought as the wall buckled and caved in. I came down on my haunches, landing in the courtyard on my feet amid screaming, dying soldiers. Granite blocks and flaming wood rained down around me. "Pity."

Henden was scrambling down wooden stairs, yelling, with longsword in hand. "Form a line! Pikemen!" His troops were scrambling over the remains of the castle wall to form a defense between me and the tallest tower in the castle. I thought to beat them to it, but my empty stomach reminded me of more immediate matters. The "princess" wasn't going anywhere, and the terrified bleats and moans of the castle's livestock had gotten my stomach rumbling.

"Yes, pikemen, form a line!" I called nonchalantly over my shoulder, slamming my barbed tail against the ground to rattle their nerves. In battle, you expect your enemy to flee from you, not to stroll away and toss a taunt without looking back. They were expecting me to continue advancing, so my wandering off for a quick supper would confuse them long enough for me to eat in some semblance of peace.

The keep's populace was already fleeing for the safety of the castle itself, so I didn't have to try tiptoeing around panicked innocents. Someone had been one step ahead in getting the people to safety. Apparently, Henden's stupidity wasn't contagious.

I knew my way to the livestock pens. A plump heifer was first down my gullet, and a pair of sheep followed her. Say what you will about these silly people living behind their huge stone walls, but they do know how to raise some fine-tasting meats. I wished I had more time to savor them, but I was there for another reason.

As I came back around the corner of the castle, the pikemen and I almost bumped into each other. Not only had they formed their line, but there were actually advancing! I lifted my head in surprise and some of them scuttled back a few yards. Henden ran behind the line from side to side, trying to get them back into formation with frantic yelling, pointing, and the occasional threat from his sword.

I craned my neck upward, looking at the tower to gauge how I was going to get into the top. It looked fairly sturdy. If I was careful about it, I might be able to scale it. I sighed inwardly as more archers appeared and moved quickly into a block formation. The fool was throwing everything he had at me. At this rate, there wouldn't be enough guardsmen left to watch the front door. Henden shouted at the archers to prepare to fire. I punctuated his order with a quick blast of flame, just enough to broil the air between us and break their lines.

The castle's main tower was tall, but fortunately I am long. Once I stood on my rear haunches, the round peak was only a dozen feet above my head. With the archers broken, my only concerns were the ring of pikemen surrounding the tower and myself, and Prince Henden's loud and uncompromising opinion of my mother. One step up the side of the tower would take care of the former, and the latter was easily ignored. Thankfully, this tower hadn't been the work of the masons who built the keep's new wall; it managed to hold me. I clung to it and shoved the wooden roof off with my snout, then twisted my neck to look down into the top floor of the tower. I managed to gaze inside with a single eye.

Your relieved sob was what drew my attention. You were cowering on the four-poster bed, looking back at me wide-eyed, wearing that pink dress and the ridiculous cone-shaped hat with the gauzy pennant. I've never understood that—the primping of princesses to look more like party favors than people.

"I know of a lonely old man who would very much enjoy the pleasure of your company," I rumbled softly, grinning behind the edge of the stone wall. That was enough to shake you from your reverie and coax you to your feet. I lowered the end of my snout through the ruined roof. "Climb atop and hold onto a horn as tightly as you can, and close your eyes." Once I felt you settle into place and murmur your readiness, I carefully lifted my head again and prepared to take flight.

Henden's indignant screams drifted up from the courtyard as I reappeared, wearing the latest in captive princess atop my head. I couldn't quite make out what he was going on about, but I'd heard more than enough. Shifting my grip on the tower, I carefully glanced down and shouted, "Save your breath, princeling! Try to spend more time drilling your troops and less lusting after farmers' daughters, eh?"

I turned my gaze skyward again, spreading my wings to their full length and leaping from the tower. I gave a powerful stroke, hurling myself into the air from a standing start. The tower leaned and then gave way under my rear legs as I took flight. It was almost enough to cause me to fall, but another quick pair of wingbeats got me clear of the keep. I turned south and managed enough altitude to look down into the keep before it was out of sight behind me. The tower had collapsed across the courtyard, right through where Henden had stood with his pikemen. If we were all lucky, Henden was dead and the people of Castle Renald would prosper under a prince who was more concerned with the events within his walls than creating events outside them. Perhaps I'd finally removed that thorn from everyone's side.

The flight back was as uneventful as the flight to the keep, if a bit slower out of consideration for my passenger. When I glided down through the valley and gently alit at the end of the lane, your father was already there waiting and your joyous reunion warmed my heart. This was where my real payment lay, not in the cattle to eat or the shiny baubles to add to my hoard, but in seeing justice served.

Why, no, of course I never turn down the tasties or the pretties. The idea that I require actual payment keeps people from taking my service for granted. It's not something I'd admit to just anyone, but you're not just anyone anymore, are you?

That is indeed the Dragon's Kiss upon your brow, and a lovely shade of blue it is. As I said, I'm old. I've felt the end of my time growing closer and closer with each passing moon. I knew your rescue would be my last, and here you are right on schedule, precisely one moon later. That is the nature of the Valley's Wager, you know. When the guardian's time is done, it falls to the last person we've saved—the most recently rescued damsel—to pick up the mantle of duty.

You still have some time yet before the change really takes hold. Go spend it with your father. You will be drawn back here soon enough, and I will be waiting to guide you into your new station, as my predecessor guided me after I was rescued from similar straits—from the very same castle, in fact. Don't look so surprised, my dear. Renald the Prime laid the cornerstone long ago, before my eyes ever saw the light of the sun. Oh, it all looked different back in my day, but the Renaldi have always been tenacious. Sometimes I wonder if their repeated attempts at expansion and my efforts to prevent them from overrunning this valley are the very thing that's kept them together as a community for so long.

I can see that you don't think much of your new station, or your new home. I had the same look on my face when I first saw this cavern. But it grows on you, just as the Kiss will grow to give you a fine armoring.

What of me? Don't worry about me. Do you see the echo of the Kiss upon my own brow? I'll have a final transformation of my own, and this old guardian will finally go home. Oh, no one's left in my village who'll remember me; I'll be some kindly old woman they take in because they've some good in their hearts, but it'll be a homecoming all the same. I'll live among them a short while, remembering what it was about them that made their wives and their sons and daughters worth protecting, and then I'll take my well-earned rest. Someday, you'll do the same.

No, no, don't dwell on that now. Dry those eyes; come now, and look. The mountain overlooks the valley with a wonderful view, and there is plenty of game to hunt. The hoard you'll inherit holds countless entertainments and diversions—centuries old, some of it—gathered by myself and my predecessors. Sorting and shining it is relaxing, and soon you'll know every piece. It will all serve you well, and I'm sure you'll serve the valley likewise. You will make your father and your village proud, protecting them and the rest of the valley with your cleansing fire of justice, and no prince will be able to harm you again.

❧

LESSONS LEARNED

Peadar Ó Guilín

VICTORIYA PRIDED HERSELF ON sharp wits, devastating put-downs, instant puns, retorts, one-liners and quips. But waking now, tied up, hanging by her feet from some sort of conveyor belt with her head all fuzzy from whatever drug they'd gassed her with, threatened to cramp her style.

She wasn't the only captive. Her whole squad swung upside down to either side of her, every one of the lazy shits sleeping through their captivity. How helpful! Brilliant!

The conveyor belt moved forward in painful little jerks—there was a pun in there somewhere and Victoriya was just the woman to find it, but a whole new set of sensations were ganging up to distract her. The noise for one: clangs and creaks and hisses; the steam for another: beading every surface, hiding the walls of what had to be a cavernous space near the edge of the ship. Nothing, however, could mask the metallic stench of blood.

Victoriya looked to the man hanging to her left. Alkaev. Handsome, and rather lovely in his way. She asked, "Do you think we won?" It was a mercy he didn't wake. She could pretend that once—just once!—he might have gotten one of her jokes.

To the other side hung Filipov, as stupid a slab of muscle as ever she'd led on a raid, with calluses inside his nose from all the picking he'd done. His great body swayed just enough to give her a first glimpse of their destination. A little man in a bloody apron was slashing the throats of her squad one by one as they passed, bleeding them out into a vat beneath the grill he was standing on. He whistled some stupid old-fashioned tune and Victoriya curled her upper lip at the cheapest of cheap haircuts clumping on his scalp. Had he actually *asked* the barber for such a style? Or perhaps he had a goat for a lover and it got peckish in the night? She could think of nothing more shameful than being killed by such a man, and she sincerely hoped that none of her squad woke up in time to see it happen.

Victoriya closed her eyes and tried to remember something—anything—about the raid and what might have gone wrong. Her mind, sharp as a tack, a knife... no! a *razor*, would not cooperate.

They'd been celebrating, she remembered that much. Deep inside the farming sector near the middle of the good ship *Lessons Learned*. The weak gravity there allowed suggestive-looking vegetables to grow to enormous proportions, and half the crop went towards the manufacture of a clear, tasteless liquid. They called it "Voyager's Friend," because only death was better at helping the ship's inhabitants forget the horrors of the journey their ancestors had begun, the ending of which only their great-great-grandchildren might ever see.

Victoriya's sponsor, Alex Maksimov, had sent over a whole barrel of Voyager's Friend to congratulate her on a string of successes and to help in the planning of the squad's coming triumph. A note in his own handwriting had been stuck just over the stopper: "Welcome Home, Heroes! I'll always have your back! Alex."

"A toast!" Victoriya had shouted. "Another bloody victory against the Engineers!"

The guys had all cheered with cries of "They'll never tell *us* what to do!" and "It's not like they *own* the life-support equipment!"

Victoriya swallowed along with the others, despite the fact that a mistake in a previous exploit had deprived her of the ability to get drunk or high no matter how much she imbibed. That might explain why she was awake now and waiting for Crappy Haircut Man to slit her throat.

The conveyor belt jerked again, putting Filipov under the knife. "Humpty-dumpty," sang the slaughter man, "you are my spinward loooove..." What an efficient butcher he was! A single sweep of the blade and Filipov was emptied out faster than...than a...damnit! She was wittier than this! But there was no time to come up with a good line because the belt was moving again and it was Victoriya's turn at last. Time to put her killer in his place.

"Hey!" she said.

His mouth hung open—Victoriya's beauty often had that effect on men.

"Do you even *own* a mirror?" He was too stupid to realise how badly he'd been pwned by a superior intellect. While his brow wrinkled in confusion, she undid the last knot holding her wrists. Before he could so much as ask her for a date, she had removed the knife from his hands and arched her body up just enough to plant the blade in his throat.

Of course, the butcher couldn't be cooperative enough to fall backwards as she had expected. Instead he dropped to his knees, spraying blood everywhere. "Not the hair!" screamed Victoriya. For once her amazing wit deserted her and by the time she had freed herself she was reduced to kicking the corpse and shouting, "You bad man! You bad man!" She retrieved the knife, not knowing what she meant to do with it, but then she heard footsteps coming through the curtain of steam behind her and she froze.

A short-stout woman stood there with a bunch of tazer-wielding guards.

The newcomer's voice had a rough, smoky quality to it. No give, no give at all. Victoriya stiffened as she realised who this must be: Dame Gogol, the most powerful woman on the ship and the intended victim of today's raid. "I don't pay you to waste no time on scalps," said the Dame. "You gonna slit some throats or you wanna hang up there yourself?"

Victoriya opened her mouth to make a cutting remark about knives, but some of the guards were already levelling weapons so she just nodded and turned around. Lovely Alkaev hung before her, his neck level with her waist. He hadn't been the sharpest tool in the drawer, but he'd been a good lover, and—

"Well?" said Dame Gogol.

Victoriya cut Alkaev's throat and watched him bleed out. The belt moved, bringing Margarita next *(silly bitch, enjoyed that one)* and then hairy Bulgakov. By now the footsteps on the walkway behind her were retreating back into the steam, but just to be sure—they might still be watching!—Victoriya did a few more of the boys. Only when she was certain it was safe did she start slicing ropes instead of flesh and kicking people awake. "How dare you snooze on the job!" she said as each opened his eyes. But not one of them got the joke. They just stared at her, dozy-like. *That's what happens when you're as gorgeous as me. Women hate you and men turn to imbeciles!*

The good ship *Lessons Learned* had helped previous generations of passengers communicate via chips grown into their brains. It was enough to think something like, "Hey, Alisa, how about you erase those recordings you took of our special time? Or do I have to come up there and erase *you*?" and the message would travel instantly through city decks and farms and engine rooms, complete with obscene images and threatening background music. Oh, yes, those were the days. But the first bulkhead war had killed off all human connections to the core AI. Now Alex Maksimov had to rely on hearing the beep from the plastic walkie-talkie of a long dead child.

"Come on, come on," he muttered to the ancient toy.

He was sitting at his desk deep in what he called his "mansion." Really, it consisted of seventeen standard cabins high up on the port-side of the *Lessons Learned* that had been knocked together after the families inhabiting them had "decided" to leave.

Maksimov was a business man, a man of action, carving a place for himself in history. People were tired of vegetables? Maksimov had found them meat—hundreds of thousands of cow embryos. Colonists might complain about this in a hundred years if the *Lessons Learned* ever reached her destination, but they'd just have to stop whining and do a bit of work, is all. Human ingenuity would see them through that future crisis as it had every other one before it.

Your home planet is out of resources? No problem! We'll preserve the human race with a colony ship! The ship is infested with rival gangs? No problem! We'll gather together a band of heroes to wipe them out! One of your heroes has become dangerously unhinged? No problem! Make a deal with your arch enemy to have her captured and killed! Heroes were all the same. Great for a while, until they turned idealistic—or, in Victoriya's case, psychotic—at which point they simply *had* to be put down. No Problem!

But Alex was beginning to think there was a problem after all. The walkie-talkie hadn't so much as peeped in two hours. It should all be over by now. Had an underling stolen the toy's batteries? But moments later he got his wish and his arch-rival for upper-level control came through loud and clear.

"Gogol," he said.

"*Dame.* Dame Gogol to you, asswipe."

Alex didn't rise to the bait. There'd be an accounting one of these days. The Dame based her power on control of the freshwater sea that filled the top side of the ship's skin. The only other source of H2O and fish came from another sea in the lower levels, but all trade with that part of the *Lessons Learned* had slowed to a crawl since their revolution. Until the Lowers calmed down, he would have to keep cooperating with Gogol.

"We got 'em all," said the Dame. "My boys found 'em unconscious like you promised, and now we have 'em hangin' an' my slaughter-woman cuttin' their throats for 'em."

"A woman? A slaughter-*woman*?"

She bristled. "What's wrong with that? Yeah a woman! Real good with the knife, but..."

"Oh no," said Alex, his stomach churning.

"It weren't her!" Gogol protested. "This one looked like she bin done over a thousand times by a blind plastic surgeon. A real Frankenstein! I mean it—I seen pictures of Victoriya, and this one weren't nothin' like—"

"Victoriya makes the pictures herself, Gogol, you hear me? She makes them. It's what she *thinks* she looks like. I handed her over to you! You were supposed to just kill them all."

There was a bit more back and forth about how plain killing was never enough to make a point and so on, but finally—for above all else, they were practical people—they got back to business. Gogol asked, "What'll she do now?"

Alex considered this for a moment. Did Victoriya know of his betrayal? If she did, her gang of murderers would be thinking up ways of killing him right now. But that was unlikely. Victoriya thought he was in love with her, for some reason. And she would be blinded by the unprecedented riches he'd offered her for the raid. No, Victoriya wouldn't suspect him, which meant only one thing. Oh God. He cleared his throat, almost afraid to speak. "She...Victoriya...she's going to try to complete her mission."

"You gave her a mission?"

"I had to invent something. I...I didn't think she would actually...You were supposed to kill her!"

"What? What's wrong? Maksimov?"

Alex's mouth had gone dry. He clutched the brightly coloured plastic toy hard in his sweating fist. "She...she's planning to vent your sea into space."

"She...She's gonna WHAT?"

Victoriya and her merry band escaped the search parties by losing themselves in the sewage baths. It was no place for a lady like her, but she made some brilliant jokes out of it: "you smell like shit," "stop shitting me," and a few that were even better. Not for the first time, she wished the group had somebody besides herself who could write properly and who would compile a book of her witticisms.

After a few hours of standing up to their necks in sludge, she felt it was safe enough to order everybody out again. She had Gurdski and Lagunov take a few of the cleaning robots apart for weapons—they were clever like that, and while robots had grown increasingly rare, these boys had an instinct for finding them.

She gathered the nine remaining squad members around her for an address, making sure to keep her back straight and her shoulders square so they could all get a good look at what they were fighting for. Let them drool, the animals, if it made them fight better.

"OK, *shit*heads..." she paused, but they were too respectful of her to laugh, "we're light enough that we must be close to the centre of the ship somewhere, but we need to get to the starboard edge where that catty bitch..." No response. Perhaps they didn't know what a cat was? "...has the fish supply all sewn up. Does anyone know a way out?"

"Alkaev might've helped," somebody muttered. "He was from around here."

"Yeah? Well *he* couldn't keep his neck shut, could he? Who else?"

But like Victoriya, most of them had been born in Lean-To, a shanty-town where people went when they'd lost their cabins and weren't strong enough to win one back. Victoriya herself had three cabins now, but hadn't yet found a man extraordinary enough to share them with.

Gurdski spoke up. "We need a console. Should be one left in the corridors a hundred metres to port."

"Exactly what I was thinking," said Victoriya. "We'll go into the old transport tube, through the air ducts and get into a residence level. Since it was my idea, I'm going to lead the way. Follow close! This is the biggest yet. Any of us that come back from this won't have to work again for a year!"

They piled into the transport tunnels, feeling their way along in the pitch black, cutting hands on broken glass and metal that previous wars had left behind. They emerged into a corridor of cabins. Vines and other plants twisted over the surfaces here. Birds skimmed overhead or settled on giant flowers to pollinate them. The few bare patches of wall that remained had been decorated with old slogans, sports team logos and that weird new circle that had been appearing everywhere lately, like a porthole with nothing behind it. Who knew what it meant? Who cared?

A sewer stench rolled on ahead of the squad like a herald. People fled before it, except for a young boy who stuck his head out of a doorway at just the wrong moment.

Victoriya whooped and stabbed at one of his eyes. Oh, the expression on his face when she missed! It was good to be alive. And she almost got to deliver a wonderful line about sticking his nose where it didn't belong, but by the time the joke had fully formed they'd passed far beyond its intended recipient.

They swept around a corner into a market district where a queue of people waited to use the console. Once upon a time, every cabin in the ship had a little screen for children to access the central AI until they were old enough to have the link inserted directly into their brains. But after the first bulkhead war when direct linking had stopped working, clever clogs like Dame Gogol had smashed most of the consoles in the areas they ran so that people would have to pay for knowledge.

Victoriya shouted at the waiting queue, "Piss off! Or there'll be nobody to *console* you!" She punched a man in the face who had failed to laugh, and all the other humourless pricks made a run for it. With her squad on guard, she sat down under the faded "Public Education Terminal" notice and spoke her demands.

"I need a map from here to the bulkhead for Sea Number One. Include all air vents, and that kind of shit."

The first thing to come up on the screen was the message: "I'M DYING, HELP ME!" Victoriya cursed. The story was that some long-ago hacker had got into the system and made it display these weird messages every now and again. Victoriya herself preferred the idea that it was the ship itself playing a practical joke on the passengers. It's what she would have done, although she'd have been a lot funnier, using the voices of a person's dead relatives to speak the words. She was creative like that.

Finally, after enduring some meaningless gibberish about "DAMAGED CO_2 SCRUBBERS," she charmed the machine into giving her what she needed: a completely safe route to the top of the ship where Dame Gogol's ocean would soon be making its final exit into space.

A voice came from just behind her. "What...what are you going to do?"

Victoriya looked up in surprise, for none of her own crowd would have addressed her in this way. A young man, completely unkilled by her supposed bodyguards, was peering over her shoulder.

She should have been angry, but a glance was enough to show that this one was no threat to anybody: rickets had bent his legs, his skin was pocked and his teeth were a hideous mess just begging to be smashed. As for his clothing, it was old and patched. He had one of those graffiti circles stitched like a target above his heart.

Neither of them spoke—she because his presence here was so puzzling, and he, presumably, was struck dumb by her beauty. All the while, Lagunov and the others looked on with big grins on their faces.

Victoriya smiled.

"I'm going to blow out the ocean," she said. The knife was in her belt and she was reaching for it slowly, slowly, so as not to startle her prey.

"It'll divert the ship," he said.

"What?" Her hand paused.

"All that water pushing out will send us off course, an' we'll never get to the colony—I mean, our descendants won't."

Her hand started moving again. He was just another doom merchant, after all—the ship was full of them and not one had a proper job as far as she could see.

"Our ancestors put the water in the hull to protect us from cosmic rays," he said. "They'll rot our skin first an' then—" He squeaked as the point of her blade pushed a centimetre into soft flesh just under his chin. Gurdski was nudging Krupin in a "wait'll you see what she does next" kind of way.

However, Victoriya wasn't doing anything just yet. Her free hand came up to stroke the skin of her face. It had cost her nearly everything she owned to look this good. Would her beauty really just rot away if the ocean was gone?

"I don't like the sound of these comic rays."

"C-cosmic, *cosmic* rays."

She shoved the blade in another centimetre. "I *know* that!" She began twisting the knife. "I...was...making...a...joke! Get it?"

The worm was braver than he looked. He ripped himself free of the blade and before anybody could react, he ran out through the back of the market on his bandy legs and escaped into a tunnel.

Victoriya felt confused. "It's our mission," she said to the others. "We could be rich. But these comic rays—"

"He was just making that up!" said Krupin. "Alex Maksimov ain't nobody, is he? He'd know about that stuff."

Krupin might be right. The smart thing to do would be to research comic rays on the console that stood right beside her. She was about to do just that when she realised something—something brilliant—and started laughing.

"What?" this from Gurdski.

"Even if what that worm is telling us is true," said Victoriya, "we can just move. We can move to the other side."

Gurdski's fat face was caked in double helpings of sewage and confusion. "The other side of the ship," she clarified. "We'll be protected by the *other* sea. The one on the lower levels."

They all got that and raised a big cheer until she hushed them up. They had a mission to complete and the console had shown her the way to their next destination.

"Through the air vents!" she cried.

The inhabitants of the sports deck had been told to leave so that when Alex Maksimov came face to face with his nemesis, both he and the Dame could stare each other down across that huge empty space, surrounded only by their bodyguards.

The Dame had been around a long time and he wouldn't put it past her to have arranged an ambush that would strike right about now. He was tempted, himself. The Revolutionary Council—whoever the hell they were!—had united the lower half of the ship and very little information was getting out of there. They'd

Peadar Ó Guilín

be consolidating their control now, throwing traitors into the recyclers. All the usual stuff. After that, without a doubt, they'd be heading updeck. Already, they had their graffiti everywhere: little circles representing some sort of who-knows-who-cares political bullshit. If Alex was to be ready for their invasion he'd need the Dame gone.

So yeah, he was tempted to have his marksmen put an arrow in her neck. But a big confrontation now would weaken the two sides, and worse, allow Victoriya to finish her mission. It would leave the whole top of the ship with no water of its own and the "Revolutionary Council" would just waltz in here after that.

The Dame grimaced at the sight of him. "She's your mess," she said.

"You wanted her dead as much as I did," Alex replied. "I gave you everything you needed to finish her. Everything."

Perhaps Gogol was going to say something then about picking a less astoundingly stupid mission for his rogue employee, but she'd been at this game a long time. He saw her shut her mouth and shrug instead. "You know the monster best. What her next move?"

He didn't get to answer—the sports deck filled with people again. It happened so suddenly that it was as if they had poured out of the air vents and the walls and the sewer hatches. They were little folk, badly nourished, skinny as sticks. But they came in hundreds and each wore a single circle stitched above the heart. They carried weapons too and without so much as calling for surrender, they began to rain down homemade arrows on both Alex and Gogol.

Alex unsheathed a dagger and spun around. A few of his men were holding their heads or other parts of their bodies as blood dribbled through their fingers. Others had fired off their tazers, but the enemy were too many for the finishing knives to get a chance. Instead they were swarmed by ugly little people.

"Form a line!" he shouted.

Too late! He felt a horrible ripping pain and his foot went out from under him. A bloody dagger hovered at his throat. "Your hamstring," said an old woman helpfully. She had enormous ears that seemed to fan hatred and foul breath right into his face.

"Welcome to the revolution. Now, where is she? How does she plan on doing it?"

"Who?" Alex sputtered. "What are you talking about?" But of course he knew.

The Engineers again, the poor Engineers. Always trying to hide away bits of technology for the day it would be needed (or so they claimed), to serve humanity.

"*I'm* human," Victoriya said to their chief, who was gasping under Kurolev's foot. She smiled and blew him a kiss to take his mind off his discomfort. "And I need some of your spacesuits. Stylish ones. I have a reputation. Oh! And some of your *blasted* explosives too!"

But for all her witty chit-chat, she knew she should hurry. There was something going on. The little people were skittish and full of whispers. Entire corridors were deserted except for birds or bats that had escaped being eaten. There were only eight of her squad left alive by now, and no matter how many bones the Chief Engineer carelessly broke—with a little help from Gurdski— he couldn't find more than five spacesuits for them. That was enough, though. She could use the remaining three lads to watch the airlock while she was outside.

She heard a sound then, like a torrent of water on metal, only louder.

"You're for it now, bitch," said the Engineer.

The 'B' word never went well with Victoriya, and her knife hand took matters into its own...no, no that pun would never do! Which was really unfortunate, because once again the queen of quips was reduced to screaming: "You bad man! You bad, bad man!" as she stabbed the Engineer full of holes. But he had been right. The rattling sound had turned into a stampede of undernourished, circle-wearing, knife-wielding humourless deck-dung losers thundering from the direction of the sports zone. At their head, running as fast as his bandy legs could carry him, was the rickets boy she hadn't gotten around to killing earlier.

Victoriya's squad turned as one and fled. They weren't far from their goal now—a portside airlock—and two of her lads managed to slow the attackers with an ill-advised bout of heroism. It gave her just enough time to don her suit and grab the explosives before a large gang of enemies arrived at a gallop and smashed into her remaining six defenders.

Even in the suit, Victoriya made a good showing. Two stabs took the eyes of an old hag; another found some delightfully squishy kidneys. But then the scrum knocked her back against the airlock and she lost hold of the explosives.

"Give up!" shouted Rickets Boy. All of her squad were down by now and the peasants were hanging back to see what would happen next.

Victoriya happened next, of course. Always.

She smashed the "open" button behind her and, as the door swung wide, she grabbed the rickety little shit and dragged him into the airlock with her.

A woman screamed, "Anton!" and nearly got her fingers trapped as the hatch closed again. *Hardly the first relationship I've split up.* Now Victoriya had a hostage and two easy ways of killing him. She could either open the far door to deprive him of air, or use her knife. He knew it too, and his bandy legs sagged.

"You look a bit weak at the knees," she said with a winning smile. "You're mine now. Tell the losers out there I'll give you back, but I want my explosives, OK? I'll open the door for just a moment—"

"No," said Anton. His wobbly knees straightened.

"You might say 'no,' but *they*," Victoriya pointed out to where the ugly woman was screaming soundlessly and her friends were banging on the door, "will *beg* for your life. Believe me, I know the type. So, listen: All I want are my explosives, and then you can go. All right?"

"W-wait," he said. "You can't do this thing, you can't. It'll be like Earth all over again. This was the only ship to escape and now you'll be condemning our children to—"

"Oh, please!"

"Just..." he said, "just drop the knife and I'll tell them to go easy on you."

She couldn't believe it. "You...you'll go easy...on me? *I'm* the one who's armed. *I'm* Victoriya! There's nothing you can do about it."

He was sweating, but he reached a hand over to one side where the red button waited—the emergency hatch-blower. Was he insane? He didn't have so much as an oxygen mask. Victoriya smiled. It had to be a bluff. Like he was really going to kill himself! Like anybody would do that for the sake of...No, it didn't make sense. It couldn't make sense.

But if Anton wasn't going to speak his own ransom note, then Victoriya would have to do it for him. She went to open the hatch where his allies waited, but it was Rickets Boy who reacted faster and suddenly they were both hurtling backwards and out, out into the black. Victoriya couldn't believe it.

Anton spun away from her, his whole body as twisted now as his legs, his face frozen in horror.

He must have been suicidal all along, she thought. Had to be something like that.

She'd been blown too far away from the ship to grab onto anything and the whole glittering mass of the *Lessons Learned* was passing away from her. It was an oddly moving sight, seeing the entire thing from space, seeing how fragile it was. Not so big, really. A little circle in the middle of nothing, framed by a billion stars. Mine, she thought, wrapping its shrinking form in her hands. All mine.

She was just hanging there now, getting left behind. It was relaxing. It was beautiful and Victoriya felt no fear. Ever. Sooner or later something would turn up. It always had before.

A check on the air gauge showed a full twenty minutes remaining. *Good.* Plenty of time to think up a great line for her rescuers. Victoriya had always been good with the repartee. She wouldn't disappoint them.

∾

BRINE MAGIC

Tony Pi

A MINNOW SPY DARTED out of the Coral Trigram Gate, calling out with his mind-voice. *Sire, the demon comes!*

We were ready for her. We had left the Pearl Empress no other escape. My spies had swum every twist and turn of the reef maze in advance, and I had mapped out the passages she must be herded through. The rest was up to my sworn brother Sword and his barracuda soldiers to send her into our trap.

Nonetheless, the warning set my company of eel-wizards on edge, their fear rippling their surface thoughts. I swam a circuit through the coral crevasses to reassure them. *Be ready to bind her when she emerges, eightfold to seal her sorcery. Succeed here and we turn the tide of war. Let the thought of victory be your courage!*

On my final word, a sickly glow lit the darkness beyond the gate. My eel-mages darted into the opening to capture our lustrous foe, but she jetted through their midst and smashed them into the coral with her tentacles.

I swam into the fray, growing to match the Pearl Empress's size. I began coiling around her, but she pulled at me with a half-dozen arms. I had only completed four turnings when two of her tentacles closed around my head. She would have torn me apart if Sword hadn't caught up to her in that moment. He torpedoed out of the coral maze and impaled the demon on his swordfish bill.

As her luminous blood clouded the seawater, she cursed us as she died.

The salt of the sea turned bitter, and we began to drown.

The gills of my eel-shape helped not at all. My instinct to breathe drove all other thoughts from my mind, and I unwound myself from the demon's corpse. My body began remembering arms, legs, and lungs, and I swam upward for air. The brine stung my eyes, and I ascended blind.

Just as I thought I would die, my head broke the surface. I coughed up seawater. Between the dark skies and the storm-churned waves, I could see nothing. The mind-voices in the sea, from the battle-cries of our legion to the mantras of chanting fish, had gone. I sought Sword's mind in hopes that he made it to the surface as well, but my will would not cast forth. I tried my voice, but the typhoon buried my voice and surged to fold me back into the deep. I fought to stay afloat, but I was tiring. I didn't know how long I could continue treading water, much less attempt another shapechange.

Then, I heard a strange rumbling sound and also voices. It took me a few moments to realize they were shouting in modern Cantonese, not the Old Chinese I learned while stranded in the past. Could that noise be a *boat motor*? A bright light dazzled my eye, and something hit the water close to me. A life preserver? I grabbed it and held on, my heart racing.

Am I back in the twenty-first century, home at last?

Hands pulled me out of the sea. In half-remembered Cantonese, I commanded my rescuers to find my sworn brother. Only then did I give in to exhaustion and sleep.

When I awakened, before I opened my eyes I felt dry, my whole body was dry like it hadn't been in seven years. Someone clutched my hand tight, and I opened my eyes and saw it was Ma. Her eyes met mine, and they were brimming with joy and tears.

"Man-Tak, oh my son, my precious child. You've come back to me," she said, planting kisses on my forehead.

I blinked, trying to clear the blur from my sight with little success, but I recognized Big Sis, her arm around Ma to steady her. Asleep in a chair beside my hospital bed was Yehyeh, snoring away beside a jungle of get-well flowers and cards. Could this be real? Was I back in Hong Kong? When the sea took me back to the time of the Three Kingdoms, I never thought I'd see them again.

"Welcome home, Lil' Bro," Sis said, the words squeaking out of her. "Dad's coming too. He cut his business trip short and is flying back from Vancouver."

Yehyeh startled awake. He grinned and ruffled my hair with a hand that stank of tobacco.

Was this an illusion, demon-made? But no, it couldn't be. I bottled the memories of them and cherished them, and the three at my bedside were true to what I remembered. The Pearl Empress could not have conjured them so faithfully...could she?

I managed a word. "Ma."

My voice broke as I said it. I hadn't sounded like that since....

I raised my free hand before my eyes. Thin fingers of a teen's hand, clean of calluses and scars of war. I was thirteen and gangly again, when I should be a stalwart warrior with seven years of relentless training. The Dragon King of the South Sea himself had fostered us!

Had the past seven years been simply a dream? I sat up and looked around wildly, nearly pulling out the IV line in my arm. "Where's Sword?"

Sis frowned. "You mean Gim-Leung? Your friend's on the other side of the curtain. He hasn't come to, yet."

Hui Gim-Leung had been Sword's name, I remembered now, before the Dragon King dubbed us Eel Duke and Swordfish Prince. The curtain was out of focus, too. I'd forgotten I was near-sighted. I lost my glasses when the ferry capsized, but I fixed my eyesight after the King taught us the Eighteen Transformations.

"I need to see him."

Sis quietly pulled the curtain aside. Sword—Gim-Leung—lay in deep sleep in his bed, likewise restored to his younger body.

"The doctors say he'll be fine," Ma said, wiping tears from her face. "Let him rest, son."

Yehyeh leaned in close, his breath smoky-stale. "They thought you both drowned, but I never believed them."

My eyes brimmed with tears. How I missed the old storyteller's voice! Once, I would've made a face in mock disgust at my grandfather, but now I gulped the scent deep and held it hostage in my lungs. "I'm tougher than that, Yehyeh." *Let this be real!*

"Good, good. But where you *been*, boy?"

His words silenced the room. A look of fear overtook Ma's face, while Sis darted a look towards the door.

"Now isn't the right time to ask such things," Ma said to Yehyeh. "This is a time to celebrate, to thank Guanyin for her mercy."

Sis fretted. "But he was gone a year! The police will want to know—"

Ma pinched Sis's arm, surprising her into clamming up. "And Man-Tak will tell us when he's ready, won't you, son?"

A year? I was confused, but nodded to stall for time. I thought we'd been sent back to the day the storm sacrificed us to the sea, fished out of the water while the same winds blew. A chill overtook me as I remembered more of that day, and I realized no one was waiting by Gim-Leung's bedside for him to wake.

"Where's Mr. Hui?" I asked. We'd been on the ferry with Sword's father when the squall hit out of nowhere. We'd lost sight of him when the waves overturned the ship and washed us overboard.

Gloom befell the room. They didn't want to answer me. Ma began to sob.

"Someone will come for him," Sis said. "I promise."

I began to fear the worst. Gim-Leung lost his mother when he was very young. Did he lose his father as well?

A thin-haired doctor entered the room. "I see our patient is finally awake," he said, smiling.

I nodded.

"Mrs. Yuen, I know you want to be with your son, but you've hardly slept at all, have you? Why don't you go home and rest?"

"I'll still be here in the morning, Ma." I squeezed her hand.

Ma squeezed back and nodded.

"We'll be back, Lil' Bro," Sis said. "You want anything from home? Your trading cards? Your Nintendo stuff?"

The offer caught me off-guard. My games had been my world, my obsession. Life under the sea had changed all that. I hadn't thought about those hobbies in ages.

"Sure, Sis."

"And I'll tell you everything missed on TV while you were away," Yehyeh said with a wink.

I gave them a reassuring smile as they left, praying to the gods that she and Sis and Yehyeh were real. I had until morning to wake Sword however I could, and maybe together we could sort things out.

After a battery of tests ranging from blood pressure to simple walking, the doctor told me I was well on the way to recovery. I asked him about Sword, but all he would say was that Gim-Leung was out of danger, for now.

At last, he left me alone with Sword. I caught a glimpse of a cop outside the door as they left. They had taken the right precautions. We'd been presumed dead, after all. What nightmares must they think we had endured in the intervening year?

They'd never believe the truth. Truth was that summer day when Mr. Hui took us to the Macau Zoo. Truth was the supernatural storm that capsized the ferry on our way back. Truth was the undertow that stranded us eighteen-hundred years in the past.

Lost in time with no way to return home, we joined the Dragon King. The Pearl Empress and her demons had challenged him for dominion of the sea, but he had no sons to lead his armies. He believed the sea had answered his prayers for aid. Under his tutelage, we learned the ways of battle, royal words, and the Eighteen Transformations. As Eel Duke and Swordfish Prince, we won the King victory after victory against the Pearl's shell-bound demons and tentacled beasts.

Together, you are invincible, the King once praised.

Tell them that truth and they'd think us mad. Well, maybe Yehyeh would believe us. He knew all the old legends by heart, like fox spirits and longevity peaches and the rabbit in the moon. But no one really listened to him but me.

I needed to prove those seven years were real. I needed Sword.

I slipped out of bed and wheeled my IV over to Sword's bed. "Wake up, Sword," I said, keeping my voice low.

No answer.

I tweaked his nose. "Gim-Leung." Nothing.

Even a vigorous shake didn't wake him. He remained dead to the world.

I slumped into the chair by the window and watched the rain drum against the glass. *Think, Eel, think!* This turn of events was as complicated as a xiangqi lesson from the Dragon King, but perhaps that was the key. The King's puzzles demanded patience, focus, and careful deliberation.

When he found us drowning in the depths, the Dragon King coiled around us and thundered in our minds: *welcome the brine.* We tasted the salt of the sea, opening the way to the ocean's magic. With it, the Dragon King changed our shape, gifting us with gills to breathe and fins to swim. Gim-Leung became a swordfish, and I, an eel. I had lived in the ocean for so long that I hardly thought about the taste. The saltiness was gone, replaced by a touch of bitterness that reminded me of the Pearl Empress's blood.

What if all I needed was a lick of salt?

I looked at my IV drip. I knew little of medicine, so I had no idea what was in it. But if I remembered right, they often used saline.

How do you catch the tiger cub without entering the tiger's lair? The old saying went. I unhooked an extra IV bag from the wheeled stand and opened a valve, squeezing a drop of solution onto the tip of my tongue.

It was salty, all right. I let the salt erase the bitter aftertaste, and tried to remember the power of sea magic. My head throbbed with pain as I forced my mind to listen for Sword's dreaming, but I kept at it. Only when I gave Sword a drop of salt as well did I hear the whirlpool of his dreams.

Sword, I need you.

His eyes opened. *Eel?*

I told him when and where we were, and how I roused him with salt.

He sat up and tested his voice. "You felt her curse too. This could be another of her tricks. How do I know *you're* real?"

"There are things here only you and I would know," I argued. "Hong Kong. Hospitals. Nintendo! No one else from that time knows anything about the twenty-first century."

"A dying curse is strong," Sword countered. "Maybe it trapped me in my own memories and you're just a figment of my imagination."

I couldn't deny that I feared the same thing. I gripped his shoulders to assure him that I was real. "When the waves swept us into the sea, we locked our fingers together and held on. The currents tore at us, and I panicked, but you wouldn't let go. We sank deeper and deeper, and I thought my lungs would burst. But then the Dragon King changed us."

"Swordfish and eel." Sword raised his hands and clamped them on my shoulders as well, thinking back to that momentous day. "It was my turn to be scared but you wouldn't let me swim away. You coiled around me and reminded me of our debt to the King."

"What I actually said was, '*Would you run if this was a video game?*'"

"And let you beat me? Hell no." He gave me an indignant look. "But it turned out very different from a game, didn't it?"

I sensed doubt ebb in his mind and the tide of his trust rise, and hoped he saw the same in me. "Our transformation lessons, remember them? You wanted to keep the bill in every form." We couldn't turn into just anything—that took Seventy-Two Transformations, and we were nowhere near that good—but the power of the Eighteen gave us countless water-breathing shapes. Sword has his favourites and I had mine. "Me, I tried a dragon-shape straight away, but got everything wrong except staying long and thin."

He grinned. "Yeah, you turned into one ugly sea snake. Even the King said so."

"Hey, I wasn't the one who turned into a narwhal in tropical waters," I snapped back.

"Only to save your sorry ass!"

We both broke into laughter. This had to be Sword!

His laughter trailed off, and a far-off look shadowed his face. "We lived through it together, so it must be real, all of it. But no one will believe us."

"So? We tell them we remember nothing. Let them think we were kidnapped, brainwashed, whatever. We're back. Nothing else will matter to them."

He stared at the flowers on my bedside table. "Why didn't my father come?"

"Maybe he's out of town, like my father," I said, but surely he was thinking the same nightmare scenarios as I was. Did Mr. Hui drown? Had he been arrested? "We can ask someone tomorrow."

"Why wait?" He grabbed a TV remote and turned the set on, tuning the volume down.

On a twenty-four hour news station, he found a report on us.

The police have identified the two mystery youths rescued yesterday morning from Hong Kong Harbour. They are Yuen Man-Tak and Hui Gim-Leung of Hong Kong, both fourteen years of age. This case has baffled police, as Yuen and Hui were presumed to be among the twenty passengers lost in the Hong Kong-Macau ferry accident that happened a year ago today. Hospital officials say that the two patients are in stable condition and remain under guard. Authorities hope to interview them soon to shed light on their whereabouts for the past twelve months. This story is particularly tragic in that only three months ago, Hui Gim-Leung's father, Hui Po-Fong, took his own life after a period of severe depression over the loss of his son.

"No!" Sword cried, hurling the remote at the TV and ripping the IV line off his arm. I felt his grief and anger surge. I reached for him, but he slapped my hand away.

Hearing the commotion, the cop outside rushed into our room, but Sword had already grabbed his IV bag, held it over his face and burst it, catching what saline solution he could in his mouth. As the IV monitor beeped in alarm, he ballooned in size and tore his hospital gown, settling into a monstrous, horned shape as the cop stared in disbelief. Sword had shifted into a haiji:

lion's body, goat's fleece, and a dragon's head crowned by a lone horn. In beast-shape he slammed into the cop and knocked him flat, then roared and tore through the room door.

"Sword, wait!" I cried, but he galloped down the corridor on cleft hooves, ignoring me. Where was he going, home? What might he find, an empty apartment or another family? No, without his father, there was no place he could go.

At least, not in the present day. Though the *haiji* didn't look it, it was a Water beast, famed for eating fire. Sword might be heading for the sea. But would the ocean take him back to the Dragon King? It didn't matter. I couldn't let him suffer his loss alone.

Sword had knocked the cop out cold. I propped a pillow under his head and wondered what form would let me catch up to a *haiji*. A *gaolung* would do the trick: the hornless dragon, lord over a company of thirty-six hundred fish, able to lead its shoal in flight.

I grabbed the extra IV bag and gulped from it. The taste of salt flooded my mouth, and I called on the power of the Eighteen Transformations. To my shock, magic surged wildly within me, tightening my skin and flesh around my bones and burning my insides like salt poured into open wounds.

I steeled my mind and tried to reason through the fog of pain. Shape-changing was tasking, but it never hurt like *this*.

My legs braided together and I fell. The IV ripped out of my arm but the pain from that was nothing. Though I tried to brace myself against the impact, my bones had turned so brittle that my arms broke in several places. I opened my mouth to scream but my cry became a throat-dry bellow.

Salt. We were always immersed in the sea, always wet with salt when we changed. Here, the magic must be drawing salt from my body to compensate, be it from blood or sweat.

Dragon scales burst bloodlessly through my skin in patches.

What had Sword done differently to save him from this agony? Perhaps nothing; in his rage he must have embraced the pain and let his instinct mould the *haiji* shape. I must do the same.

I emptied my mind save for the shape of the *gaolung* and my need for it: crocodilian head, scales of white jade, and putrid saliva. I accepted the pain of transformation and felt the power of flight begin to buoy my now-sinuous body. Though I was not fully formed, I reared like a cobra, smashing the window. Rain moistened my scales and I drew strength from that, forcing my *gaolung* shape into adequacy.

I flicked the air like a living whip and flew through the window, seeking Sword. I didn't know which hospital this was, but I scented the sea very close-by.

A scream and the sound of breaking glass drew my attention towards the second-storey. *Haiji*-Sword had escaped the hospital through a room window, landing on the asphalt with a thunderous clack. When he had his bearings, he galloped for the nearby shore.

I gave chase. *Sword, this might not be a curse!*

He wouldn't answer me. He bounded atop a parked car, dented its roof but kept going, single-minded in his steeplechase.

The obstacles on the ground wouldn't impede me. I intercepted him in the maze of shipping containers in the docklands between the hospital and the water, fell on him from the sky, and wrapped a coil around his middle.

Sword roared and bucked, but I held on, twisting a second coil.

The Dragon King prayed for help against the Pearl Empress, and the sea brought us, I thundered in his head. *Now she's dead, maybe it's our time to come home.*

It's a curse and the King may need us still, he snapped. He rammed me against a metal container, trying to dislodge me. *Here, I have nothing to live for.*

The impact rattled me, but I added another twist around him. *I'm devastated to hear about your father, truly I am. But years ago we helped each other when we thought we might never again see our families alive. Let me help you.*

You have your family. He changed his tactic and continued towards the sea, fighting my attempt to keep him from it. *Here I'm an orphan, but in the Dragon King's court, I am a prince!*

I bound him further, now at four coils like our fight against the Pearl. Four more and I could counter his transformation. *Would you run if this were a video game?*

Nice try, but I'm not the boy I was seven years ago. I will not be less than the man I already am. He dragged us to the edge of the water.

Then where's your vaunted courage, Swordfish Prince? Yes, it's a scary prospect, to live your youth again without a father. But you are my sworn brother, and so you are my family. I'll move the heavens to make my family take you in.

Five coils and we fell into the water together. The touch of the sea soothed the pain of the dragon-shape and gave me renewed strength, but it quickened Sword as well.

A chorus of timeless whalesongs arose from farther and deeper into the harbour.

Hear that, Eel? They're calling us. He began to change again, taking on the shape of a great swordfish.

I wound my sixth coil.

Come with me, Sword pleaded. *We were meant to stay in the past, Eel. Why else would the sea leave us this power if it were done with us? The brine welcomes us back. Together, we are invincible.*

Entwined, we sank further, but I paused on the seventh winding. Maybe this was the sea giving us a final choice: stay Eel and Sword or be Man-Tak and Gim-Leung again. I could reclaim a life of magic and adventure or let go and return to a normal life with my family.

Sword stopped struggling. *The whalesongs are fading, Man-Tak. Finish your binding or let me go.*

Perhaps that's what the Pearl intended with her curse, to break the bond between us. The choice was mine: fulfill my duties to my family, who still thought me a child, or choose to remain the man I had become in the Dragon King's court and never look back again.

If I returned to the past, I would break my family's hearts again and lose them forever. But what if the Dragon King did need us? What if Sword died because I wasn't there?

In the end, I uncoiled from Sword. *Go, Sword, but I cannot follow you.*

Freed, Sword swam out from my rings but did not rush away. *Why? We had a grand adventure together, and I loved every moment of it. But sometimes you have to turn off the video game and live in the real world, even if I'd rather slay demons at your side. Maybe that's part of growing up: things change, and you learn to accept and go on. That, I feel, is the right choice for me, just as it is right for you to choose the sea. I will never forget what we have taught each other.*

We will always be sworn brothers, Sword said.

Besides, you're going into the past, I said. *Find some longevity peaches and try not to die, OK? Maybe one day, if the sea will have me, I will swim at your side again.*

Sword laughed. *The brine will welcome you, even if I have to move the heavens myself to see it done. Until we meet again, brother Eel.*

He swam for the depths where the whalesongs played on.

There'd be many strange things to answer for when I returned to the hospital, but I'd make something up. Yet Yehyeh deserved the truth because he would believe it.

I waited until I could see Sword no more before I surfaced and took to the air. To my surprise, thousands of fish leapt out of the water and schooled behind me in flight.

༄

THE LEGEND OF GLUCK

Marie Bilodeau

GLUCK THE BARBARIAN DRAGGED the maggot-ridden, oversized head of Klar the Dark through the forests of the elves, the mountains of the dwarves and the ridiculously dull flat lands of the peasants, to the swamplands of his forefathers.

The elven sorceress Alara lurked somewhere near, he knew, even if she was currently hiding. She had followed him the entire return journey, insisting the head might yet prove dangerous. Gluck grinned at the foolish idea. Alara was powerful and a proven ally, but sometimes he feared that the perfumes she favoured affected her judgment.

She remained hidden in a cloaking spell, following Gluck's advice. Few of his people had ventured from their land in the past few generations, and their legends now labeled elves as tricksters and thieves. Just as Klar the Dark was said to be the greatest enemy to have ever walked the lands.

"If you were so great," Gluck muttered down at the head, "you would have been called Klar the Black, not just the Dark." A giggle came from within the trees, though its origin was lost in the breeze rustling the leaves.

Damn witch. Doesn't she know how to be quiet?

He shifted the great leather straps that were tied to Klar the Dark's large head. At first he had carried the head on his shoulders, but after a week of travel he swore the head was growing heavier. He had then dragged the head by its oily, thick black hair for a while, but soon the strands were ripping off, along with large chunks of rotten scalp. He still needed the head semi-recognizable so that he could stand with it before his chief and tribal council, so he had tied leather belts in its mouth and around its forehead, opting to drag the head along the ground. Its remaining gray skin and the red spheres that peered through its maggot-eaten eyelids would be enough to convince them of its origins. It was certainly nothing spawned from their land. And it certainly couldn't be his grandfather. His family's name would be cleared by sunset, with this monstrous head as proof.

He only wished the head wasn't getting heavier all the time. *Unless months of chasing the evil-doer down claimed my strength?* Gluck scoffed at the idea.

"I don't see why you have to bring this monstrosity back to your council," Alara's silky voice danced on the wind around him. "If you hadn't saved our king's life..."

"Twice," he grunted before she could continue.

"Well, yes, twice. But if you hadn't saved his life, he never would have granted such a strange request."

Gluck snorted. "You're the one who requested to accompany me, sorceress. I asked for no escort, and would have brought the head back to you when I was done with it. Does my word mean nothing to you?"

"Hardly, foolhardy barbarian. But I worry. Klar the Dark was powerful in his time." She paused. "I suppose I can't wait to put this whole business behind me, too."

Her voice faded away. He didn't bother answering, concentrating instead on dragging the head the last few miles to his home, where he could finally prove his grandfather's innocence and restore his family's line.

Gluck approached the settlement. He knew the moment he was spotted. A shadow to the left vanished behind a tree. A sucking noise nearby indicated a foot being pulled out of mud. He gritted his teeth and straightened his back, despite the growing weight of the head.

The settlement was comprised of rock houses thatched with

wood—simple and practical, with a touch of iron and fire, like his people. The houses didn't outline roads, but were instead strewn about, their location based on the barbarians' complicated system of barter, social rank and battle prowess. A scent of pig fat mixed with fresh mint teased Gluck's memories to life: growing up in the village, learning to hunt, to fight, to destroy, listening to elders tell legends and histories around bonfires.

Dark-haired, bronze-skinned settlers were coming out to greet him. Children recoiled, either from the sight of him or from the head, he wasn't certain. Women looked appreciatively at him, and he found himself hoping that Alara wasn't around to witness their lingering, assessing gazes. But it was the warriors who held his attention. The heroes of his youth. They stood nodding to him in camaraderie, and he returned the gesture, fighting a grin. He tried to spot his favourite warriors, eager to share stories of heroism and strange lands with them.

Hiding his fatigue and keeping a firm grip on the leather straps, Gluck entered the Great Hall. Its walls were formed of stones piled on top of one another, then layered with wood, so that every few years, the hall had to be torn down and rebuilt when the wood rotted through. Legends said it was a way to ensure they would always stay powerful, as each generation rebuilt the hall and claimed it as their own. After bearing witness to the ancient cities of the dwarves, Gluck now suspected the Great Hall's plight was due to poor workmanship coupled with laziness.

He decided he would not participate in the next rebuild, not unless they hired a dwarven architect. Which they never would. Dwarves were seen as treacherous cowards. But Gluck had seen their endless stone buildings, carved out of the mountains themselves, he had received their hospitality and kindness, and he had fought in enough battles beside them to know none of those stories were true.

"Gluck!" The chief called from where he sat. His dark hair was loose about his shoulders, and he wore the skins of his position, not the simple loin cloth that most of his tribe favoured. Gluck approached him and, pulling on reserves of strength, picked up the head and dropped it on the floor before the chief. The walls of the hall trembled. The chief jumped to his feet, eyes wide.

Gluck did not wait for permission to speak, angered by his leader's lack of control. If he was terrified of a decomposing head, Gluck wondered how he would have acted in combat.

"I bring you the head of Klar the Dark, fiend of the lands, Great Destroyer of the Faeries and enemy of the elves, the dwarves and our tribe!"

Seeing that the chief was still recovering, Gluck continued. He wasn't interested in babble. He wanted to get the head back to the elven king so that he could throw this ugly business behind him.

"This proves the innocence of my grandfather, Gluck the Seventh. He did not flee the lands to become Klar the Dark. This creature was never human. I claim back my rightful name of Gluck the Ninth, and my family's ancestral home!"

The chief had recovered slightly. He sat back down and stared at the monstrosity. Maggots slid from the eye sockets. The eyeballs, still red but shrinking, moved from time to time as insects writhed within.

"This proves nothing, Gluck," said the chief, Lurp the Eighth. Gluck's anger consumed him quickly, from toes to fingertips to the roots of his hair. He felt lighter and his fatigue left him. Lurp was intimidated by Gluck's greater standing, being ninth of his line. He clearly feared a power struggle. Not that Gluck was at all interested. He just wanted his rightful name and his home back.

"Do you really believe," Lurp continued, apparently unaware of the tension in Gluck's limbs as the warrior's muscles began to throb with unspent anger, "that I would allow for such poor proof? We need something more concrete."

Lurp smirked, shattering Gluck's remaining control. Gluck leaned down and picked up Klar the Dark's head, lifting it high over his own, ignoring bits of rotten flesh trickling onto him. Lurp fell off his chair trying to escape, but was too slow to avoid a direct hit. The head knocked into his chest and threw him back, covering him in liquified brains.

"Gluck, be careful," he heard Alara say. She stepped out of the shadows a moment later, the strands of her spell slipping away.

She was taller than him, thin and pale, as frail looking as a birch tree. Her hair was long and tied back, dark to contrast her skin, and her eyes always seemed to conceal a joke. She looked like she would be easy to defeat in her simple white robes, but he knew from fighting at her side for months that she could easily destroy most adversaries.

He growled. "What are you doing, woman?"

She ignored him as she walked towards the head.

She hissed. "Look." Gluck bit back a retort and looked, the sorceress' warnings having saved him often.

The head of Klar the Dark was rocking back and forth. The eyes were looking at him, and a glow grew within them. Before he could speak, a recovered Lurp the Eighth pointed accusingly at Alara as he struggled back up.

"You dare come here, elven woman? Gluck, you have dared to bring one of our ancient enemies into our very land?"

Alara gave a short laugh. "The only meeting our people have ever had, Barbarian, was a small trade dispute that you ungraciously lost. And we actually keep written records, unlike you, you illiterate oaf."

Lurp growled and turned to Gluck. "This is a much greater betrayal than your grandfather's! You are exiled from these lands!"

Gluck's heart pounded in his chest. He took a step forward, but before he could reach Lurp, the head of Klar the Dark slammed into the chief and rolled over him. The chief's bones snapped, crushed by the impact. Gluck grabbed his axe—the double-edged weapon was covered in nicks, but still sharp.

"Wait," Alara shouted, but Gluck ignored her, rushing forward. He embedded the axe in both Klar's eyes with a cross hit. Dark liquid gushed forth. He rolled out of the way and jumped aside.

"Don't let it touch you!" Alara screamed. Then he heard the familiar chanting of a spell, like a whisper on stormy winds. The head hovered before him, the axe slowly dislodging from the rotting skull.

"You're even more disgusting in death," Gluck said, careful to stay between the hovering monster and Alara. He would have to move fast once she was finished her spell, but he knew she was unable to defend herself while casting.

For a moment, though the lips had already decomposed to reveal the sharp teeth, he swore the head smiled. Then it launched itself at him. Gluck braced for the blow, his left leg thrust back to absorb the impact, but it still sent him sprawling to the ground. The head hovered over him, the glowing red eyes holding him fast.

Welcome to your future, Klar the Dark's voice boomed in his mind. Sweat rolled down Gluck's face as he fought to move, but he was trapped, as though his body was no longer his own.

Alara finished her spell. "Not this time," she hissed. The head turned and tried to strike Alara down, but she was too quick. She sent nets of fire around it, constricting and cutting it up into hundreds of criss-crossed pieces, to burn into fine wisps of black fire until nothing was left of them but a rising red smoke. Alara held her hand out and the red smoke gathered in her palm. She covered the wispy orb with her other hand and closed her eyes, her lips barely moving, her drawn features betraying the danger and drain of her spell.

Barbarians streamed into the hall, fully armed. When they saw the broken body of their leader, they turned on Alara.

"Kill the elven sorceress!"

Gluck picked up his dripping axe and stood between his countrymen and Alara, testing his left arm as he did so. Hurt, but not broken.

"Gluck," Glar—his second cousin—spoke. "You would protect an elven sorceress, a witch of the sworn enemies of the Barbarians?"

Gluck snorted as he looked at them. Their skin was flawless with barely a scar, while his was crisscrossed with sword marks and puncture wounds, and two of his toes were missing. Their blades showed no nicks or signs of battle.

He sought out the men he had admired as a child—Klinix, Slayer of Dragons; Grotso, Eater of Death; and his childhood hero, Trillo, Puncturer of Pain. He met their eyes and could see fear and hesitation in them. They held their weapons weakly, betraying their lack of battle prowess—or, more likely, experience.

He set his jaw and let his muscles relax, lowering his weapon. These lying cowards didn't deserve to be faced with respect.

"What do you even know of elves, Glar?" He spat. "I'll tell you what I know of them. When Klar the Dark threatened all of the lands, including our own, the battlefields that held off his armies were littered with the bodies of elves, dwarves, and the last remaining faeries. Nowhere in that battle did I see a barbarian wield iron against the enemy." He took a step toward his cousin, his axe held loosely at his side. He knew the firelight caught every scar on his bronzed body, and his eyes showed more steel than even his axe. "So, cousin, I will stand by those who stood by me in combat. That is the warrior's way. Or have you forgotten?"

His cousin was about to answer but his eyes darted past Gluck instead. "She's gone." He took a step back.

"Cowards." Gluck mumbled. He walked out of the hall, shouldering past the barbarians, not interested in engaging them in combat the way he once would have. He had since fought much worthier foes. Outside, the rush of cool air made quick work of his blanket of sweat. He avoided the settlers and walked into the woods, away from their staring eyes and pathetic cries of victory.

Alara had either been consumed by her spell, or she had simply cloaked herself again to avoid conflict. Frustrated, he hollered into the surrounding woods. He hoped his people would hear him, and fear. Real fear would be a healthy change for them.

His land was beautiful, he now knew. It was wild and overgrown. It could at once be dry and wet, lush and dead, strong and weak. It could be flat one moment and a cliff the next, desert could lead to the ocean, settlement to cemetery. It was old and wild, like his people, except that it kept growing, unlike them.

Anger still pumped in his veins, fueled by the recent battle and by the months of fighting beforehand. His new-found allies falling beside him, battling an evil seemingly too great for them. The mourning songs of the faeries echoing at night as they gathered their dead, before the last one was slain. His voice rising with the elves and the dwarves to mourn the end of that race. Preparing for battle with true warriors by his side, jesting with them, choosing tactics, being taken into the confidence of kings and queens, heroes and true legends. Months of fighting were over, and he had nothing to show for it. Nothing, except perhaps the death of Alara, one of his last remaining allies.

He grabbed a nearby birch sapling, pulled it free of the earth and swung it into another tree. He tackled a bigger birch and wrestled it out of the ground, clenching his teeth and growling from deep within his thorax. The trunk snapped before the roots were pulled free. He grunted as he fought to keep his footing.

"Redecorating, barbarian?" a familiar soft voice said, each syllable like a fresh note of spring. He smiled despite himself.

"Alara. You should know better than to sneak up on a warrior."

The elf stepped out of the shadows, and Gluck's smile broadened.

"Is your homecoming so dull that you rip trees out of the ground to entertain yourself, or is this a ritual I'm unfamiliar with?" She arched an eyebrow.

He let her words float a moment on the air about him.

"What happened to Klar the Dark?"

She shrugged. "His essence lived still, and was attached to you. I suspected it after his defeat, but my king granted your request for the head before I could warn him. I figured I would simply follow and be ready for the final strike. I've trapped his energies." She held up her hand to show him the perfectly spherical red stone that lay in her palm, seeming to glow from within.

"Attached to me? Klar the Dark? That's nonsense, woman."

She met his eyes and he was surprised to see hesitation in them. He had seen her destroy the elven uprising against her king with no second thought, and those had been her people. Yet here she hesitated for a moment before holding the stone out to him. "This is yours, by right."

Gluck almost asked what she meant, but then he understood. There was only one reason for her to utter those words.

So many other stories of his childhood were lies, but the legends of his grandfather were true. He was Klar the Dark. Which meant his family's dishonour stood, and all of the last few months of fighting and bleeding, of seeing his comrades fall around him, of fear and pain, had been for nothing.

Nothing.

He couldn't reclaim what he believed had been his birthright. He had no birthright save the dead riddling the battlefields of the lowlands. The blood of Klar the Dark's victims was on his hands, no matter his fighting, no matter his actions, no matter that he had been hailed by many as a hero.

Gluck breathed hard as he looked down at the stone, the final remnants of his family.

Alara put her slender hand on his arm, her skin milky white beside his. "Your legend will long outlive your grandfather's, Gluck. I will make sure of that." He looked deep into her hazel eyes. He had believed many lies in his day, but she spoke truth. He knew as much.

He took the red stone in his palm. He could feel the dark whispers of Klar the Dark echo in his mind. He blinked and put it away in his pouch. He didn't need or crave any of this evil magic. He took a deep breath and looked at Alara.

"I promised your king I would return the head. I intend to do so, in whatever form it now holds."

Alara nodded and the two began walking in silence, the sorceress not bothering to cloak herself.

He knew without a doubt that this time, when he left his land, he would never come back. He had sealed his fate the moment he had left his home in search of—and had found—honour, and answers.

But he didn't mind.

He would forge his own legend with fire and steel.

ONE AND TWENTY SUMMERS

Brian Cortijo

FINALLY, THE DIGGING WAS over.

Danor had always hated this part the most. Toiling for half the night with a trowel and only one good hand, only to look at the simple oak plank that separated a man from the earth. A ward against fell spirits possessing the dead. A doorway to the heavens, when the soul was finally prepared to depart the world.

It turned his stomach still, after twenty digs.

Despoiling the graves of comrades of war was not what Danor the smith had been bred for. Yet still he did it. It was a duty he had long prepared himself for.

After twenty digs, the routine had become natural.

He slipped the hammer from his belt. Despite not being at his forge, Danor always carried his hammer—except to sleep, when he left it hanging on the bedpost. The smith spun it once in his left hand. Only two fingers and the thumb still answered the demands of his mind, but he would not use his good right hand for the task. That hand had held sword and spear with this man. Viccam deserved better than to have his coffin defiled by the same sword arm that once defended him.

Bending down to kneel in the dirt, Danor struck. A simple blow to the corner, and the first panel squealed and creaked in protest. A second swing followed, this time from the bottom, and the long nail came loose.

It was never difficult for Danor to know where to strike the wood. He had, after all, been the one to build these coffins, day after day, until they all were buried. Good men, each of them, interred with their arms and armor.

Good iron and steel that their families now needed.

Had there been another way, any other, Danor would have taken it. But there were no men skilled and old enough to take to the mines, and so no iron for smelting or silver for trade. The only smith left, and the only man remaining from those better times, he did what he must. The village needed plows and pots, axes, and the occasional spear for taking down a stag or a boar. Someone had to show they still understood duty.

He could not tell, in the dim moonlight, whether it was his tear or the hammer that struck the wood first.

"Look at him. The old man is mad, I tell you."

Edvard glanced over toward the old smith, who gripped the wooden tankard in his gnarled left hand, and then looked back at his friend as though he had spoken in another language.

"Mad, Micu? He fought in a war less than a dozen men survived, for a corner of land no one was left alive to use—and that wasn't worth the dust to bury them under. You would be mad, too."

"Aye," said Micu, scratching at the itchy spot where his first full beard was finally growing in. "Maybe, Vard. But remember: our fathers died there, yours and mine both. That one was at least lucky to survive the battles."

"Lucky indeed," muttered Edvard, and looked down into his empty cup before raising it in mock toast to his friend. "May such luck find its way to other men's doorsteps and never yours, all the days of your life."

"Some friend you are." Micu frowned at him, understanding clearly lacking in his eyes. Edvard merely shook his head, and waved the tavern mistress over for another drink.

At least she had wits enough to know that the only sorts that drank so early in the day were bored wastrels like him and Micu, or lived lives of crushing sadness, like poor Danor over there.

Finally, it was done, the last hammer blow fallen and the ringing of metal on metal stopped, at least for the afternoon. Danor lifted the tongs—it was never easy anymore, with his fingers so mangled—and considered the slim edge of the curved blade. Nodding, he turned and thrust it swiftly into the trough of oil, smiling in satisfaction as the hissing began.

Yes, it would make a fine blade for Tora.

Once, years ago, a fine blade meant a spear head or a sword. Now it was plows and shears. Or a scythe, like this one. Good, tempered steel, that wouldn't rust in a pair of threshing seasons and need to be replaced. Again.

After the long count of ten, Danor put his hammer down on the anvil and hefted the tongs in his right hand. The blade was coated now, and he set it aside to cool.

This would be last time he would need to hammer such steel, pried from the cold, dead hands of his brothers in arms and melted into something less warlike for use by their wives and sons. Those sons were old enough to work the fields and tend the mines, which meant trade. And trade meant metal, of all kinds, flowing into coffers and molds.

It also meant that men from farther villages would be coming, to seek local girls as wives, or conquests. That much was already beginning, and seeing the younger women begin to swell with children brought a strange sense of pride to Danor's heart. Not that any of those offspring would be his—oh, no—but at least *life* was returning.

Danor would be able to rest for a while. Perhaps take an apprentice, when these new boys were old enough. The last generation had lived at their mothers' skirts, tending fields and little more. Tora's boy, Edvard, was bright enough. Too easily distracted, perhaps, but that could be trained out of him.

A deep, rueful sigh shook his broad shoulders, and Danor rose to look in the small plate of polished metal he used as a mirror. Lifting his chin, he checked the thick, blond beard for any embers that might have jumped up as he worked. Seeing none, he stared a moment into his own eyes, searching for something of the idealistic young man that once went off to war thinking his one blade could change the world.

He saw nothing. No pride. No hope. Not even disgust at what he had done.

Taking a sword from a dead man to use its metal so that his widow could eat brought nothing to his heart. No pain, no shame, no pride. He was a smith, and a smith's duty was to forge whatever metal he could find into tools that could be used.

Hurling the mirror across the smithy, he smirked as it jammed into the wall with a loud clunk. He had never been so skilled when it mattered.

Lifting the boar brush, he moved off to the blade, to scrape off the oil before it settled too thick on the metal.

Viccam's widow deserved a scythe that could be sharpened properly.

The men were crouched among the brush at the edge of Edvard's mother's lands. It was a short walk to the house and from there, to their prize. His companions looked at their leader like he was a man possessed. Which wasn't far off from the mark, considering how well he had been paid for this service.

"Now listen closely, Olev. You and Bjartr will sneak in the back and grab Tora while Ragn and I are chatting with her at the door. Once she's tied up—and with a hood, mind you, so she can't see us work—we can set to recovering the banner Viccam took in the war."

Tora's husband had been one of the few to survive the war. He came home clutching a banner that represented something, and then the fighting stopped. Then he died of his wounds a scant week later. Bjartr did not remember much else of the tales. It was hard to recall so many details. He was barely a season old when the fighting started. All he knew for sure was that Viccam was a hero who died saving their village.

"But—" Bjartr, the large, dumb one of the bunch began, only to have slim, grasping fingers suddenly around his throat.

"Bear," growled the eldest and cleverest of the group, calling Bjartr by the name they had used as children, "do as I say. We have been offered gold—not silver, but golden coins—to recover this little scrap of cloth not fit to wear as a cloak. If some idiot wants it for an hour's work, he can have it."

Bjartr's large hand wrapped around the wrist at his neck. There was fear in his eyes, but there was more than enough strength in his thick, meaty fingers to pry him free.

"Edvard is our friend. I'll not hurt him, or his mother." Bjartr stared menacingly. If his childhood friend felt any fear, he did not show it. The Bear was not wise enough to know the difference.

Olev and Ragn were wise enough to say nothing.

"Edvard is off east, and will not return until the morning. Go with Olev. He'll show you what to do."

Bjartr, chastened, could only reply with the same response he held for every rebuke his friend had tossed at him for the last decade and more.

"Yes, Micu."

It was near dusk by the time Danor arrived at the path leading to Tora's small home. From the short wooden fence he saw the door opened wide, but no light spilled from the windows. This close to sunset, surely Tora would have the hearth fires lit and a lantern ready.

Horror crossing his face, Danor dropped the cloth-wrapped metal and pulled his hammer as he ran for the doorway. Three figures ran off into the woods behind the house as he approached, each in a different direction. Fear boiled up in his heart and fury rose in his ears as he stepped over the threshold.

A dagger, sharp and steel, met his arrival, gouging a slash in his shoulder before clattering against the doorframe and falling to the floor. Looking down, the smith saw the weapon glitter in the waning sunlight.

"You gallop like an ox, old man."

His gaze rose to a tall, slim man. A mask of black canvas covered his head but for two small slits for his eyes. He was refastening his breeches as he spoke. Around his waist, a fine belt of brown leather secured a sword. He drew it slowly.

"Keep your nose out of my affairs, if you care to keep it at all."

Danor hefted his hammer to advance, but the hooded man raised a finger and pointed to his left. A woman's foot—Tora's foot—peeked out from behind a doorjamb.

Before the smith could even look up, the man was already running. Danor threw his hammer, but it struck a post and spun away harmlessly.

Tora lay sprawled on the wooden floor, her skirts raised well above her knees. Small cuts littered her hands and arms, along with a few on her face. There was blood soiled into her dress, in her dark hair, across her lips.

Leaning down, Danor listened. She was breathing, though only barely. He used a thick, calloused thumb to raise one eyelid, but she did not respond.

He hefted her up and carried her into the back, placing her into the first bed he found. Whether it was Tora's or Edvard's, he neither knew nor cared.

"I am sorry, Tora, that I did not come sooner," he said.

The last hero of the nameless war, so slow as to be unable to protect against a single masked coward.

He would lament that fact later. First, he needed to tend her wounds. That skill, at least, he still retained. He only hoped it would be enough to keep her alive until her son returned, and he could go and ferret out the bastards who had done such a thing.

It had been a long, long time since Danor's hammer had tasted flesh instead of metal or wood. And it was hungry.

The small fire was set in the hearth beneath the pot. It would be hours before the meat was tender enough to try and feed the stew to Tora, and she slept soundly. She did not see the banner missing from above her mantel. Danor did, though.

Danor was a smith, not a hunter. That the hart had wandered too closely to Tora's home and was now being cooked as her supper—or breakfast, more likely—was the result of fortune and not skill. But he would not seek the vagabonds, hours gone and fled through the wood. He was headed for the marsh.

As he walked south and a bit west through the Reaching Wood, the hills that surrounded their village receded as though swallowed by the earth. Twice he nearly fell, and only the strong grip of his left hand let him hold himself up from sliding down towards the long-dead river that formed the blood of the marshes. The pain in his shoulder reminded him that though the bleeding had stopped, he would need to be careful as he walked.

She would be here, he knew. Unless the old tales lied, and the crone was not some ageless, undying thing, the witch would be there.

Gunda would have an answer for him.

Edvard stopped short when he saw the small fire ahead. He was taking the back ways home, small, winding paths that cut out much of the tedium of travelling from the village. Convenient as they were, only the boys of his generation knew of them. Bjartr would not be out so late without prodding, which meant that it was either Olev and Ragn, or…

"Micu," Edvard said dryly, looking down to see whose hand was holding a blade to his throat.

Micu stared his friend in the face for a long time before lowering his steel, and gesturing toward the fire.

"There was a…an incident."

Edvard narrowed sharp, dark eyes at the older boy.

"Someone attacked your mother's home."

Edvard took a deep breath, looking over Micu's shoulder to see Olen and Ragn laughing by their small fire. He turned, to head south and east towards his home.

A hand on his shoulder stopped him.

"She is all right, Edvard," said Micu. "We chased the fiends off into the night, and slew one of their number before the other escaped. Here," he held up a small pouch, "gold from the murderous bastard. Will you come with us to hunt down these villains?" Micu's green eyes flashed for a moment in the flickering firelight.

Edvard stared at him. He should care for his mother, not follow these fools on some errand to chase down men that had a whole night's start.

"Vard?"

Edvard's sharp, black eyes narrowed.

"Who," began Edvard, as calmly as he could, "is with my mother?"

"The smith, Danor, was arriving as we chased them off. If he has any wits about him, he will care for her until you return."

"Danor is an honorable man. He will stay," Edvard said thoughtfully, and sighed. "Two days. If after two days we find nothing, I am returning to my mother."

"Of course," said Micu, smiling broadly. Edvard looked down to notice the sheath at Micu's hip was empty. The short, slender sword he carried was something new. He did not bother to ask after the missing dagger, following his taller friend over to the fire. It was cold, and he was hungry.

"So, Vard. Let me tell you about the gold these men carried..."

It was well past midnight when Danor saw the small, orange glow at the foot of the massive oak. Such a tree should not have been able to grow so tall and lush there, if at all, yet there it was, and at its base was the shriveled woman he had come to see.

Gunda—if that was her name—had been a legend when Danor's grandfather was a boy. An old woman who lived alone in the marshes, who told the future as though it were past. She demanded little price for her wisdom, but for some, the horror of knowing the truth was payment enough.

Danor approached the small mound of earth around the oak's base. Had it been an island in the midst of a raging river, once? Or did it come after?

"A bit of both, dear boy," came a high, screeching voice from behind him. It sounded like someone trying to sharpen a horseshoe with a file. He blinked twice, shook his head, and turned.

"Oho," said the voice again. This time, his head did not feel like it would burst open. "Prettier than the last one, this one is."

The woman stood in a simple cloth shift that hung to her ankles. Her skin was pale—not green, like he had expected—and strands of white, fluffy hair descended from her balding scalp like pulled sheep's wool. Her nose curved slightly down towards her upper lip.

"Dark things has Danor done," cooed the crone, caressing the skull in her lap as though it was the scalp of an ill child or a listless lover. "Dark and shameful and needful. It is no wonder that he comes to Gunda for help."

He stared at her for a long moment, and then drew a deep breath, anxious to share the details he had hidden from everyone for two decades.

"Gunda does not want a confession, pretty man. She wants payment. Payment for visions is the bargain, as it was when your grandfather was a boy. Payment or…" she held up the skull like a trophy, "…recompense."

"And what if I believe nothing of your visions, crone?" His voice wavered, but only barely. Gunda smiled a near-toothless grin.

"If Danor did not believe, then Danor would not be here. He would be home at bed with his pretty wife, or teaching his strong, healthy son." She laughed then, and stared white, sightless eyes at the smith. Her tongue darted out to wet cracked lips in hunger.

"You know well enough that I have neither of those, woman."

"Ahh, but you might, before the day is out." Gunda laughed, and shook her head as she walked, slowly, to the stool she used as a seat. She slapped Danor's gnarled left hand away when he tried to help her down onto it.

"The woman will live, pretty man. You do not need to worry for her." She stared at him, those white eyes piercing into him. "Are you afraid of me, man?"

"Yes," Danor replied. "But only so far as a man with his wits is afraid of what he does not know."

"Good," came the crone's shriek, her voice booming through the small valley. Bird wings flapped all around as owls and worse tried to flee her.

"I am older than these marshes, lovely boy. I knew the river when she died. I can see more than you would like me to." She leaned forward, resting impossibly long fingers on her knee and dragging her shift just a little higher, like a woman trying to use her allure. "I ask again. Are you afraid?"

"Yes," said Danor. This time, he was truthful.

"Good," she whispered. "Then know this: there are no vengeful spirits here, come to take your bones and hammer them into blades and bowls and plowshares. Your friends are dead. Their iron is theirs no more. Better their wives and sons and daughters have it then it lies to rot and rust."

"But…"

"Gunda is not finished, boy." Spittle flew from her lips as she hissed at him, and then leaned back. "The woman will live. The spirits are quiet. But one problem remains."

"And what," he asked, "is that?"

"You, pretty man."

She reached those long, slender fingers behind her, and pulled out a small satchel. Shaking it twice, she sniffed at it, nodded, and tossed it at him. He caught it in his right hand, dropping the hammer he forgot he was carrying for protection. The crone grinned.

"Place this in your supper pot. Let it simmer until morning, and drink a full bowl when you wake. Feed some to the woman. It will help her heal."

"And your…payment?" Danor did not wish to know what she would come for if he tried not to pay her price.

"Leave a bowl out for me, with a lock of your beard in it." She winked, and grinned again. "For luck."

Danor's face showed his revulsion. Gunda was quick to correct him for it.

"Here stands a man who for twenty years has raided the graves of comrades he buried with his own hands, in order to get metal to keep their widows and orphans fed. He wants Gunda's help to find peace. One way or another, he will have Gunda's tongue, too."

She extended that sickly, purplish muscle down toward the skull in her hand, and laughed mightily.

"Go, man," she said, and tossed the skull to roll into the darkness surrounding the roots. "Gunda likes her venison hot."

The smith did not consider himself a wise man, but he was not foolish enough to remain any longer. He turned, bent to retrieve his hammer, and began the trudge up the slope that once made up the eastern bank of the river.

Gunda watched, smiling, and reached behind her. She examined the brown, shriveled thing, opened her mouth, and took a bite.

The sound reached Danor's ears. He was glad he did not stay to find out what she was eating.

Edvard was still shaking. After a full morning of searching, it was over so quickly, so suddenly, that he had not even had the chance to pull his axe from its harness before the men were dead.

Two men, older than Edvard and his friends by at least a dozen years, hunched over the carcass of a freshly slain bear. Micu shouted at them in rage, and by the time Bjartr fell on the larger man, Olev and Ragn already had knives in the smaller one's gut.

"Micu," Edvard finally said, when the others had cleaned off their blades. "Are these them?"

The taller boy—no, not boy. Each of them was past twenty summers. These were all men, and capable of killing, now, too. The tallest and eldest among them rose to full height, and thrust his weapon into the ground.

"Yes, these are the bastards," he spat, and tossed a sack to the ground. Coins of silver and gold spilled out onto the soil between them. "Paid good coin to rob and slay."

"But for what, Micu?" Edvard asked. "We have nothing anyone could want."

"We have pride, Vard. And we live." Micu knelt to tie up the sack. "They did not wipe us out in the war, as they had hoped. Now they finish the job."

"*Who* will?" Edvard's voice was angry. "There are less than a hundred folk in our village. The people that killed our fathers are so few as to not even merit a name. What use could they have for revenge?"

Micu took a deep breath. "The Ingrii," he said, as though the name would jog a memory for his friend. "Or rather, a faction of them. They recruited our fathers, in the war. Their battle was over some inheritance of land. Two brothers decided to fight over a stretch of land, and we were caught in the middle. Luckily they called a truce before the whole village was killed. We have your father to thank for that."

"And now they're after us again?" Edvard's voice had the familiar ring that told Micu he thought him a liar.

"Not anymore," said Micu. "Their failure should end their seeking."

"Good," replied Edvard. "Then let us get home."

"Aye," chimed Ragn. "But first, a drink!"

Edvard would not deny that he needed one.

Danor woke with a start to the sound of a spoon clattering in the bottom of an empty wooden bowl. His blue eyes darted around the unfamiliar surroundings as he stood from the chair in which he had slumbered.

Tora's house. Of course. He had returned at full dark, added the herbs to the stew, and sat watch over Tora until he could no longer keep his eyes open. Now, as he awoke, he saw the bed was empty, and rushed out of the room.

There, sitting at the small table where she took her meals, was Tora. Her bowl was empty, and she looked satisfied. The cuts on her face were nearly gone, and those on her arms looked to be healing well.

Perhaps Gunda's satchel of herbs worked after all.

"Good morning, Danor." Tora sat upright, and though she still had bruises, she seemed to be in little pain. The smith smiled meekly.

"I am glad to see you well, Tora." She had always been too beautiful for him to look at for very long. He turned away, and saw the gouged wood where her assailant's dagger had struck. His eyes fell to the floor, and to the dagger tucked in the corner by the door. Danor squinted, and knelt to lift the weapon.

Its pommel was familiar, and the guard, if he remembered right, should have a nock in it right…there. Mikkel carried that dagger until the day he died. When his son turned four, Danor had given the boy his father's knife. It was a ritual that he had kept with all of the boys of the village. There were so few of them, and none knew their fathers beyond tales at their mothers' knees. To have something metal, something real, from a grown man who knew their fathers, was the most he could give them.

"Tora," he called, "will you be well enough if I head to the tavern for a spell? I want to ask Kaja for more herbs for you."

At the tavern, he was likely to find some of the younger boys.

Micu, son of Mikkel, had much to answer for, but not before Danor left a bowl of stew at the rear door.

"Thank you, Kaja." Micu beamed as he handed the buxom young woman a gold piece, and drank deeply of the mead she handed him. The girl smiled, slipped the coin into her bodice, and winked as she walked away.

"You see that, boys?" His green eyes flashed as he looked to each of his companions. "Silver eases roads, but gold helps hearts. If we can earn more, we'll each be wed by harvest."

"Earn more how, Micu?" Olev's face was skeptical. "Trade is slow, and the mines won't pay nearly this well."

"Well," said Micu, leaning forward to share his plan with his fellows, "we can take up arms with a faction of the Ingrii."

"Like father did?" Bjartr's eyes were wide, sad things, as he remembered a father he had never met. Tears welled and he sniffed, looking away before his friends could see him verge on weeping.

"Aye," Micu said. "They pay well for stout warriors. And we have no prospects here."

"No, Micu." Edvard was angry, and the ale had made his tongue loose. "I'll not leave my mother to starve while I head off to be a fool hero. Our fathers did enough of that for all of us."

"But, Vard…"

"No!" Edvard's shout cut him off as he rose to stand. He stumbled, drunk, toward the door, and right into the broad chest of Danor the smith.

"You," he slurred, pointing up at the larger man. The tip of his finger brushed Danor's beard. "Why are you not caring for my mother?"

Danor looked down at him and sighed. "I see the young wolf has learned to drink." He leaned back as he spoke, the smell more than he was willing to bear after such a long night. "I came to ask Kaja for some things to aid your mother. And why are *you* not home caring for her?"

Edvard straightened. "My mother was attacked." He waved towards his childhood friends. "We went out to find her attackers. Micu led us to them."

"Ahh," said Danor. The smith's eyes narrowed as the group of young men rose from their table. Bjartr had grown even larger since the last time he saw him. He stood nearly a head taller than Danor, and was broader, too. His hand went to his hammer as he saw Olev and Ragn reach for the knives at their belts. "Micu led you, did he?" He placed a hand on Edvard's shoulder, patted twice, and nudged him towards the door.

"Run home, boy. You'll not want to see this."

Edvard stood, silent, as Danor slowly pulled the short, heavy hammer from his belt. Micu was already pulling his sword.

"Old man," Micu cautioned, "have a care what you say."

Danor shook his head. "I'll say what I wish. A man earns that right, when he acts like a man and not some craven coward."

"I will…"

"You will do nothing, boy." Danor turned his hammer in his hand. "You assault a woman of this village, steal something her dead husband bled for, lie to her son, and then challenge all our honor by drawing steel here."

Ragn and Olev started forward, then stopped. On each of their shoulders was one of Bjartr's large hands, pinning them like mice beneath a bear's paws.

"Micu," said Bjartr, "what did you do?"

His friend turned to face him, cheeks beginning to grow red. "I did what men do, Bear. I took what I could to gain what I wanted."

When he turned back, he was nose to beard with the elder smith. He did not see Edvard pass through the door and begin running home.

"Boy," came the voice he had known all his life, "a man works. He sacrifices to feed his family. He bleeds to protect his kinfolk and his neighbors. At times, he does shameful things, but never because he chooses to."

"And in doing what is needful, his shame is lessened."

"What do you know, old man?" Micu took a step back, and held his sword out to the smith's throat. "You're a coward that survived a war no one else saw the end of."

"I am the man who buried your father, Micu. He was never the bravest of men, but he found death on his feet." Danor shook his head solemnly. "And he was no murderer."

"Micu?" Bjartr's voice was a whisper.

"Yes, Bear. Those men did nothing to us."

The largest man's hands tightened, and Olev slumped unconscious to the floor. Ragn struggled for a moment, and then fell atop his friend. Bjartr turned away and strode from the tavern.

"Micu," Danor said. "Put the blade down. I don't want to hurt anyone else."

"Hurt me?" Micu looked around, but the tavern was empty. Even Kaja had left. Only he and Danor remained. "An old smith with only one hand, who was not brave enough to fight with a spear and armor, is going t—"

Steel cracked against Micu's jaw as Danor's hammer struck, and he fell, limp, at the smith's feet.

Lifting him by his belt, Danor carried the boy outside, dropped him, and continued on his way.

"Hand me that ingot, Vard."

Edvard scampered across the dirt floor to grab the bar of iron. He was an eager learner, if a bit too excitable.

"Danor?"

"Yes, Edvard." More questions. This time, he was sure, about how many times to pump the bellows.

He was sure, but also wrong.

"It's been three weeks, now. Why won't you tell me how you knew it was Micu that…"

Danor interrupted him, as he always did. "How is your mother?"

"She is well," said Edvard. "Far better than Kaja would have guessed. How did you—"

"Secrets, boy." The smith tapped his temple with his hammer. He took the slab of metal from the younger man with his left hand. Those fingers, long dead, were responding better to his commands. More of Gunda's magic, perhaps. He did not care.

"She asks after you, sometimes."

Danor smiled, but he did not mention Tora again. "Micu forgot his dagger when he threw it at me." His voice was low, and sad. "There are a great many weapons in the village that only I remember."

There were other things only he remembered. Like the war. The last reminders were gone, now: the banner was taken, Viccam's sword was hammered into something useful. Even his hand was returning to use.

Lifting the ingot towards his face, the smith took a long breath.

"This was Varg's axe, once," Danor explained, gazing at the metal reverently. "A massive man—Bjartr is smaller than his uncle, if you can believe it. He swung it in one hand, like a twig. Until last month, it was a pot in Sohvi's kitchen."

Edvard's head tilted, like a child hearing a new language. He would understand, in time. He always asked the right questions.

"And what will it be tomorrow?"

Danor smiled.

"I don't know, boy." He thrust its end into the coals. "Let us find out together."

∾

THE BLUE CORPSE CORPS

Jim C. Hines

HALF THE GOBLINS UNDER Jig's command died over the course of the battle.

Given that goblin casualties were usually double that amount, and more importantly, that Jig himself was in the half that survived, he wasn't going to complain.

The rest of the survivors showed no such restraint. They had gathered in the shade of some stunted pine trees on the way back to the lair. Jig sat a short distance from the others, dumping rocks and dirt from his boot as he listened to their grumbling.

"It's not natural," said Valkaf, a younger warrior who had lost her left ear during the fighting. "What do we care about renegade human wizards and outlaws? Let the humans kill each other. Just as long as they stay out of our tunnels."

"The only reason the king hasn't sent his army to kill every goblin in the lair is because of the treaty," Jig pointed out.

Valkaf laughed, a nasty sound that brought back memories of Jig's younger days. Jig had been a small, scrawny muckworker, and had spent most of his childhood learning how to survive the torments of the bigger goblins...which included pretty much everyone. But those lessons had served him well as a small, scrawny adult.

"So instead, we do the human king's dirty work," Valkaf said. "Hunting his criminals."

"Only the ones who hide on our mountain," Jig mumbled.

Heat wafted from Jig's right shoulder as Smudge, his pet fire-spider, reacted to the growing hostility in Valkaf's words. Not that Jig needed the warning. The other goblins had already begun to split into two groups. Most gathered by Valkaf, the only exceptions being Braf, who appeared oblivious, and Skalk, who had taken several nasty wounds during the fighting.

Jig couldn't blame them. He was the one who had signed the treaty with King Wendel, naively hoping it would end the fighting between goblins and humans. Instead, it had simply shifted the war to a different front, one for which goblins were ill-prepared: politics.

Pages and pages of obligations. Taxes to be paid, and duties to be performed...including the defense of goblin territory against all outlaws. To neglect that duty was to violate the treaty. So the fighting had continued, only the goblins now paid taxes for the privilege. They were tired of it, and none moreso than Jig himself.

Braf scratched the inside of his nostril with his little finger. "At least we got to burn a human camp. And I got to punch a horse."

One of Valkaf's supporters laughed. "That was no horse, you idiot. That was a donkey."

"I thought it was a cow," said another.

Braf's expression was a carefully crafted mask of vacant confusion. "Well, it was a *big* cow."

It was enough to break the tension. The goblins began to relax, boasting about their triumphs over the wizard and his magically cursed warriors who had refused to die. Jig caught Braf's eye long enough to give him a tiny nod of thanks.

"Hey, Skalk stopped whining!" Valkaf kicked the wounded goblin in the side. "Good timing. I'm hungry."

"We'll be back at the lair before nightfall," Jig said. "We could bring him back and let Golaka roast him properly, with that spider egg jelly she makes—"

"I'm hungry now," Valkaf shouted. "Unless *you* want to haul his carcass up the mountainside? Let's build a fire and toss him in."

"Save me some palm meat!"

"I want a leg. No, wait. How bruised are the arms?"

Jig's mouth watered. He was hungry after the battle, and—

Heat seared Jig's cheek. Smudge was growing hotter with every passing moment. The palm-sized spider paced a tight circle on Jig's leather shoulder pad. When one hairy leg brushed Jig's ear, it was hot enough to raise blisters.

Jig tugged the shoulder pad further from his face, nearly dislodging his spectacles in his haste. He perked his good ear and searched the woods, but he neither saw nor heard anything dangerous. So what was Smudge reacting to?

"Looks like one of the humans already started in on him." Valkaf pointed to a nasty bite on Skalk's shoulder. The blue skin had turned black, and blood oozed from the wound. "Let Jig have that part."

"This might not be a good idea," said Jig. He stepped closer to the body. A tiny wave of red fire rippled over Smudge's back in response. "I've only seen Smudge this scared a few other times."

Braf hesitated. "But Skalk's so well-tenderized from the fighting."

Jig backed away. He didn't bother to argue further. They wouldn't listen. They might follow his plans in battle, because they knew he was good at surviving, but this was *food*.

Braf scowled and rubbed his stomach. "I'd better not. I had some bad dwarf yesterday, and my stomach hasn't recovered. If I eat Skalk, my trousers will regret it before the day's over."

Jig's stomach gurgled as the others began roasting Skalk's body. He scowled at Smudge. "You'd better be right about this..."

Despite Smudge's fears, they reached the lair without incident. Jig relaxed somewhat as he left the moonlit sky for the security of the obsidian tunnels. His warriors exchanged boasts with the guards as they passed into the wide, sour-smelling cavern which was home to more than two hundred goblins.

Green muckfires burned around the edge of the cavern. The scent of fresh meat made his mouth water as he passed Golaka's kitchen, but that smell was soon overpowered by muck smoke, goblin sweat, and fouler things.

Jig kept his head down as he made his way toward a smaller cave at the back of the lair where goblins fought for sleeping space. He claimed an old blanket in a bumpy corner nearest the crack connecting this cave to the lair.

Sleep refused to come. Images from the day's battle blurred through his mind. Groaning human warriors who refused to stay dead. The memories blurred into fights from months and years before. No matter how many battles Jig survived, there was always another enemy. Dragons and pixies, humans and orcs, and of course his fellow goblins. He had survived for years on trickery, cleverness, and luck, but it wouldn't last forever.

The chief's voice echoed through the lair, jolting Jig from his memories. "Where is that runt Jig?"

The other goblins in the sleeping cave moved away as Jig groaned and stood. Whatever the problem, they wanted nothing to do with it. Smudge grew warmer as Jig trudged into the main lair.

"What is that?" Trok demanded, jabbing his sword toward the entrance where Braf, Valkaf, and one of the guards were fighting a battered goblin.

Jig adjusted his spectacles. "That's...that's Skalk. But he died."

"Does he look dead?" Trok was a fierce figure of a goblin, strong and well-armed. He had taken to filing his fangs lately. The tips were white and needle-sharp. "What happened to him?"

"We...kind of ate him. The other goblins did, I mean."

Skalk looked like a rag doll that had been devoured by tunnel-cats, then hacked back up. One leg was missing; the other ended at the knee. His left hand was gone as well. He was filthy, and the fingers of his right hand were bloody. He must have dragged himself back to the lair.

Blackened skin cracked and oozed as he fought the other goblins. The few uncooked areas of skin were a sickly blue-gray. Jig could see a whitish film covering his eyes...just like the human zombies they had fought before.

"If you're hungry and want to eat one of your wounded, that's one thing," Trok yelled. "But *kill him first!*"

"We did!" Jig protested. "I mean, he was!"

Skalk groaned as Braf rammed a long spear through his ribs. It didn't slow him down. He reached out, trying to pull himself along the spear toward Braf even as Valkaf hacked off his other hand with her axe.

"The humans we fought were the same way." Jig swallowed. "When that human bit Skalk, it must have infected him somehow. You'll have to burn him or cut him into pieces to stop him."

Trok pursed his lips. "Warriors who don't die."

"They die," Jig said. "It just doesn't slow them down. They keep—Oh, no." He recognized the calculating look on Trok's face.

By now, Valkaf had grabbed the other end of the spear. She and Braf lifted Skalk off the ground. He let out a confused moan as his body slowly upended. His head swung to and fro over the floor. The stumps of his arms reached uselessly for the spear.

"Imagine an army of goblins who can't be killed," Trok said.

"Because they're already dead!" But it was too late. Others had overheard.

One of the closest goblins sprinted toward Skalk. "I want to be unkillable!" He tried to shove his arm into Skalk's mouth, but Braf kicked him away. More closed in, pushing and yelling in their eagerness to become zombies.

"You have to stop them," Jig said. "They'll attack anything, even their own kind. They won't obey orders. They don't care who's in charge. All they do is kill and eat."

"So they'll be no different than most goblin warriors," Trok said. He waded into the middle of the crowd, tossing the other goblins aside. He started to speak, and then his gaze fixed on Valkaf.

Skalk had gouged her arm in the fighting, but the wound wasn't bleeding like a normal injury. Instead, the cut oozed dark, mudlike blood...just like Skalk. Valkaf glanced down as though surprised.

"You're like him, aren't you?" Trok tapped Skalk's head with the toe of his boot.

"But she wasn't bitten," Jig protested. His stomach tightened. Valkaf *had* eaten plenty of Skalk the night before. No wonder Smudge had warned him against it.

"Behold the first of my zombie warriors," Trok shouted. "We'll call them Trok's Trudging Troops! The Blue Corpse Corps! An unstoppable army of blue death!"

"That's true." Valkaf's words were slightly slurred. She dropped her end of the spear, slammed her axe through Skalk's neck, then turned toward Trok. "You can't stop me, can you?"

"Oh, dung," Jig whispered.

Valkaf raised her bloody axe. "I challenge Trok for leadership of the goblin lair!"

Goblins had no rules regarding challenges for leadership. Indeed, often the challenge wasn't even announced until after the challenger finished stabbing the former chief in the back.

Valkaf charged. Trok swore, grabbed the nearest goblin, and flung him into Valkaf's path. She struck the poor goblin aside, but doing so tied up her axe long enough for Trok to draw his own weapon, a two-handed sword with brass spikes on the hilt and crossguard.

Jig pushed his way to the back of the crowd, where he could watch the fight through a protective layer of goblin spectators. Trok had already hit Valkaf twice, cutting her left arm and stabbing her through the gut. Neither wound affected her as far as Jig could see.

Jig frowned as he watched Valkaf fight. Against the humans, she had been vicious and gleeful, fighting with her own unique and terrifying style. Now that joy was gone, and her attacks were as straightforward as those of a child. Straightforward but powerful, and she showed no sign of weariness.

Trok backed away, earning jeers from the watching goblins, but Jig saw what Trok was doing. Every step he retreated brought him closer to one of the shallow muck pits, burning with foul-smelling green flame. If swords wouldn't stop Valkaf, fire would.

Heat pulled Jig's attention to Smudge, and then to the four goblins beyond who had broken away from the crowd. They gathered around the body of the hapless goblin Trok had flung into the path of Valkaf's axe.

Braf saw them as well. "Stop that," he shouted. "Wait until Golaka has the chance to cook him. And save some for the rest of us!" He started to reach for one of the goblins.

All four snarled, and Braf jumped away. Blood and worse dripped from the goblins' fangs, and they shared the same vacant, hungry expressions Jig remembered all too well from the human zombies.

Jig didn't move. He tried not to breathe until the goblins slowly turned their attention back to the corpse.

"Who starts with the head?" Braf whispered, sidling closer to Jig. "Ears are a chewy treat, sure, but there's so much better meat on the body. Brains are too slimy for my taste."

"The dead humans were the same," Jig said. "Unkillable, but they kept stopping to eat the corpses, especially the brains."

It had been a good thing, too. Ultimately, Jig had laid out five of his fallen goblins and waited for the dead humans to feed. Once they were all gathered together, it had been simple enough to encircle them in flames.

But these goblins were more alert than the zombies Jig had fought. Maybe they hadn't completely succumbed to whatever magic sickness they had eaten with Skalk's body, but all too soon they would be the rotted, mindless killers Jig had faced before.

The zombies snarled again, but this time their hostility was aimed inward. One jabbed a knife into another's chest, distracting him long enough for the first goblin to sneak in and snatch a bite to eat. They were like tunnel cats fighting over a meal.

"What do we do?" Braf asked.

"They're not the only ones we have to worry about." Jig searched the crowd. Where were the other survivors of his last battle? They would all be dying from the inside out as the magic took them.

The commotion was attracting attention away from Trok and Valkaf. One of the younger goblins pointed to the zombie with the knife in his chest. "Hey, there are more!" Before Jig could react, the young goblin ran toward the zombies. "Bite me, too!"

Jig caught Braf's eye. Braf inclined his head ever so slightly. As the goblin sprinted past, Braf extended the butt of his spear. The goblin hit the floor with a crack, but it was too late. Others were closing in, hoping either to be bitten or to eat the zombies, whatever it took to become undead.

Cheers broke out on the far side of the lair. Jig glimpsed Valkaf stumbling forward, bathed in green fire and missing an arm, but still fighting. If one zombie was giving Trok this much trouble, more would pretty well wipe out the lair.

"I've been bitten!" A gleeful goblin waved his arm in the air, showing off two bloody fang marks. "I'm unkillable! I'm—"

Jig stabbed him in the back. The other goblins froze. The one Jig had stabbed looked down, gurgled, and fell. Two of the zombies immediately broke away and began to feed on his body.

"Maybe he wasn't bitten hard enough?" one goblin suggested.

Braf punched him in the head.

Jig raised his voice. "These zombies can't make you unkillable. They're not...um...they're not ripe yet."

Braf sniffed. "They smell pretty ripe to me."

"Help me get the zombies to the kitchen," Jig said. "We can keep them in Golaka's slaughter pit until they're ready." The pit was as secure as any dungeon, both by nature of the pit itself and because anyone who escaped still had to get past Golaka.

"How do we get them into the pit without getting bitten?" Braf asked.

Jig glanced at the two corpses. He grabbed a sword from another goblin, jumped in, and swung, severing the closer corpse's head. "Jab the head with your spear and toss it into the pit. They'll follow."

"Gross." But Braf obeyed. He returned a short time later, wiping goo from his spear. "Golaka isn't happy about this. I told her it was your idea."

Jig grimaced. One more confrontation he wasn't looking forward to, but at least the immediate threat had passed. Over on the far side of the lair, the fighting was finally coming to a close.

Valkaf had lost her weapon and three of her limbs. What followed wasn't so much a battle as simple butchery.

He reached up to pet Smudge, who was beginning to cool now that the zombies were gone.

"I've changed my mind," Trok yelled, wiping sweat from his face. "Kill every last one of those walking corpses."

Good. Let Trok finish cleaning up this mess. Jig would return to the sleeping cave and—

"And anyone who could have been exposed!" Trok added.

Anyone who could have been...Jig's chest tightened. He looked at Braf.

As one, they turned and fled.

"This is the stupidest plan in the history of plans."

"Shut up," whispered Jig.

"It's not even a plan." Braf picked at the grime on the floor. "Of all the places to hide, you picked Golaka's slaughter pit?"

"Nobody's found us yet, have they?" Jig rubbed his knee, which had been badly bruised from jumping into the pit. Fortunately, one of the zombies had broken his fall. They were still squabbling over the brain of their last victim, but that wouldn't last long.

"And how do we get out?" Braf stabbed a finger toward the faint green light overhead. "The walls are too greasy to climb."

"I'm working on it!" Jig leaned back, banging his head against the rock. Braf was right, of course. It was a stupid plan. It hadn't even been a plan. More like blind panic. Eventually either Golaka would find them and toss them into her pot, or else Trok would figure out where they'd gone. At least Golaka would be quick, and she generally kept her knives sharp, so it shouldn't hurt as much...

In the end, it was Trok who peered down into the pit. "Not so clever after all, are you?"

"We didn't eat Skalk," Jig protested. "Neither of us has been bitten. We're not going to turn into zombies!"

"I'm not taking that risk. You saw what happened with Valkaf."

He rubbed his shoulder, which looked like it had taken a nasty cut from her axe. "The last thing I need is an undead Jig walking around causing trouble with his zombie spider."

Jig's heart pounded so hard he could barely breathe. Braf's spear had broken in the fall, so he couldn't reach Trok. Jig had his knife. He could try to throw it at Trok, but that still left them trapped in the pit. Not to mention he had never had much luck with thrown weapons. On the other hand, it wasn't like things could get much worse.

Trok disappeared before he could try. A short time later, another body tumbled into the pit, landing with a sickly crunch. Several others followed, corpses and zombies both. Smudge flared to light, illuminating the groaning survivors from Jig's last battle.

"Now what?" Braf muttered.

"I don't know." Jig sagged against the wall. He had fought more battles than he could count, but nothing ever changed. Kill the humans, and the goblin zombies tried to eat you. Get rid of them, and Trok sentenced you to death. It never ended.

"Get that filth out of my slaughter pit!" Golaka's shout echoed through the cavern.

"We will." Trok peeked back into the pit. "We were going to burn them all, but it was stinking up the lair. Easier to leave 'em down there to rot away."

Jig threw his dagger. It missed Trok by a wide margin, then clattered back down into the pit, nearly striking Jig's foot.

"Stupidest plan in history," Braf repeated.

Jig nudged Smudge's fuzzy thorax, trying to scoot him up the wall to safety. Smudge kept climbing halfway up the pit, then scurrying back down to stare at Jig, as though wondering what was wrong that Jig wasn't following.

"Will you stop worrying about the stupid spider?" Braf snapped. The zombies were licking their fingers and fangs as they finished off the last of the corpses. One drooled as he studied Braf, who shook his broken spear in response. "Eat Jig first. Everyone knows his brain is too big."

"But Braf's meatier," Jig countered.

"Eat," said the closest zombie, slurring the word. She started toward Braf, who clubbed her back with the butt of the spear.

"Even if you eat us, you'll still rot down here," Jig pointed out. Flies had already settled on the zombies. Normally Smudge would have been in paradise, pouncing from the wall to cook the hapless insects, but he wasn't going anywhere near those goblins. "There won't be anything left but maggots and bones."

"That's your plan?" Braf asked. "You're trying to reason with the dead goblins?"

Jig sniffed the air. Over the putrefaction of the zombies, the scent of cooking meat filled the pit. The spices made Jig's eyes water. Golaka must have overspiced the meat, trying to overpower the rot from the pit.

The others smelled it as well. Undead or not, they were still goblin enough to prefer Golaka's cooking. They pressed against the wall, arms stretched upward.

"Probably leftover bear," Braf guessed. "Or maybe leftovers from the hunters who died killing the bear."

Jig's stomach gurgled. On top of everything else, he hadn't had a decent meal in at least a day. He had fought more battles than he could remember, and *this* was how he would die? Hungry and miserable, devoured by the rotting remnants of his own warriors? Meanwhile, with Jig gone, the treaty with the humans would follow. Trok would drag the goblins into all-out war within weeks, if not days.

"I know that look," said Braf.

Jig wiped sweat from his nose, then replaced his spectacles. "Hey, Golaka?" He called again, trying to pitch his voice so it wouldn't carry beyond the kitchen. After a third attempt, he heard footsteps approaching, and Golaka peered into the pit.

Golaka was the largest, strongest goblin in the lair. She could have killed Trok one-handed, but she had no interest in being chief. Her straggly hair had thinned in recent years, and her face was like cracked blue leather. She wore a heavy apron so stained it probably carried a meal's worth of food all by itself.

"You know the rules, Jig," she called. "If the food can't keep quiet, I dump the grease pot on its head."

"Wait!" Jig tried to force his voice down to a less frightened pitch. "You know you can't eat these goblins. They'll be rotting for weeks. It will stink up the whole kitchen. The smell will probably even get into your food."

Golaka said nothing. But she wasn't dumping hot grease on his head, which was a hopeful sign.

"Get me out of here, and I promise I'll—Ouch!" Jig rubbed his arm. "Get Braf and me out of here, and I'll take care of the zombies."

"How do you intend to do that?"

"I'll need you to cook something for me. One of your specialties..."

Jig crept out of the kitchen, both hands clutching a covered clay bowl. The buzz of voices died down as the nearest goblins noticed him.

Braf followed, clutching five leather leashes with both hands. Each leash was secured to the neck of a zombie, and all five strained to reach Jig.

He heard Trok's roar from the far side of the lair. Goblins split a path as Trok stomped toward Jig, flanked by armed guards. "I don't believe it! How in the name of all that's edible does a scrawny, miserable runt like you survive these things?"

A flicker of anger stirred in Jig's gut, or maybe that was just hunger. He straightened.

"You thought you'd try to turn the zombies on me, eh?" Trok eyed Braf and the leashed zombies. "You know they'll rip you apart before they even reach me."

"You think it's an accident I'm still alive?" Jig asked softly. "This scrawny runt has survived more battles in this past year than you have in your entire life."

Trok's eye narrowed. "Sure. Battles against *humans*."

"And orcs. And hobgoblins. Even a dragon." Technically, someone else had killed the dragon, but Trok didn't know that.

"That will make it more impressive when I run you through."

"I'm not scared of you." To Jig's amazement, it was the truth. He had fought too many opponents, survived too many times, and Trok simply didn't frighten him anymore.

Trok pulled out his sword.

All right, maybe Jig was a little scared. Mostly though, he was just tired. "I challenge you for leadership of the lair!"

Trok laughed. "You don't even have a weapon."

Jig yanked the cover from the bowl. Steam rose from the red-gray sludge within. He flung the contents at Trok, doing his best to avoid splashing anyone else. Especially himself.

Trok wiped his face. His skin was a vivid blue, but the burns weren't serious. He raised his sword. "If you think hot gruel is enough to—"

"It's not gruel," Jig interrupted. "It's pudding. Minced bear brain pudding, spiced with fire-spider eggs."

Braf released the leashes.

Smudge seared Jig's ear as the zombies rushed past on either side, but they ignored Jig completely.

"I survive because I'm smarter than you," Jig muttered. He doubted anyone heard over the screams.

The next battle came a month later. This time it was a band of human mercenaries, led by a young human in garish colors. Jig popped a fried lizard tail into his mouth and crunched happily as he watched them approach.

"How long until the attack?" asked Braf, settling in beside him.

Jig offered him a lizard tail. "Don't ask me. You're the chief."

"Don't remind me." There was just enough hostility in Braf's voice to make Jig scoot sideways. Jig's reign as chief had been the shortest in goblin history. He had named Braf the new chief before Trok's blood was even cool.

In a way, Jig owed Trok thanks. If not for Trok, it would be Jig himself down on the mountainside preparing for this battle. Instead, Jig got to watch from a small outcropping high above the lair, protected by rocks and gnarled trees.

The mercenaries reached the mouth of the lair. Jig heard shouts from within.

"There they are." Braf pointed to a handful of goblins running down a trail. Each carried a small, goo-filled bladder which they flung at the humans.

"We should find a better way to throw those," Jig said as the makeshift missiles exploded, splattering cold pudding on the mercenaries. Slings would be too messy. "Maybe handheld catapults?"

One goblin took an arrow to the stomach, and the rest scattered, earning taunts from the humans.

Braf snickered. "They think the goblins are running from *them*."

Jig could already see the first goblin zombie shambling up the path. "They look pretty well-preserved."

"Keeping them up in a colder cave was a good idea."

"So were the spiders." Jig had gathered all the spiders he could find, releasing them into the cave where the zombies were leashed and guarded. No fire-spiders; the cave was too cold for them anyway. But there were plenty of others to help protect the zombies from flies and other insects.

Jig reached up to pet Smudge. Trok might not have thought things through, but Jig had. Enthusiasm at joining the living dead had died out once the rest of the lair saw a few zombies in more advanced states of rot. Few were willing to risk their important bits falling off.

One zombie stopped to eat the fallen goblin while the rest closed in on the mercenaries, who had stopped laughing.

"You're sure they kept enough pudding in reserve to get them all back to the cave?" Braf asked.

Jig shrugged. If not, each of the zombie keepers carried a

pointed skull-cracking hammer to use on whoever was responsible for forgetting. "They'll find a way to lure the zombies back."

"It won't last forever, you know."

"I know." Goblin plans rarely did. Sooner or later a zombie would escape, or one of the keepers would get careless, or the humans would find a way to destroy the zombies. When that happened, Jig would deal with it.

But until then, he intended to sit back, eat a few more lizard tails, and enjoy the well-earned rest.

∾

Maggy —

Have wonderful
journeys!

Rosemary
Sue

ASHES OF THE BONFIRE QUEEN

Rosemary Jones

RED MOLLY SPUN WIDDERSHINS in the ash and cinders as the trains rumbled blindly past. She trailed her fingers along the bare ground. Above her head, the smoke of the yard veiled the cracked yellow face of the moon.

Confusion, disorientation, and obfuscation, all this she whirled into the dirt between the train tracks. Then, carefully moving so the darkening moon remained on her left and never crossed her path on the right, she readied herself for a jump into the next empty boxcar.

Beyond the barbed wire and high steel fence, the silver hounds howled their frustration.

Red Molly smiled. She was lost to the robot dogs' red eyes and sensitive ears, hidden with the clanking heart of the freight yard. Magic hedged by metal, moving metal, ruined the perfection of their fine plastic noses and disguised her scent from the sharp-toothed seekers.

The clack on the tracks alerted her to the passing of a wooden boxcar. Red Molly spat on her shadow to pin a bit of herself in the coal dust, another tactic to baffle her pursuers, and then launched herself through the air in a swirl of black lace skirts and silken scarves.

She misjudged her own strength or the desperation driving her flying spell, soaring like some giant bird straight into the boxcar. As soon as she crossed the threshold of its door and lost sight of the moon, her magic broke, shattered by the shadows within. She fell from her flight, fighting against gravity and twisting like a cat in midair to keep herself upright.

Her scarlet boot heels struck the wooden floorboards with a bone-jarring thump. Red Molly lost her balance and slid across the boxcar's floor, skidding like a child on an icy pavement, slipping towards another open door on the opposite side. She flung herself down to anchor her body inside the boxcar. Her painted fingernails scrabbled in the dirty straw littering the floor as she tried to slow her slide.

A scarred hand reached out of the shadows and caught the collar of her leather jacket. Yanked back to safety and nearly choked by her rescuer, Red Molly rolled herself upright and shook her long braids out of her eyes.

Her rescuer stared at her.

She met his stare with her own even gaze. His face was as thin as a boy's but he had a man's beard shadowing his high cheekbones and a man's width to his shoulders.

"Are you one of hers?" asked the young man, with an old man's voice full of rust and tar smoke. "One of the Bonfire Queen's?"

Given her plethora of scarlet scarves and the crimson flames adorning the back of her leather jacket, Red Molly doubted he'd believe that she followed the Shadow Boys.

"I know the Bonfire Queen," she admitted.

"They say that she burned inside her own spells." He sounded sad, but Red Molly didn't know if that meant he mourned the Queen or regretted the missed chance to kill her. Numerous factions jostled for power in this war. The ragged man squatting on his heels before her wore the blue canvas trousers of a soldier but his faded orange vest once belonged to a prison. Red Molly knew jail garb when she saw it.

She'd heard the county's POW camp had been scoured by floodwaters a few days before. According to all the official broadcasts, no escapees survived the raging of the Wide Muddy. But the train tracks ran perilously close to the river's banks and the announcers on the static-choked radio rarely told the truth.

"There's plenty of rumors swirling through the air," she compromised.

Then, because she liked to have control of any situation, she said, "I call myself Red Molly. Do you admit to a name?"

"Turtle," he answered, which meant he wasn't one of the Nameless Sons of the Rose. But blue trousers constituted part of many uniforms, everyone from the North Wind's Wards to the Lost Dogs.

She waited to see if he would tell a little more, but Turtle scooted further into the shadows. He settled into a slump, swaying comfortably with the movement of the boxcar, seemingly as calm as his namesake.

"You riding south?" she asked.

He nodded, a movement that she could barely see in the dark.

Red Molly tried a couple more questions but got no answers. It seemed as if he'd spent all his words for the night.

So she scooted herself as close to the open boxcar door as possible, aware of Turtle in the shadows but also watching the barbed wire and broken-down fences bordering abandoned backyards. Since they'd left the main station, she'd sensed no further pursuit, but she didn't want to be taken unawares.

The train rattled out of the city, leaving behind the shining lights and the glass towers occupied by the men with mechanical hearts. The stars filled the sky and ran down to edge of the black fields. Once or twice Red Molly heard the far off barking of a flesh-and-blood dog or it might have been a coyote hunting rabbits.

The rhyme of the wheels singing over the steel tracks became a lullaby urging her to sleep. But every time her head drifted down, she jerked it back up. Turtle never stirred from his spot on the center of the boxcar.

Time drifted, like wood smoke out of an autumn fire, and she lost sense of herself in the wider night, until she was dreaming of battles fought in sputtering flames amid rolling houses of black metal.

The smell of hot mud and rotting vegetation woke her the next morning. The air blowing into the boxcar weighed humid and heavy on her tongue, laced with the acid tang of the train's smoke.

A dawn mist, pink as the blood spray from a fresh wound,

oozed out of the swamp bubbling below the embankment. The train ran on its bed of steel and concrete, just high enough out of the wet to keep the tracks clean. Something green and scaled slid off a half-submerged log and swam away, powered by the sweeping strokes of a powerful tail.

"When did we cross?" Red Molly asked her boxcar companion.

"Just after the moon set," Turtle answered, raising his head from where it rested on his knees. He rubbed red-rimmed eyes with one grimy hand. "You could see frost on the field stubble one moment, glittering white in the moonlight. Then the dark came and the wind whirled up, full of green swamp." Consciously or unconsciously, the rhythm of his words matched the clack of the wheels turning below them, making his story into an incantation of location.

"Border is shifting again," she said, keeping her own voice flat and her vowels clipped. Magic flourished too easily in this sultry atmosphere, just as the mechanicals ruled in the cooler climes north. She didn't need the full moon here. If she wasn't careful, she'd spell something just by making conversation.

A few months earlier, it would have taken several days for the train to reach this fetid place. But the Belle Verde Girls seemed unperturbed by the electric fences and concrete barriers set by the machine men, pushing steadily north in their expansion of their territory. Only the train and its tracks remained free of their encroachment, the old treaties still holding the last of the travel ways open to all, even stowaways like herself and Turtle.

Red Molly unwound a couple of layers of scarves and tossed them on the boxcar's floor. She'd rue the leather jacket's weight by noon, she knew, but she didn't want to give up the protections painted on its back and sleeves in red-inked tongues of flame.

"Heard the Kudzu Kid rules this part of country," volunteered Turtle, who seemed equally reluctant to shed the wool vest that he wore, even as the sweat darkened his fair hair and ragged beard. "That the mechanicals won't follow the train because of him."

"Vine, swamp, and general rot. It's a tough combination to beat and it plays havoc with their pistons and gears. Trouble is, that same rot gets into everything. If the Kid isn't careful, he can destroy his own armies just as easily," she replied. Then, as the humid heat of the boxcar continued to increase, she added, "Do you have any water?"

Turtle shook his head.

"Then we drop off at the next station."

"Do you think it is safe?"

"No," she answered truthfully. "But it's better than dead of thirst in this rolling hotbox."

The train hooted, a long whistle and short, signaling the upcoming stop. Molly poked her head out the boxcar door, trying to determine if it was just a crossing or something more populous. The track curved out of the swamp and into a cleared area bounded by trees. A water tower and concrete platform with a corrugated iron shed stood in the center of the clearing. Coming closer to the station, she could see a pile of boxes on the platform along with a black coffin propped up on two trestle legs. Somebody was shipping a corpse home.

"Mail stop," Red Molly reported over her shoulder to Turtle.

He nodded and rose from his crouch, swaying to the opposite side of the boxcar to look out the door facing away from the station. "Scrub grass, a few vines, and a dirt road leading into the trees," he said.

"Anyone out there?" She kept her eye on the station as the train slowed. So far, no sign of guards or any passengers waiting for this train. The stationmaster was probably napping the morning away inside, hoping nobody would call him out to help load the bags, the parcels, and the coffin. She kept forgetting how lazy folks got this side of the border, acting like there were no wars swirling north and east of them.

Turtle scanned the opposite field. "Nothing," he said. "Nobody at all."

Red Molly joined him at the boxcar's door. The train slowed to a halt. Muttering a spell to prevent an awkward fall, she leaped straight out. The dry grass crackled beneath her crimson bootheels as she struck the ground. Keeping the train between her and the station, Red Molly sprinted towards the trees shadowing the brown clay road. Behind her, she heard a thump and the sound of a man running.

Once she was safe under the tree branches, Red Molly glanced over her shoulder. Turtle cleared the field just steps behind her, crowding close once he came into the shade. Sweat glistened on his face.

"Nobody saw us," she said, to reassure herself as much as him.

"Don't think so," he panted as soon as he'd caught his breath back in his mouth.

The train made a mournful hoot and chugged out of the station. The coffin was gone from the platform, as were the other boxes and bags, but nothing had been left behind. The yellowed lace curtains covering the station's grimy windows hung straight down and prevented Red Molly from seeing anyone inside.

She waited for a few more minutes, just in case somebody would emerge. But nobody came out the station door and the only sound was the buzzing of the insects in the branches above.

"Seems safe," said the man slumped at her feet.

With a start, Red Molly turned to Turtle. He'd folded himself into the hollow made by a pair of jutting tree roots, blending down into the shrub and browned grass. If it hadn't been for the orange vest that he wore, she might have lost track of him altogether.

"You should ditch that vest," she said. "Makes you too clear a target."

"Shirt underneath isn't much better," he answered.

"The war is behind us," she said. "Folks down here won't care so much."

He shrugged and grabbed the vest, pulling it up and over his head. As she suspected, the gray shirt underneath was stenciled on both front and back with the name of the mechanicals' prison camp.

"So the floods didn't drown you all," she said.

Turtle shook his head. "I grabbed a log and rode it down the current," he told her. "Until the river dropped me off near the trainyard." He rolled the vest into a neat ball and tucked it under his arm. "I might want it later. If it gets cold."

"It never gets cold here," Red Molly replied. "Never cools. The nights stay hot and the days grow hotter."

"You sound like you've been here before."

"Back and forth across the border before I left my mother's womb. And many times since." She stepped out on the brown clay road, with one last check over her shoulder to make sure that nobody was watching. "I can't say I like the heat."

The road twisted out of the meadow and up a small hill and then twisted so sharply back that Red Molly was afraid they'd end up walking in circles to where they began. But another bend deposited them on a log bridge crossing a sluggish stream.

With a sigh of relief, she hopped off the bridge and onto the stream's bank, dropping to her knees to scoop the water into her hands and down her burning throat. It tasted like mud, but she didn't care. Turtle didn't seem to mind the brackish taste either, matching her gulp for gulp at the stream's edge.

With the worst of her thirst cooled, Red Molly climbed back onto the bridge and peeled off her fancy boots and silk stockings, thrusting her bare feet into the water below. Again, Turtle followed her example and the pair of them dawdled there, paddling their feet like children in the creek.

"What's that?" Turtle finally said, pointing to a mound of metal at the far end of the little footbridge.

A belly full of muddy water hadn't stopped her hunger pangs. Red Molly was thinking hard about how soon they might find a farm or a town than what lay just beyond the bridge. But she followed the line of Turtle's pointing finger, only to start cursing the minute that she saw what he was looking at.

Although covered in kudzu and rust, the sentinel on the other side of the bridge still had a green light glowing on top of its knobby head. Which meant that its one round lens eye had caught her picture when she first walked up to the bridge and had sent it flying off to the satellites beeping high above them. And for the last ten minutes, she'd been sitting causally in front of its spying eye, making it clear to all the machine men back in their glass towers that she was still alive and quite easy to find.

Red Molly almost let loose a spell that would have melted the little sentinel into a puddle of iron and glass. But then she thought better of it. Pictures transmitted out of this region often blurred, fogged by all the random magic misting in the air. So they might not see her clearly or be certain of her face. She picked up a stone from the creek bed and walked up to the sentinel, smashing its lens as any offended woman might.

"Come on," she said. "We'd better get off the road now."

Turtle unfolded himself from the stream's bank, straightening and straightening until he was taller than her. It was easy to forget his height or the breadth of his shoulders. He tended to fold in on himself when they were walking or roll himself up tight when he was sleeping, like last night in the boxcar.

But now he stood with his shoulders back like a soldier, and the look on his face etched lines from his nose to mouth, lines of pain. Red Molly felt her own face settle into a look just as grim, but she didn't want to say anything. Didn't want to say that she was scared, that all the long, long nights and days of running had been useless, ever since the great bonfire up north.

"Who is coming?" Turtle asked, each word more distinct and clipped than she'd ever heard drop from his mouth.

"With luck, no one," she said, turning off the road and heading under the trees. The ground was sticky, slick with mud underfoot, and every step treacherous. Red Molly slung her boots around her neck, knotting them together with her long stockings. On ground like this, it was safer to go unshod than risk getting a heel caught in a trailing vine or twisted tree root. She walked such woods barefoot all her childhood.

Turtle ducked when she ducked, turned when she turned, apparently still willing to go where she led. She almost warned him off, sent him back to the road. But then she told herself that he was safer with her. And it was safer for her too. If the men with mechanical hearts caught him, their probes and needles would quickly find her image in his eyes and memory. That clear a picture she didn't need broadcast throughout the world.

Since his one question at the stream, Turtle held his tongue and kept his thoughts to himself. Which left Red Molly with lots of time to listen to the chatter inside her own head. "Her doom came upon her." Where had she heard that line before? Some lecturer in a little red schoolhouse, going on and on about a silly poem in a tattered book, a poem about a woman too foolish to try to save herself. She hated stories like that. Such tales were even worse that the "what if" talk you heard in cafes and bars. "What if the Wizard Lyman hadn't opened the gates between dreams and time, what if his rituals had failed, what if the new world was as free from magic as the old world was sodden with it?"

Old poems and silly speculations never stopped any spell or turned aside even a single tick-tock robot dog. The world was what it was. You learned to live in it before it chewed you up and spat out your bones on the dung heap. That's what her mother always said, and Red Molly was yet to discover any grave containing the old harpy.

To survive in these chaotic times, a woman must take a side. Magic or Science. The art or the artifice. She made her choice, fought her fight, and now they were hunting her down because of it. But she could survive this chase, just as she had survived all the battles of her past.

Besides, every step, every brush of bare skin against earth and vegetation grounded her. Held her closer to this place. Magic ran like lighting up and down her body until her hair fairly crackled with it. Until she almost burst into flame.

Behind her, Turtle gave a grunt. She whirled around, already searching for a possible attack. Turtle held a hand up in front of his face, as if to shield himself from the heat of her gaze. The rest of the woods were silent and empty. The man had only stumbled on a vine. She needed to calm herself. She needed to remember that her war was done.

"It's all right," she reassured him. "I only burn what I want to burn."

"Tell me about the Bonfire Queen," he said. "What she beautiful?"

She blinked. She hadn't expected any such question from this raggedy young man shielding his eyes with one scarred hand.

"I'm no judge of that face," she answered as truthfully as she could. "I know others thought the Bonfire Queen beautiful, especially when she sizzled the wires at the Stockyard and let the wild ones run free. The Wolf Ladies all howled that night to the moon about her face being brighter than any star."

"I heard the moon grew jealous then, and whispered her whereabouts to the mechanicals."

"That's a fairytale," said Red Molly, hopping over a twisted root and scrambling up a small hill. "Truth was, and this I know, being there, the Bonfire Queen grew careless, forgetting how far north of the border they were. The drones overran the Army at dawn and chased them to every point of the compass rose. The great, superior, shining Alliance Army smashed, and its fine general with her grandiose title, blown away like ash before the wind."

"We never made it to the Stockyard," Turtle said, talking slow, measuring out words like coins from a miser's purse. "They captured us at Cicero and sent us south to the stockade."

"So where were you marching from? And what were you looking for?"

"We were coming from Upstate, to the east, and looking for the Bonfire Queen's coalition."

"Upstaters have no magic," she said. "Too far north, much too far."

"I know," said Turtle. And then, so softly that Red Molly barely heard him, he added, "But some of us had dreams."

At the top of the hill, the trees thinned enough for her to see the ramshackle fences marking the overgrown outlines of once cultivated fields. Down in the hollow, a log cabin squatted, chimney looking cold and devoid of smoke.

"Empty, probably abandoned when the border shifted," she speculated as she headed down the hill. With luck, the place hadn't stood empty too long and there would be something worth eating inside.

Behind her, Turtle held to her zigzagging line through the trees, following close but never uncomfortably close.

Halfway down, she could see the cabin door was standing wide open, but the shadows hid anyone who might be inside.

"Howdy," she sang out. Just in case the place wasn't empty.

The shotgun blast burst through the air in answer to her call.

Red Molly hit the dirt, tasting clay in her mouth, as her heart beat as wildly as the birds winging frantically from the trees above them.

Turtle slammed down beside her. A second blast, the gun's other barrel, kicked up dust far too close to her nose.

"Damn it!" Red Molly yelled. "Hold your fire. Friendly folk here."

"How do I know that?" A man's voice, echoing out from the cabin.

"Because I'm not burning you where you stand," Molly muttered into the dirt and heard Turtle grunt beside her. Louder she cried out, "Just traveling through. Hoping for some well water and bite of something. We can pay."

"I have no cash," Turtle whispered in her ear, sounding worried.

"Neither do I," answered Red Molly. "But there's always barter."

"Sit up, so I can see your faces," yelled the man in the cabin.

"You come outside, where I can see that shotgun and know where it's pointing," Red Molly wiggled herself cautiously forward, poking her head out of the grass.

The man clumped onto his porch, shotgun still held tight to one shoulder. He was dressed like a dirt farmer, overalls and worn checked shirt underneath. From where she hid in the grass, she couldn't see his face clearly, but judging by the grey in his hair and beard, he wasn't some young soldier.

Red Molly stood carefully, holding her hands wide from her body in a gesture meant to show that she held no mechanical weapon. The magic burning up from the soles of her feet and tingling down her arms to her outstretched fingers wouldn't be so obvious to a regular man.

"I burn when I want to burn," Red Molly whispered softly, barely letting the beginning of the spell breathe through her lips. "I burn where I want to burn." The magic raged against her control, twisting its flames through her body, but she stayed steady, hoping the man before her was blind to her power. She didn't want to kill a man for protecting his home.

The shotgun stayed pointed straight at her for one heartbeat, two, three. She took a deep breath. Then the barrel of the gun pointed down. The farmer on the porch broke it open and hung it harmless across his arm.

"Come on up," he said. "Don't got much, but there's stew from yesterday and the bread's still fresh."

"I burn when I want to burn," Red Molly told her magic, letting it run back into the dirt, the dried grass, and the open sky above her. Only the palest spark leaped from fingertip to fingertip. She tucked her hands under her jacket to hide that.

Behind her, Turtle straightened out of the grass slowly.

"That last shot was close," he observed.

"Too close," she answered as they crossed the yard to the cabin. "Didn't come all this way to be cut down by some farmer's shotgun."

"Funny close," Turtle continued, sounding worried. "If it had been me, from there, I would have hit one of us."

"How so?"

"We used to sit on the porch and take out rabbits in the vegetable patch with a double barrel like that. If we missed the first shot, we hit with the second. Da beat that into us."

"Easier to shoot a bunny than another human being," Red Molly said. Easier to burn a life away when you couldn't see the face or hear the screams, she could have added, but didn't.

"Maybe," said Turtle, but he didn't sound convinced.

On the porch, the farmer looked as ordinary as his cabin. Grey hair, grey beard, grey eyes, a middle-aged man worn by the sun and the wind.

"John Porter," he said with a nod and no offer of a handshake.

"Red Molly," she answered, "and this here is Turtle."

The two men nodded at each other, and then looked at her.

"Food?" she asked, because that was foremost in her mind.

"Got no room inside," answered Porter, "but you can sit here and I'll bring out a bowl for each of you. There's bucket and dipper by the pump if you want water."

"I'll fetch it, sir," said Turtle.

Porter nodded, "It's back of the cabin." Turtle hopped off the porch, disappearing around the corner.

Porter went into the cabin, shutting the door carefully behind him. A few minutes later, he came out with two straight back chairs. He set them down in the shade of the porch. Then he went back inside, door shut tight behind him again, but no sign of the shotgun.

Red Molly, seeing as nobody asked her to do anything, leaned back in one of the chairs and whistled through her teeth. The sky was blazing blue above, no clouds at all, but something in the air felt like thunder. The lightning tasted four or five hours away to her, and she was more than a fair judge of such things.

Porter came out, juggling two brown pottery bowls of stew with a hunk of bread and a pewter spoon balanced across the top of each bowl.

Red Molly accepted hers with real thanks. Turtle rounded the corner with a full bucket of water and the dipper. He set the bucket between the two chairs and took the stew from Porter.

"Good pump you've got," said Turtle to Porter.

The man shrugged. "Guess so."

"Must be a deep well, the water's almost cold."

Porter shrugged again.

"I could water your garden if you want, to pay for supper."

Porter frowned. "No need."

"It's looking dry. You'll lose those peas soon."

"No need," the farmer said with more force, and went back into his cabin with a slam of the door.

"Maybe he doesn't care for peas," said Red Molly, stirring her stew with her spoon. "Looks like meat, onions, and beans in this."

Turtle tasted his stew and frowned. "Army rations, canned."

She stirred it again and ate some more. Meat cooked tasteless, but too much salt, too. "Canned? You sure?"

"This is what they fed us every night in that prison," said Turtle. "Bread's not fresh, either."

She tore out a hunk and dipped in the stew. "We're strangers, tramps, he might give us yesterday's leavings."

"The vegetables are dying out back. No water for a week or more, but there's plenty coming out of the pump."

Red Molly stared hard at the closed door of the cabin. "No room inside," she muttered, as much to herself as to the man raising doubts in her mind.

"Maybe we should go," said Turtle shifting in his seat.

"And take two shots to the back when we walk away," Red Molly argued. "Besides, I want to know what's inside that cabin that's so important a man will let his farm wither around him."

"Nothing good," Turtle guessed.

The door opened and they both started. Porter came out with two blankets dangling from his hand. Black wool washed so many times that it had turned rusty brown. Common enough, the type of blanket that Red Molly had seen on the shelves of most general stores in this area.

"Here," said Porter, dropping the blankets on the porch. "You can sleep in the barn tonight. If you want to help me with chores tomorrow, that's payment enough."

"We're much obliged," said Red Molly because Turtle seemed to have gone silent again. He sat hunched down in his chair, slumped in such a way that the prison printing on his shirt wasn't obvious, staring at the worn boards of the porch and not looking at Porter.

Porter lingered a moment or two. Red Molly waited for the inevitable questions: Where are you from? Where are you going?

But the farmer said nothing. Just turned his face to the sky, looking north into the blue emptiness. Maybe he could feel the same approaching storm that tasted electric hot in her mouth.

Then he turned back into the cabin without a word. The door clicked shut and a bolt snicked home.

"So do we go or do we stay?" Turtle asked his boots, but she knew the question was directed at her.

"I'm staying," said Red Molly.

"Then I'm staying too," said Turtle.

With food in her stomach, and several dippers of cold well water to wash it down, Red Molly felt too restless to stay on the porch. She hopped off, wandering back and forth in front of the cabin, wondering if Porter would emerge again. But the man stayed firmly behind his locked door. All windows were shut tight too, with flour bag curtains drawn across the glass. It reminded her of the closed-up stationhouse.

The sun dropped below the trees, but the heat continued to rise. Porter must be sweating something hard in his wooden box of a cabin, Red Molly thought. As it was, she stripped off her heavy leather jacket, the sticky shirt underneath, and only kept her lace-trimmed camisole to preserve Turtle's modesty. She'd caught the fine red blush tipping his ears when she peeled off her shirt and grabbed the bucket off the porch.

"I'm soaking my head under the pump," she told him. "You watch that door."

Turtle nodded, and dropped his eyes to his boots after one quick glance.

Red Molly marched around the cabin. A few good strokes of the pump handle and the water began to gush out cold and clear across her hot head and shoulders. She hit the pump handle a few more times, careful to keep her magic from fouling this simple mechanism.

Back north, they had water piped into their tall glass towers, hot showers cascading from multiple outlets in marble bathrooms. She lived with such luxury once, but it hadn't felt as good as this cold well water hitting the back of her neck and making muddy puddles around her bare toes.

Cool and feeling clean, Red Molly ambled over to the vegetable garden. As Turtle had observed, the ground was cracked dry and the plants drooped in their places. Odd waste with enough water close to hand. She walked the rows, stealing a peapod off the vine and popping the raw peas in her mouth. At the far end of the garden, she found a spade sticking in a pile of dirt.

Red Molly plucked the shovel free, frowning at the accumulated grime along the edge of the blade. Porter had as little care for his tools as he had for his vegetables. Down here, people knew the value of cold iron, hard to forge and harder still to keep from the magical rot that ate away all good man-made items. Just letting a spade sit out in the yard was a sure way to ruin it.

Red Molly looked more closely at the pile of dirt in front of her. Six feet long and at least three feet wide, the mound had a familiar feel.

"Aw, hell," said Red Molly, who had dug far too many graves. She struck the blade into the center and began to shovel. It only took a few strokes and she hit something soft. Red Molly dropped to her knees and brushed the dirt from the cloth-wrapped bundle.

With a steady hand, she pulled aside the winding sheet. The face staring up at her was less than a week dead and perfectly recognizable. Grey hair, grey beard, wide-staring grey eyes. It was John Porter in the grave behind his cabin.

With a curse, Red Molly stood up and kicked dirt over Porter's face. Slipping the shovel back where she found it, she hurried around the cabin. Turtle was where she left him, slumped in his chair, looking asleep in the long red rays cast by the setting sun.

"Turtle," she hissed. "Turtle."

The man didn't move. Red Molly reached out to shake his hand and it was icy to her touch. She sucked in her breath and fumbled one hand against his throat. A slow heartbeat moved the sluggish pulse beneath her fingers. She ran her hand along the side of his neck and found the little needle dart that she half expected.

The door to the cabin clicked open and Porter stood there, a Northern needle gun held loosely in one hand. His eyes gleamed with their own pale light in the growing gloom of the evening. Red Molly knew if she placed a hand on his artificial flesh, she'd feel the beat of a mechanical heart.

"So," said Red Molly, "were you just sitting here, waiting for me?"

"You," answered the mechanical man, "were not in our original calculations. This outpost was for spying upon others. We expect the Belle Verde Girls to be heading south again and meant to catch them as they passed. We did not expect the Bonfire Queen herself to jump the train at a station that we controlled."

The little stationhouse, curtains drawn across every window, with a mechanical man sitting inside, waiting and watching. Red Molly wondered if the real stationmaster had been in the coffin propped up on the platform.

"My mistake. I thought I'd left your kind far behind," said Red Molly, backing away from the mechanical and feeling with her bare feet for the edge of the porch. She needed to get off the dead wood and put the dirt under her to call on the best of her magic.

Porter raised the gun. "Stop. Now. We know this poison will work upon your kind."

"Proved that when you overran us, didn't you," said Red Molly, staying still, unwilling to be dropped like her followers back in the Stockyard. Her grand Alliance Army, destroyed through her pride and certainty that no mechanical weapon could breach their magic.

Porter gestured with the gun. "We prefer you conscious when the copter arrives. They will want to question you and the drug will keep you sleeping for nearly a day."

The electric storm soiling her mouth wasn't thunder and lightning heading their way. It was the black blades of the mechanicals, chopping through the air.

"You will be flying over the border," Red Molly said, slumping like Turtle, trying to look small and defeated, and shifting one step closer to the porch edge.

"The border is moving, it is not stable yet," said the mechanical Porter. "Our calculations show that it will move again tonight and this area will be flyable until dawn."

"Know that for certain?" asked Red Molly, trying one more shift of her body weight and feeling the porch edge under one heel.

"We have taken our measurements," said Porter. "Tonight is best night for flying. If you went to the barn as we instructed, this would be unnecessary." He raised the needle gun again. "We would have taken you there."

"So why shoot him now?" she nodded at the frozen Turtle.

"He tried the door," Porter replied.

"Stupid mistake," said Red Molly, and flipped herself off the porch. She hit the dirt with a shoulder roll, chanting even as the needles flew toward her: "I burn where I want to burn. I burn when I want to burn. I burn who I want to burn."

Fire crackled around her, igniting the dry grass and licking greedily toward the cabin. Porter roared and fired his needle gun repeatedly.

The glittering darts burst into flame at the wave of Red Molly's hand as she pulled her magic out of the center of the world's burning heart and channeled it through her tingling body. She shouted her own commands and the fire crackling across the porch circled around Turtle, leaving him isolated in a ring of flame.

Porter lurched back, beating at the flames with a hand that dripped plastic into the fire and showed the gleaming steel beneath.

Red Molly yelled and the fire circled Porter's thrashing body like red-hot chains of barbed wire, rolling him back into his cabin where the mechanical man's measuring devices began to overheat, pop, and explode.

Leaping back onto the porch, Red Molly chased the fire inside even as she pulled the unconscious Turtle over her shoulder. With a grunt, because the man was heavier than she expected, she lugged him off the porch and into the ash left by the dying flames.

She slapped him with one hot hand, putting a sharp tingle of magic into each slap, just enough to burn the cold poison out of his veins. At her third strike against his icy cheek, Turtle grunted and blinked his eyes open.

"There's something inside," he started to say. "Something clicking."

"I know," said Red Molly, "time to go before they come looking for their missing mechanical man."

Turtle stumbled to his feet, blinking at the cabin now a roaring blaze, lighting the night sky and blotting out the stars.

"Was that what he was? One of the face stealers?"

"Yes," said Red Molly, moving around the cabin to make sure that false Porter had not escaped out the back and to fetch her boots and jacket from under the pump. "There's another one back at the station."

"Thought it was too quiet," said Turtle. "What are you planning?"

"Burn it out, same as this one," said Red Molly, slinging her boots under her arm. She wanted to keep the dirt under her feet, better to feel the border when it started shifting.

"And then?"

"He said the Belle Verde Girls are heading this way. Sounds like they could use a little help."

"From the Bonfire Queen?" said Turtle, still watching the cabin as the roof collapsed inward in an explosion of sparks and black smoke.

"My name is Red Molly."

"That's not what he said, not there on the porch."

"How would you know? You were frozen solid."

"Could still hear. Just couldn't move, couldn't scream when the fire started."

Red Molly shook her head, seeing again the flames circling bright around Turtle as he sat frozen in his chair. Amazing that the man hadn't died of a heart attack right there.

"The fire only burns where I command," she told him.

Turtle nodded. "They said it was beautiful. Deadly. But beautiful, when you lit the night skies with your flames. That's what I was looking for."

"I never wanted an army," she said. "I never wanted to lead them. I just wanted to set the magic free. Wanted to stop the mechanicals from stealing people's faces and their lives."

She headed up the hill, backtracking the path that they had taken. Behind her, she could feel the beating of the copters' black blades. But the border hadn't shifted yet and by the time it did, they'd be long gone.

Turtle came after her, close but not too close, falling into step, following his dream. Red Molly stopped at the top of the hill, waiting for him to catch up.

"No more armies," she said. "Not for me."

"How about a friend? Somebody to watch your back? Like you helped me back there," asked Turtle. "I keep surviving and you keep fighting."

She cocked her head and looked up at him, a tall, grimy young man wearing the ragged remains of a prison uniform. A man that the Wide Muddy couldn't drown, that a mechanical man couldn't poison, that she couldn't burn.

Red Molly laughed, spat in her palm, and shook his hand hard. "That's a deal, my friend," said the Bonfire Queen.

Then they turned and headed down the hill together, walking swiftly side by side.

∾

KEEPING TIME

Gabrielle Harbowy

THE TWIN DIGITAL DISPLAYS were set flush into the wall, side by side. Here in the lab, just like in the mess and in my quarters, the blocky red digits on the left sped through the date and time back on Earth. The right-hand display, local time on *Overture*, crawled along in comparison.

I glanced down at my hands. It had become habit to do so, every time the left display cycled to June. The exposed slice of white skin where my ring had been didn't seem to fade from one anniversary to the next; but then again, back at full acceleration as we were, June came about once a week now.

"Dr. Perry?"

I started, jerking my gaze up from my hands and turning just a little too quickly. I had to reach for the counter to stop my momentum, and a warm burn spread up my cheeks. Without gravity, there were no footsteps; without footsteps, it was impossible to hear people approach. I hadn't heard a footstep in years, but my startle reflex was too ingrained to fade. I forced a smile. "Dr. Kimura."

Jason's lean frame hovered in the open hatchway, slender fingers resting lightly on the grab bar with the thoughtless grace that proved his tales of being groomed for the ballet as a child. The physicist had shaved his sparse stubble, and that meant he was preparing for vid.

Capturing the mission for posterity was one of our least favorite tasks, but regulations, procedural manuals, and automated reminders had impressed upon us that it was our bound duty. Especially while we were out of signal range, everything that happened aboard fell into one of three categories: important, potentially important, or potentially interruptible by something important.

In the time that would pass on Earth before we were again close enough to beam the data back, an entire psychology curriculum would be developed and refined, leading to a team that would be chosen and groomed to study the backlog of every waking moment of our voyage. I'd never been one to seek out the spotlight—or the receiving end of the microscope—so the thought sat uneasily in my stomach.

"We're at full speed, homeward bound. Everyone's gathering in the mess to celebrate."

"I know."

His brown eyes softened, searching mine. When he looked up, it was to check the clock on the right. "Trying to be fashionably late?"

My smile was weak, but real. "Yeah." I glanced down at myself. My white regulation jumpsuit and scuffed sneakers were almost identical to his, save for the department designation and rank on my sleeve. "I just can't decide which pumps go with this dress."

He spared a glance down the corridor, then pushed off lightly and drifted closer, dropping the friendly formality we kept up in public and lowering his voice. "Wear the red ones and I'll dance with you all night."

I laughed and reached out to his smooth cheek, brushing my thumb across his jaw. Touching him brought comfort, and comfort lowered my defenses. "I'm kind of socialed out," I admitted quietly. This party was a celebration of our—of my—success. It was also an excuse for us all to mask the unspoken flutters in our bellies about what we'd be returning to after so long away. But primarily, it would be for the camera: for Earth, not for us.

I was pleased, but I still felt completely drained. I didn't have the energy to summon enthusiasm on command; given my way, I'd go curl up and have a good cry. I'd spent a lifetime in preparation and eight years in transit for this. Though it was done and we were heading home, I didn't feel ready to celebrate yet. I still didn't quite believe that it had all been real.

Jason was real. This close, he smelled of toothpaste and soap. "I know. But you're the hero of the hour, Monica. The rest of us...all we did was get you out here. You're the xenolinguist who made humankind's first contact with aliens—the first interstellar diplomat. You averted a misunderstanding that could have wiped out our world...and even managed to get them to like us." He said it like he was rehearsing it for the camera, but gently. He was preparing me for the way it would sound out loud.

It was true, and that was why I flinched from it. Those words would be my tagline, my subtitle, my legacy. They'd be ringing in my ears for the rest of my life.

"So...*do* you dance?"

Jason laughed and tightened his arms around me instead of answering. We hung together in our improvised double sleep sack, strapped in vertically so that we couldn't float away during the arbitrary night.

"What?" I asked, laughing too. I was glad I had gone, after all. The warm reception I'd gotten from the entire crew had done its part to erase any lingering melancholy. The heady alien wine helped too, aiding the grin that tugged at my lips. The words had flowed so naturally, once I'd understood the basic construction of their language. Going over it all again in my head brought an even warmer flush of pleasure than the wine.

He nosed aside a black curl that had drifted free of my hairband, and kissed my temple. "I do. Pretty well, I'm told."

Jason and I had circled so slowly, like two planets turning toward each other just a little more with each revolution around some common sun—as inaccurate as he would tease me that such a description was. And he had been so patient with me, waiting without complaint until I was unquestionably a widow before he'd even kissed me. When he finally learned my body, his eyes had misted and gone hard each time he discovered another little white scar. Fading marks and a band of pale skin around my finger were all that remained of my marriage now.

Aaron hadn't danced. It was beneath him, and a waste of precious networking time. He used to say that by the time he was elected to a high enough office that he'd be expected to dance, he'd be powerful enough to be able to ban dancing from official functions.

I glanced at the clock, then down to my bare finger. I had finally removed the ring a few months ago, when our slower ship-side calendar had inched around to its eighth June. Senator Aaron Perry was long dead by now, and I had done what was necessary to save myself from his indifference and his temper.

I hadn't told him that I'd been picked for the mission. I was too choice a trophy and too convenient a punching bag; he would never have let me come. But the existence of the Mirai had been classified, and that had helped. It meant that our crew and our launch had gone unmentioned by the press, and that our extended training sessions were officially just "research symposia." It meant that, as the preeminent expert on something even I had never thought would be more than a theory, my clearance was higher than his. The day I left on a government shuttle for the Cape, I could step out the door with my briefcase like it was any other day, with the butterflies in my stomach soothed by the knowledge that I would never have to go home to wrath and rage and the demeaning names he loved to call me, ever again.

"Hey," Jason murmured against my cheek. "Safe now. I've got you." It was what he always said when my body tensed for flight in that way that told him I was thinking too long about the past. I breathed deeply and willed relaxation into my shoulders, my spine, my curled toes.

Calmed, I rested my head on his shoulder. "I really do have red pumps, you know." It was empty conversation, but so much of our conversation was. We daydreamed about the life we'd make together. There was so much possibility, so much unknown, that thinking about it too long was like trying to listen to too many voices at once, all speaking different languages. A word or two peeked out of the mumble, but mostly it all blended into a single anxious buzz.

"And a flowing black dress to wear them with. And assuming Earth still grows grapes, we'll dance to old jazz and sip champagne till dawn."

It was the Earth I'd missed out on and had always pined for, and it did strange things to that buzz in my stomach to think that out here, among the stars, I was closer to it than I'd ever been.

Without gravity, tears don't fall. Trapped and glistening in my eyelashes, they were impossible to hide. "Do you promise?" I whispered.

Jason's thumb moved slowly up my cheek and brushed a tear out of my lash line. He pulled his hand away, holding the droplet there like a tiny, precious pearl. "You can face down a whole alien diplomatic faction without breaking a sweat, but the thought that I might want to dance with you makes you cry," he whispered back. "I love that about you. I do promise."

Shifting his wrist, he eased my teardrop airborne to hang before us like a little star. I made a wish on it.

A few years on, Junes didn't zip by so quickly anymore. The closer we got to home, the more noticeable the growing synchrony in the speed of time became—just as it had when we'd started deceleration for our arrival at Mirid.

It had only taken a couple of years for the impression of my ring to fade. By the time we slowed through a mere half light-speed and marked our last two years of deceleration toward Earth, it was long gone. And so was the habit to watch for the passage of June. Developing the Mirai language primer consumed my artificial days, and making sure I exercised and remembered to be sociable once in a while filled my off-shift hours. And my nights were Jason's.

I traced my hand across his slim back and he turned, catching me around the waist and letting his momentum pull us both into a slow twirl that bumped my shoulder harmlessly into the padded wall. "Imagine if we'd taken the gravity refit," he mused with a distant smile. "We wouldn't be able to do this anymore."

I pushed off with my foot, letting the next impact be his. "Houston will have enough of a fit over what we let them do to our engines." Our mission parameters allowed us to accept plans and information, but forbade us from accepting any alien technology that might "hasten, impede or endanger" our return. Yet we'd arrived into the distant world's orbit with a slow fuel leak, and we'd all agreed that it would be more dangerous to refuse the generous aid extended to us than to risk not being able to make it home.

I had presented it all to the Mirai representatives: the restriction, my reservations, and my concerns for our safety. "The spirit of the law," I explained. It had been a long, complicated session, but they had responded compassionately, pleased that we wished to keep our word but not to the point of jeopardizing all we had come to do. It had been a breakthrough: reaching understanding on that abstract concept had led to the discovery that it was indeed one of the core foundations of their society. Everything before had felt like a test, but the "spirit," as Captain Weiss had joked, had "set us free." As a result, we were bringing back shiny new propulsion technology that was simple, clean, and efficient. It would significantly extend humanity's interstellar range.

Jason let out a playful "oof" and drew his fingertips to my ribs, only threatening to tickle because he knew I wasn't ticklish. "For all we know, that'll all look like kids' toys by now." He grinned. "I keep imagining the poor grunts who still have to train on our archaic computers, so that they'll be able to talk with us when we get back." His grin faded a moment later, and I nudged him with my foot to kickstart the curve of his lips. It didn't take.

We all worried that we'd be returning to a broken promise. A couple hundred years was a long time. Maybe they'd forgotten about us, or forgotten how to communicate at our primitive level. Or language itself might have evolved, political boundaries might have changed...and that was all assuming that humanity hadn't blown itself out of the sky entirely. But now, we were so close. I refused to let that be possible. I needed to believe that there would be dancing, and champagne, and jazz.

"Hey," I said gently, nudging him again. "Best xenolinguist in the universe right here—Dr. Monica Perry; made first contact with the aliens, remember? You just leave those humans to me."

At 1530-local, the right-hand clock went dark. The twin time-keepers had been synchronous for an hour, yet so wildly off from each other that my fingers itched to reset one—specifically, the crazy one that reported a passage of years far beyond what we'd experienced. But that one stayed. Earth time was the only time that mattered now.

Signal strength had boosted over those years. The comm crackled to life farther out than we expected it to. "Houston to *Overture*. This is an automated beacon and it will repeat. Please respond. Houston to *Overture*..."

Hearts pounding in our throats, we responded.

Nothing.

It was an automated beacon that had outlived its creators, some argued. Our own signal simply wasn't strong enough to reach them at the same distances, others countered. The days were tense and the nights were long, while we waited to see whether the optimists or the pessimists would win the bet. Jason and I sidestepped it completely. We talked quietly in the darkness, weaving our daydreams about wine and music and culture like a shield, avoiding anything that would keep us from drifting back to the reality of doubt.

And still we kept responding, until one day we were close enough for them to hear us.

"Loud and clear, Houston. You're on the shipwide. Tell me, does New York still have two baseball teams?"

The mission controller laughed, a hearty, happy laugh, and rigid tension eased a notch through the shoulders of everyone crowded into the mess to listen in. Our laughter was nervous and halting, tentatively hopeful. Through the open channel, we could hear the cheers of the mission control team back home.

"Is that the most pressing question you have, Captain Weiss?" the controller chided teasingly. In the mess, we didn't have a screen like they did in the cockpit, so we could only hear the smile on the woman's distant face. Her speech was a bit different in the vowels than I'd ever heard. I understood her easily, but I couldn't have discerned where she was from. Analyzing it in real depth would have to wait, but at least it gave me something to turn over in my head while I waited with held breath.

Dave Weiss laughed in return. "Well, not exactly, Houston, but we all agreed with Dr. Perry up here that it'd probably tell us the most about the state of the world in the quickest time."

The tinny voice still chuckled, and her answer was warm. "Mets and Yankees, Captain, and you can still get a dog and a beer, though I suspect the price has gone up a bit since your day."

Jason caught me around the waist with a whoop and a fierce hug, and I slumped just as happily against him. If there was still a New York, still baseball, still hot dogs and beer, then nothing too drastic could have happened in the interim. It was still, in some ways at least, going to resemble the world we knew.

"It's good to hear you healthy and in good spirits, *Overture*. You can bet there's a lot of people who have questions to ask you, or who can't wait to welcome you all home. Especially, well...Here. Let me give you to the top brass."

"Good afternoon, Captain Weiss, and congratulations to you and your crew. I've waited a very long time for this pleasure." The syrupy, razor-edged voice hadn't changed, and it hit me like a shock of ice water to the veins. "This is President Aaron Perry."

Ice turned instantly to steam. I clamped my hands to my ears, digging my fingernails into my hair, but it didn't help. It couldn't be. It couldn't. Hundreds of years, and...and I'd waited, and taken off the ring, and...

And I'd thought I was safe. But now even through my trembling palms I could hear his laughter, and the stunned stammers of the captain, grasping for something to say.

"Don't let us give you the wrong idea, now," Aaron's voice continued smoothly. It was the same playful tone the mission controller had used, but with the dose of smarmy condescension Aaron always poured on for the people he didn't consider his equal. He spoke slowly, almost in a sing-song, as though graciously making it easier for us to understand the language. "Let me tell you just how different Earth is from the home you know. Technology's come a long way, *Overture*. Cryo-suspension, for example, was perfected in 2025. And its first volunteer? A prominent politician who wanted to save his future to spend with his loving wife. Welcome back, *Overture*. And welcome *home*, Mons."

The dangerous edge in his confident voice wasn't my imagination. That voice. And that name I'd thought I was finally free of...I'd accomplished so much, felt so valued and proud a moment ago, and now he'd reduced me to a mere vulva with a simple syllable, yet again. My cheeks burned and my eyes stung. Not least because Jason had heard the one humiliation I'd wanted to keep from him.

A few others turned to me, pale and uneasy. Perhaps at the mere fact of his existence, if not at the promotion he'd received in the interim, or concern about what this would mean for two of their crew. Or maybe they also heard the rancid oil dripping through his tone. Jason's arms, still tight around me, were all that kept me from floating through the floor. Or toward the airlock.

The mission controller's voice started again, then abruptly cut off. As though a glance from Aaron had denied her permission to speak. Aaron had always had that power.

"Mr., ah, President, sir," the captain started, then cleared his throat. "It's an honor, sir, to speak to you personally and offer my congratulations on your success, and to, ah, relay that Dr. Perry is healthy and in good spirits. I...ah..." His voice trembled uncharacteristically, his words halting and reluctant. "Unfortunately she's not in the cockpit at the moment so I can't put her on with you, but I'm sure she'll...that is, I'm sure you've got plenty to catch up on, once we and mission control get some housekeeping matters taken care of."

Jason's hands had gone clammy over mine, but he hadn't let go. I turned my head, searching his eyes and letting him see the panic in mine. His were distant; unreadable. "Really him?" he whispered. I didn't trust myself to do more than give a shallow nod.

It was Aaron, all right. Cuts, burns and barbs, but never where they'd show. Conversation made of daggers so delicately poisoned and carefully aimed, under such a smooth façade, that you'd think the sting your own imagination. Michelle, Jason's technician, gave my upper arm a supportive squeeze. "God, he must be so... relieved, to have you...back?" But the look she gave me was a frightened, uncertain one. It turned guardedly protective when her gaze shifted to seek out Jason's reaction.

There was a laugh, a slimy, knowing laugh through the shipwide, and I realized I'd blocked out Aaron's voice and missed something. "Come on," Jason murmured in my ear, and he nodded toward Michelle and the others, too. He pushed off toward the hatch, keeping me solidly cradled against him.

I flicked off the camera in the lab. I'd claim malfunction, and it would be years before anyone sorted far enough through the data to know it had worked that morning. This way, I didn't have to be alone. Jason and the whole science team were with me.

I took a breath and flipped the record switch on the audio, then connected to the private channel. "Hello, Aaron," I said.

"Mons. My little Mons. How I've waited for this moment." He had dropped the lonely martyr act now that he thought we were alone, the channel secure, and his voice dripped with malice. "So, you did it. You snuck out on me, left me for aliens. And you found them, didn't you?"

I hesitated, but he didn't let me hesitate long. "I've got top clearance now, remember. Your president asked you a question."

"Yes," I answered. "We found aliens."

"That's yes *sir*, Dr. Perry," he snapped.

I said nothing. The comforting touches on my arms and around my waist drew tighter.

His voice softened again, like heated butter. "Think carefully now. Was it worth the beating you're gonna get for leaving me behind looking like an utter fool while you rushed off to play interplanetary whore? Is that how you greeted them? The international language of ass raised high and legs—"

Jason's open palm slammed down on the button, killing the signal. Silence echoed through the lab. I opened my mouth, but my throat had gone too dry to speak.

"Dick," one of the techs muttered. A quiet round of nervous laughter broke the tension; as if they'd all wanted to say it, but no one had wanted to say it first.

I sat alone in the mess, fingering an unopened pouch of golden alien wine and staring at the dark half of the clock. Ship time, the measure that had been real to me, was gone. There was only Earth time now, as though nothing that had happened aboard *Overture* had been real—or, at least, as though none of it counted now. But it had, and it did. I had the pouch of wine and the unmarked skin of my bare ring finger and the words of a new language to prove it to me.

At my elbow, fastened to the table, sat a thick binder of printouts that mission control had uploaded to us to help ease the disorientation of our return, but the glossy photos of unfamiliar skylines and smiling faces with unnatural tans only widened the gulf between us and the home we had once known. Racism had been stamped out by mandatory genetic engineering; everyone's skin looked the same perfect shade now, symbolizing brown and white and yellow blended and joined together without distinction. One look at any of us—Jason with his pure Japanese blood, me with my roots in the Mediterranean, even Michelle with her porcelain sunburn-magnet skin—would make it plain that we didn't belong, archaic holdovers from another time.

My jacket was tied over my chair, leaving me in jumpsuit pants and a white tank top. I'd always kept my arms covered, and when Captain Weiss entered and our eyes connected, I could see that he understood why. One round white pockmark might be a smallpox vaccination scar, but I had about a dozen of them on my olive skin. Burns and barbs, always where they wouldn't show.

He floated to a seat across from me and strapped in, peppered hair floating up at the edges of his Brooklyn Dodgers cap. "He turned sweet as day again, the moment he was back on the public comm," he reported quietly.

I lifted a hand, absently rubbing the goose bumps from my other arm. "He always did."

"What are you going to do?"

Behind him, the others started filtering in quietly, one by one. I glanced up with a watery, grateful smile, but it faded as I shook my head. "I don't have many options. It's not like I can ask you to drop me off somewhere on your way. He's right—I did sneak out on him. He's not going to let that go lightly. We have that recording of him threatening me, but he'll just suppress it, and it'll be my word against his. He'll give the press that winning smile—you saw it—and do whatever he wants." I lowered my gaze to watch the light pass through the wine.

"What about Dr. Kimura?"

"I love Jason," I answered hollowly. "You know that. But Aaron's...vindictive. If I try to divorce, if I give him an inkling that there's another man, he'll...I can't. Jason's got a good career ahead of him. I'm not worth jeopardizing that." I lifted the pouch, opened it and took a tiny sip, holding the wine on my tongue before releasing it to soothe its way down my throat. "This was supposed to be so easy. Back home, happily ever after. What the hell happened?"

The crew shifted anxiously behind the captain—Michelle and a dozen others. Apparently their spokesperson, Dave pursed his lips. "You know...we do have Daddy's keys and a full tank of gas, as it were."

I looked up at him, searching for a hint of cruel hoax in his eyes. They were genuine and kind, as they'd always been. "And," he continued, "as far as we know, all the people *we* left behind had the grace to fade away on schedule. So, we've got nothing to rush back to."

Dave's face grew blurry, and I swept tears away with my palm. "You know there's no way I could ask any of you to do this for me." Of course I'd thought it—hell, I'd thought about taking my chances with the airlock and a parachute—but I couldn't ask a whole crew to abandon their chance to go home for my sake.

Dave took the wine from me and drew a finger along the clear pouch, watching the liquid sparkle in his wake. "We all know that we're going home to be lab rats. We've paved the way, we made it possible, but they'll retire us all with big shiny medals. They'll cite some medical crap about another voyage being too risky, or say they need us grounded to study us for long-term effects of zero-g, or they'll spool out the red tape and make the approval for another mission drag on till we're justifiably too old. We know none of us will ever get a chance to come back out here again. Or...as our other option, there's a planetful of friendlies out there that've extended us an open invite, and that we're all pretty eager to learn more about. None of us want to let some damn rookies finish what we've started."

"Safe to say," Jason's voice added from behind me. His touch was warm on my bare, scarred shoulder, "all of us want a chance to finish what we started. You owe me a dance, Dr. Perry."

That hollow feeling was back, from my throat to the pit of my stomach, but it was different. Instead of a pit echoing with the absence of hope, it was a shape longing to be flooded with it, but afraid to let it in. I covered Jason's hand with mine. "So... what?" I asked with a sound that was supposed to be a casual laugh. "We just turn the ship around, go back to Mirid, and say, 'Hi, we're home!'?"

They smiled, all of them. "Well," Dave said, and cleared his throat, "we'll...ah, kind of need you to say it for us, you know. If you'll do us the honor, that is."

I looked from face to face, from one pair of shining eyes to the next, all regarding me with the same eager promise they'd shown when we'd lined up for our preflight press photos so many years ago. They all felt as alienated, and as trapped, as I did, if for their own reasons. They wanted this, too, every bit as much. Slowly, I extended my hand across the table.

"Captain Weiss, the honor would be mine."

An hour later, the last of the data from our mission was transferred; our last obligation to Earth was fulfilled. An hour after that, our final checks were complete. We severed communication with Houston and the captain brought the ship about, initiating acceleration. If first contact was the overture, then this was the beginning of the first act: our return journey to our new home on the far end of the universe.

At 2100 local time, the display on the left went dark. Moments later, its neighbor flickered to life: 0300 hours, July 1. According to shipboard time, June was over. And shipboard time was the only time that mattered now.

SCAR TISSUE

Chris A. Jackson

I STAND IN FRONT of a thousand people, and they watch as I am eaten alive.

They don't know it, of course, but I do. I know the little monsters are inside me...devouring me.

A woman wearing a flowered dress closes her eyes and tilts her head back, radiant in the summer sun. A man in uniform sits with his head in his hands, his shoulders heaving gently. A barefoot boy runs across the grass, enthusiastically waving a small flag, too young yet to appreciate its sentimental value...its power. They look at me up here on the stage and see a hero—a man whole and hale, rebuilt from a pile of human wreckage—but they don't know what's inside me.

Ten billion little monsters chewing away, eating me alive, twenty-four hours a day.

My stomach clenches and I feel a wave of familiar nausea. I close my eyes and breathe deeply, trying to banish the images that my imagination conjures. *They're not there*, I recite my silent mantra. *They're not there. They're not—*

"Lieutenant Gary McAnders."

The general's voice snaps me out of my reverie and I open my eyes. He stands tall in front of me, his back ramrod straight, his blue uniform crisp and pleated; the epitome of military dignity and protocol. He knows what's inside me; he's got them, too. He must have the same doubts—the same fears—that I have, but he hides his emotions well behind a wall of pride and honor. I want to ask him if he ever worries that the little monsters will just keep eating until there's nothing of him left, but this isn't the time and he isn't the person I should ask. He's holding the medal that will go over my head: a long blue ribbon with thirteen stars, tipped with a larger bronze star that will rest against my chest. I bow from the waist at full attention, and he puts the ribbon over my head.

"In reward for valor under fire…" he continues as the medal comes to rest against my chest. My reward for saving forty-two Marines.

My reward…

For a moment I consider the reward my country has bestowed upon me. Ten billion little monsters eating away at me. If they stop, I'm a dead man.

By all rights, I *should* be a dead man. Take one V-lifter, add an enemy surface-to-air missile, five hundred feet of altitude and a rocky hillside, and you have a recipe for death and disaster. But behold the miracles of modern medical technology.

The docs brag that if you have brain waves, they can save you. Heart, lungs, limbs, bones, internal organs, *external* organs—yes, before you ask, I lost that, too—can all be repaired or replaced. Nano-interface prosthetics were wired directly into my nervous system, a bundle of carbon-fiber nanotubes for each of my severed axons. There's no bulky computer interface, just my brain doing what it's always done, telling my muscles to move, so there's no limping or limited movement. Organs were grown from my own stem cells and used to replace their injured counterparts, as easy as inserting tab A into slot B. Real skin, seeded from my own and grown as wide, thin sheets in the lab, was lovingly shaped and sewn to conceal any external vestiges of synthetic construction. A seamless latticework of man and machine.

Whole again…that's the real reward. I see it in the faces of the Marines I flew out of that hell hole, the soldiers who lay in the beds beside mine, and the uniformed heroes sharing the stage with me. They all know the real reward, and it doesn't hang around your neck by a fucking ribbon.

But every reward comes with a cost, and ours is scar tissue.

The human immune system doesn't like foreign stuff, and every non-organic prosthesis accretes scar tissue. That's where the little monsters come in. I remember when I got them, when I was *infected* with them.

"Good morning, Gary. You look terrific!" the nurse said as she barreled into my room.

Now, after five weeks of surgeries—thank the god of pharmacology for the drugs that keep me from remembering—a month for the neural interfaces to grow and integrate, and nearly four months of rehab, people can't stop telling me how great I look. No one would tell me exactly what I looked like when they recovered me from the wreckage of my V-lifter, and I don't think I really wanted to know.

"Hey, beautiful! When are you going to jump into bed with me?" I teased, enjoying the smile that spread across the nurse's chubby face. "'A healthy sex life is important to the patient's psychological well-being...'" I quoted as I grabbed for her well-padded behind.

"Well, your sex therapist should have covered that during rehab," she said, expertly evading my grasp. "You can practice all you want when you get home. I've seen that pretty wife of yours."

"Alice," I said, and thought longingly of my homecoming. The sheet over my legs twitched and rose; the neural interface between my dirty mind and my new organ was fully functional.

The nurse was injecting a milky fluid into my IV bag. It looked viscous and not at all like something that should be going into my veins. "What's that?"

"These are your nanites, honey." She emptied the syringe, extracted it, and dropped it into the sharps waste box. "Little machines that eat up your scar tissue. And boy, you better believe you've got some scar tissue after all the work the doctors did, so it's a good thing these guys are hungry! I wouldn't be surprised if you lost ten pounds. I wish I could lose weight that easily."

Then with a squeak of the cart wheels and a whoosh of the closing door, she was gone. And the monsters began to eat me.

"Take them out!" I insisted. Dr Kliegen stared at me while he took off his glasses—metal rimmed, with some of the chrome chipping off of one corner—cleaned them with the hem of his white coat, and reapplied them to his nose.

"We can't take them out," he said in an exasperated tone. Patients were plentiful at the VA, and it's not like we could go somewhere else, so the docs didn't need to cultivate a bedside manner. "As I told you, this is the standard treatment. The ablative nanites facilitate the removal of fibrous connective tissues that accumulate around your prosthetic interfaces. With all your implants, your own immune system would kill you within a year."

"They eat the scar tissue."

"In a manner of speaking, yes. We used to try to solve this problem with immune suppression, but that creates more problems with infections. And since your body will always fight against the implants, you'll always have scar tissue to be removed. So the nanites are there for good. We couldn't remove them if we tried. What's that?" He leaned down to look at the back of my hand.

I followed his gaze and saw that I was absently scratching the site where the IV needle had been—where *they* had been injected. The skin was raw, and I had blood under my fingernails.

"When you get home, apply some antibiotic ointment and a bandage—and stop *scratching* it—and it should be fine. Well, I've got to go; surgery in twenty minutes, and I haven't had lunch yet. Goodbye Gary, and good luck." The doc turned to go without a handshake—afraid of germs, no doubt—then glanced back with a broad grin. "By the way, you look terrific."

I bolt upright in bed, heart pounding, eyes wide to the dark, and tear away the sweat-damp sheets. I look down, half expecting to see the phantom of my nightmare; a corpse crawling with nanoscopic mechanical maggots, no *me* left, only bone and the bare metal of my prosthetics…and *them*. But the pale, unblemished skin of my body glows against the dark sheets; I'm still whole, still healthy.

I slip out of bed in the dark, glancing at Alice, sleeping, oblivious to the hoard of tiny monsters chewing away right next to her. I haven't told her about the nightmares. I told my psych doc about them…once. He said that bad dreams were normal.

Normal?

During my eight trips from the LZ to the base, I watched an entire company of marines get chewed to shit. I was transporting five wounded soldiers when the missile found us. We went down in a ball of fire, and only two besides me survived. But do I have dreams about that? No, I dream about being eaten alive by the billions of nano-machines that keep me ticking. That's normal?

He asked me how I *felt* about it. That was the last dream I told him about.

I pad across the dark bedroom to the bathroom, towel off the sweat, and study myself in the mirror. I trace a finger across my goose-bumped flesh, imagining that I can see the lines where I stop and the prosthetics begin, the lines of internal scar tissue where the little monsters are chewing away at me. Will they keep chewing until there's no me left? Maybe that's what they're supposed to do.

"Gary? Are you okay?" Alice's worried voice slides under the door, startling me.

"Yeah!" I call back, but it's a lie. Morning light streams through the bathroom window now, and I'm standing in front of the mirror, a pen in one hand, lines inked across my chest and legs where my flesh borders with the prosthetics. Are the monsters gaining ground?

"Can I come in?" Alice asks.

I grab a robe and pull it on, then open the door. "Hey."

"Couldn't sleep?" she asks, slipping past me to use the toilet.

"I slept," I say, leaving the bathroom to give her some privacy, and to hide my own discomfort. I ditch the pen and go to the closet, donning an old sweatshirt and jeans before she is finished. On my way through the living room toward the kitchen, I run my hand over the cracked leather of my favorite old chair, feeling its scars. I wonder if it feels mine; if my nanites would eat the old marred cowhide, leaving a new chair behind.

"I think I'll work in the yard today," I say as Alice enters the kitchen. I stand in front of the sink, leaning toward the open window above it that overlooks the back yard, inhaling deeply, the corners of my mouth tugging upward. The scent of fresh-cut grass wafts through my olfactory senses—thank you Dr. K for the new nose—raising happy specters of my first job long years ago. I raised enough money cutting lawns that one summer to take my first flying lessons. It's all automated nowadays. As if on cue, our robotic lawn mower buzzes around the corner of the house and whirls about in its supposedly random pattern, chewing the grass like one of the little monsters chewing at my scar tissue. I think of billions of lawn mowers all around the planet, eating grass, eating the earth's scars. The back of my hand itches, but I refuse to scratch. I gulp the last of my coffee and toss the cup clattering into the sink.

Alice eyes me. "You okay?"

"Yeah, I just need something to do. Something to take my mind off…things." A passenger jet taking off from Logan roars overhead—when the wind is from the south we're under the flight path—and I look up, wondering if I know who's flying it. I used to know all the pilots that flew out of Boston. I used to be one of them.

"You still upset because they won't let you fly?"

"A little," I lie. I never used to lie to Alice, but it seems that's all I'm doing nowadays. For some reason, I don't want to tell her what's really bothering me, but I don't even know why I don't want to tell her. Maybe I'm afraid she'll start looking at me the way I look at myself in the mirror. "I'm going to have to get a job somewhere soon, even if it's not flying." I prop my arms on the sink and stare out the window. "But today, I'll pull weeds and trim the hedge."

"Well, if you need a break, let me know." Her hands slip under my shirt, and I jerk a little. "Oooo, jumpy!"

"Sorry. Your hands are cold." That's no lie, at least; Alice's hands are perpetually cold. In reality, feeling her fingers passing over the interface between me and my prosthetics is a little disconcerting. Can she feel the scars? Can she feel the little monsters chewing away beneath her fingertips?

"I know something that'll warm them up," she teases, slipping her fingers under the front of my belt. "And it might help take your mind off things."

"Maybe after I've taken a shower," I say, gently drawing her hands out, bringing them up to my mouth to kiss her fingertips.

"Suit yourself," she says hesitantly. Before, I never would have turned down an invitation like that. I imagine she's following Dr. K's instructions: "Take things at his speed. Don't push." She kisses the back of my neck and withdraws, oblivious to the real reason I refused her.

Afternoon sun plays over Alice's breasts, glittering on the tiny beads of sweat as they heave up and down with her breathing. She clutches my hand, but it's too hot for post-coital snuggling. Her scent is strong in my nostrils, her taste on my tongue. I thank God and Dr. K once again for restoring the billions of nerve connections between my brain and my prostheses, and wonder how chemical and electrical discharges can result in such pleasure. With a jolt I remember the ten billion little monsters eating away at me, and wonder if any of them are now swimming around in her, looking for something to chew on. I know there aren't—at least, Dr. K said it was impossible—but I still wonder.

I watch Alice's breathing slow into sleep, watch the sweat dry, watch her nipples relax, broaden and become flaccid. I close my eyes and my mind drifts…

Alice screams, and my eyes snap open.

"They're in me!" She's clawing at herself, her nails leaving crimson trails as she scratches and screams. Blood flows from between her thighs and screams tear from her throat. "Get them out! Gary! Help me!"

She looks at me, but my eyes are fixed on her pubis. The flesh dissolves, and she screams again. Nano-sized maggots writhe through the skin, eating her alive, and all I can do is stare...

"Gary!"

I bolt upright, sweat pouring off my body. My eyes focus, take in the scene. Alice is sitting up beside me, worry painting her face with wrinkles. One hand grips my arm, the other clenches the sheet to her breast. There is no blood; no monsters.

"Gary? Are you okay?"

"Yeah." I roll up out of bed, heart pounding, hands shaking, and head for the bathroom. "Bad dream."

"I'll say." She drops the sheet and follows me. "You sure you're all right? You want to talk about it?"

"It's...difficult." I splash cold water on my face, then scrub it off with a towel. "I don't think you'd understand."

"Try me." She puts her hands on me and catches my eye in the mirror. "Please."

"The psych doc said that nightmares are normal in my... situation. I appreciate you trying to help, babe. Really. But I don't know what to do about it other than to try to work it out on my own." For a moment her eyes widen, as if I'd slapped her, and I have to lower my gaze in guilt at having hurt her when she's trying to help.

"What..." she begins tentatively, "what about talking with someone who's been through it? You said you got an e-mail from one of the guys you rescued. The local guy? He even said he'd buy you a beer, right? I know you said you weren't ready to face any of them yet, but I think that, well, maybe you should take him up on it."

I consider it. Someone else with monsters.

Alice's fingers flutter like butterflies against my back. She taps them when she's anxious...and she's anxious about me. No, she's anxious for me. I might not be transferring monsters into her body, but I'm sure as hell putting some into her head.

I turn toward her and take her hands in mine. "Sure, I'll e-mail him, go out for a beer. Talk. If it's okay with you."

"Of course it's okay, hon." Alice smiles. I can see that it hurts her, realizing that there's nothing she can do to help me, but at least she can smile. "I don't care *where* you get the help, Gary, as long as you get it."

"Thanks," I say, and I mean it.

The beer tastes flat. Dirty taps. The bar is a bit of a dive: two pool tables, darts, and an electronic slot machine that hasn't been touched by a human hand in probably a year. There's no AC and the air's thick, even with the door open and a box fan blowing in from outside. I watch a drop of moisture work its way down the side my chilled mug, eating the smaller droplets and getting bigger, gaining momentum…eating and growing…eating and growing…

"You're thinkin' too much, Gary," Wills says, downing the last of his draft. "Not good for ya."

"I know." I sip, grimace and swallow. I look over at Wills, down at his legs. They're prosthetic from the knee down. I know. I saw him lose them. "The legs doin' good?"

"Better than the originals!" he says with a grin. "I had two bad knees from football, ya know. The new ones don't hurt at all. Of course, I can't play pro ball now because they'd say I'd been enhanced." He puts air quotes around the last word, then laughs. "Then again, who wants to deal with all that shit: contracts, millions of dollars, trophy wives…" He looks me up and down. "Heard you lost a bit more'n me. All the new parts workin' okay?" He looks me up and down again with a stupid grin and I know he knows exactly how much has been replaced.

"Ask your wife," I quip without missing a beat. I know Wills isn't married, but the joke works anyway, or maybe it works *because* he's not married. He laughs, and buys another round.

"I have nightmares, Wills," I admit, sipping my second flat beer. "Not about the combat but about…other things."

"The bugs?"

"How'd you know?" I look at him, but he just barks a laugh utterly devoid of humor, the way you laugh when you find out your utility check has bounced and you don't get paid again for another week.

"You're a Nipper, Gary," he says. I'd heard the term for people with nano-interface prosthetics, but no one has ever used it to my face before. I can see why. "I'm a Nipper. Every Nipper has nightmares." Another humorless laugh. "Anyone who says they don't is a fuckin' liar."

"My psych doc said—"

He interrupts me with a loud raspberry. "Fuckin' egg-head shrinks think they know everything. They don't know fuck!" He drains his mug and stands. "Come on, Gary. Let me show you somethin'."

I leave my half-full beer and a decent tip, and follow Wills out the door. He flips one of his tree-trunk legs over his bike and fires it up. "Hop on." He tosses me a spare helmet. I catch it and shrug.

"Where we going?" I put the helmet on and climb aboard. I'm not too worried about Wills having had two beers; he weighs about twice what I do.

"Up Blue Hills. I wanna show you somethin'."

"Okay."

"Hang on."

The bike thunders up the street and through the neighborhood. I don't really follow the route he's taking, but I know the way. Every male who grew up in South Boston knows the way up to the Blue Hills overlook, and can drive it with one hand on the wheel and the other on a pretty girl's knee. It's a nice ride once we get out of town and onto the twisting shaded road, and I try to enjoy it.

The seat jackhammers my ass as we slow over the big cobblestones of the parking strip, and the bike rumbles to a stop. The afternoon sun is behind us and Boston spreads out before us. Wills just stares out at the city, not saying a word. I look out and try to discern details.

Construction cranes and half-rebuilt skyscrapers reach into the sky like skeletal robot fingers. Most of the North End is still rubble, dozens of bulldozers scraping up the wreckage of century-old homes; it's amazing the damage an LNG tanker does when it explodes. There are still workers at Logan Airport, swarms of dumptrucks and skiploaders rebuilding the runway out into Boston Harbor. This is the first time I've seen the reconstruction effort as a whole, and it stirs something in me; so many people working to rebuild what was destroyed.

"It's like us, Gary," Wills says finally as he turns to me, pointing to the city with one hand and tapping his knee with the other. "The little guys are doing the work down there, and in here." His thick finger now taps my chest.

I look out again, and an idea clicks in my head.

"Ten billion little monsters..." I mutter, "...healing scars."

We stand in silence for a long while, then Wills snorts.

"I guess ya could consider me one of your little monsters," he says. "I got a job in construction now. We tear down the damaged buildings, clean up the mess, so rebuilding can start."

"You're eating away the city's scars…"

"The way I see it," Wills says, flipping a leg over his bike and kicking the monster to life. "Scar tissue's not healthy. It makes ya think back on the bad things instead of movin' forward toward the good. That's no fuckin' way to live."

I look back at him, then out at the city. Ten billion little monsters, some working together, some not. Maybe he's right. Maybe it's time to start eating up the scar tissue. Maybe it's time to start healing.

❧

COWARD

Todd McCaffrey

LIEUTENANT MONET EYED HIS security detail as they fanned out, ensuring that they took exactly the positions he'd prescribed. Overhead, the roar of the dropship grew louder and louder but neither he nor the rest of his platoon paid it the slightest attention, even as wisps of dust began stirring on the concrete paving beneath their feet.

Wind rose and roared as the dropship hovered for a moment, extended its wide legs and landed. The hardened landing pad seemed to lurch slightly under its weight. The roar of the jets ceased and their sound was replaced by the mechanical noise of the ramp being extended, lowered to the ground.

Monet raised his eyes, glancing beyond the dropship to the four heavy assault ships arrayed strategically around the edge of the landing field.

Enemy assault ships.

His government had demanded it, had insisted on the protection that it, now demilitarized, could no longer provide.

For the heroes were coming home.

The Star Ranger Division, Rhone's finest, were finally being returned.

Monet was not there for them, however. He and his security platoon had only one purpose, one man: The Coward of Corair.

A noise from inside the dropship caused him to look toward it. The skirl of bagpipes, an honor guard, formed and marched down the ramp, colors flying.

Of all the Divisions of Rhone, only this one had been allowed to keep its colors after their defeat by the Empire.

Behind him, someone cleared his throat loudly. "They're turned out well."

Monet's shoulders stiffened involuntarily. No matter how hard he tried, he couldn't prevent the reaction. It was one thing to know that the field was guarded by Imperial assault ships, quite another to have to remember that their commander was standing right behind him.

The honor guard marched clear of the ramp, executed a textbook rear-march and halted, bagpipes still skirling, colors raised high as another troop formed up and marched out of the rust-stained, battered combat dropship.

"Are they disembarking by *platoons?*" Monet cried, the words surprised out of him as he saw the first small group move into sight.

"By battalions," the Imperial general behind him growled, contempt for Monet evident in his tone.

The Star Ranger division was composed of three independent brigades, each composed of three battalions. A spaceforce battalion numbered between six hundred and seven hundred and fifty combatants.

"I'd heard they'd been decimated," Monet said, as he picked out the colors of the first battalion, the 1st of the 1st—the famous Iron Battalion of the equally famous Iron Brigade.

"So your government said," the general replied. Monet turned enough to meet the Imperial general's eyes and saw the cold flint in them.

"This looks like *only* a tenth survived," Monet protested.

"That's correct," General von Kampf agreed, turning his eyes back toward the dropship and the next formation exiting it.

Monet copied him even as more questions began to nag at him.

The government of Rhone had made it very clear that it had been the arrant cowardice of the Star Ranger's commander which had caused the surrender of the wormhole to the Imperium.

At first the news reports had been full of praise for the gallant Star Rangers and General Cowan. This was the premiere division of the Star Army of Rhone, the front-line defense against any aggressor. The Star Rangers had the best of men and the best of training, the best equipment and the best positions.

As the Imperial attack continued, however, the news reports changed. Fort Clarion had been lost—one of the three largest of the three dozen forts guarding the precious wormhole transit point. Then Fort Alphonse, Fort Beauregard—all of the front-line fortresses.

The Star Rangers, according to the reports, clung bitterly to the remaining forts and even set up special fortifications amongst the asteroid fields surrounding the wormhole. For two weeks the news was good. The government announced that the Star Division, well-supplied, at full strength, was able to hold the enemy up for a month or more—certainly long enough for Rhone to convince the nearby star systems to bring aid.

Then Premiere Algonquin spoke to the planet with terrible news: *"Nous sommes trahis!" We are betrayed.*

Forty-eight hours later, the Imperial battleships entered orbit and the red, white, and green flag of independent Rhone was ignominiously hauled down from the capital.

Shocked, betrayed, and desperate, the government lost no time in assigning blame for this terrible defeat. Clearly, the loss rested in the hands of the one man who commanded the most powerful force in the arsenal of Rhone—General Cowan, now named the Coward of Corair, after the last remaining fortress of the wormhole—the fortress from which he had negotiated the surrender of the Star Rangers.

Monet looked impassively at the ranks of that famous division. If they only knew! Would they turn on their commander? Would they tear him from limb to limb for his treachery?

He made a hand signal to his men as the ninth battalion—another remnant little larger than a platoon—stood to attention and the tone of the bagpipes changed.

At first he did not recognize the tune—he was no fan of Celtic music, preferring the rich tones of Rhone and the distant symphonies of France—but it was one that was familiar and haunting.

Londonderry Air.

As one, the Star Rangers removed their classic black berets, berets adorned with the three stars of their division, raised their hands to their brows and saluted.

They saluted as the Coward of Comair and his headquarters battalion descended the stairs.

The color drained from Monet's face as he saw their numbers. Headquarters battalion for a division numbered no fewer than eight hundred. Eight hundred of the toughest soldiers ever to have donned a spacesuit.

Down the ramp came seven.

In front of the other six was one man, his leg in a cast, his right arm in a sling.

He paused at the top of the ramp and removed his beret. He stood as best his could and saluted, left-handed, holding his salute with a trembling arm until at last, his eyes running with tears, he lowered it again.

Finally! Monet thought to himself. Now we can finish this farce. He nodded toward Chevarre, his trusted adjutant. Chevarre's jaw tightened, one eyelid lowered fractionally to show that he understood his orders. Good man, Monet thought to himself.

General Cowan spotted Monet and nodded to himself. One of the men behind him rushed forward, pointing toward Monet, and spoke quickly in Cowan's ear. Cowan seemed to listen politely, then shook his head, emphasizing it with a hand gesture. The man seemed ready to argue but Cowan shook his head once more. The General's aide or whoever he was, raised his head and called out in a loud voice that carried throughout the field, "Division! Present Arms!"

As one, the twelve hundred and twenty-seven survivors of Rhone's finest division moved with exquisite precision. Even the wounded shifted, raising themselves where possible to sit up and salute while those more wounded raised their arms—those who still had them—to honor their commander.

General Cowan, visibly moved, returned the salute and held it for a long moment before walking down the ramp toward the waiting detachment. He didn't get far as the troops broke ranks and surrounded him, heedless of the calls to order from their superiors.

Slowly, General Cowan moved through the mass of his troops toward Monet and his detachment. When he reached them, Monet stood still, not raising his arm in salute. Behind the General, the troops of the Star Rangers murmured ominously at the dishonor.

"General Cowan, commanding, Star Ranger Division," Cowan said as his gaze brushed over Lieutenant Monet's nameplate.

"Sir, I am requested and required to inform you that you are under arrest pending a court martial on the handling of your division," Monet told him crisply, signaling to his men, who moved toward him.

They did not get far, finding themselves blocked by burly Space Rangers.

"The Division will stand down," General Cowan said loudly, his eyes still on Monet.

Reluctantly, the burly soldiers moved aside, allowing the less intimidating security detachment to surround the General.

Cowan smiled slightly and raised his hands to the Lieutenant. "Sir, I surrender myself into your custody pending the inquiry into my actions."

"Court martial, sir," Monet corrected him harshly. Behind him one of the security men murmured, "Coward."

A movement from behind Monet distracted them at that moment. General van Kampf stepped forward, his hand outstretched.

"General Cowan," the Imperial general said, clicking his heels together sharply as he extended his hand.

"General van Kampf," Cowan said, his lips tight.

"I am sorry for your losses sir," the general said. He nodded to the division beyond. "Your division fought with exceptional gallantry."

Cowan accepted that with a sharp nod. Then he noticed something. "I see that you have the honor of commanding the Imperial's finest."

General van Kampf turned his head to survey the colors of the guard behind him. "Yes, I have the honor to command the Emperor's Own Kashtreya."

Cowan nodded. "Perhaps one day you'll explain their history to the Lieutenant."

General van Kampf clicked his heels together once more. "It would be my honor."

Cowan turned back to the lieutenant. "Very well, Lieutenant, I am your prisoner."

His words flowed back to his troops and there was an immediate cry of outrage.

"Where are you taking the General?"

"Leave him here, with us!"

"They're arresting him!"

"Arresting the General, why?"

"They're going to court martial him!"

Quickly the mood turned ugly, then uglier, and Monet motioned for his detachment to form close around the General as they shuffled slowly toward the waiting ground transport.

The discipline of the Star Rangers shattered and they started pummeling the guard detachment. The guards grew scared and drew their weapons. There was a sudden, loud *crack!*—a single shot.

General Cowan slid slowly to the ground.

Monet looked over toward the sound only to see Chevarre, his pistol drawn, with a look of triumph on his face. Without thinking, even before the troops of the Star Rangers could react, Monet drew his own pistol and shot his trooper—a head shot: direct, deadly, final.

Chevarre's body crumpled to the ground beside Cowan's and Monet raised his pistol. "It was an accident! Stand down! Star Division, stand down!"

A wave of shocked silence swept across the field. Slowly, the men of the Star Rangers drew close to their commander. A group of men gently raised the body, raised it high and carried it back toward the dropship's ramp and the remaining staff.

As he regained control, Monet gestured to his men to gather up

Chevarre's body, grabbed his comm and tersely relayed the news to his superior.

A hand clapped his shoulder and Monet jumped before he realized it was the Imperial General.

"Well done," General van Kampf said. "That was a difficult situation and you handled it well." He gave the lieutenant a very bitter smile. "Your superiors will doubtless be pleased."

"I lost my man," Monet said.

General van Kampf shook his head. "You don't fool me, Lieutenant."

Monet gave him a sharp look.

"Let me tell you about the Emperor's Own Kashtreya," General van Kampf said. "After all, I'd promised General Cowan and I'd like to keep my honor."

"I don't see—"

"No, of course not," van Kampf interrupted. "You follow orders, do your duty and hope for promotion." He pursed his lips sourly. "Your superiors tell you that Cowan is a traitor and you believe them."

"But—"

"Do you know how many troops fought against your Star Rangers?"

"A weak, understrength division, everyone knows that!"

"A full corps," van Kampf corrected. "And that was to start. A full, battle-hardened, assault-trained Imperial Guard Corps." He shook his head. "We wanted a quick victory. Do you think we'd commit inferior troops or numbers?"

A look of doubt entered Monet's eyes.

"In the end, we had to commit ten full divisions to the assault," van Kampf said. "In the end, it was the Emperor's Own Kashtreya who broke through the command center, who took the General and his six surviving staff—all the headquarters company had been destroyed."

"But—he surrendered! He never fought! He didn't try!"

"Ten divisions," van Kampf repeated, shaking his head. "And our casualties were appalling. This was the worst battle in the history of the Empire." Monet shook his head, refusing to believe. "It was. This was worse than the Battle of the Forlorn."

"The Forlorn?" Monet repeated, surprised. The Battle of the Forlorn was legendary, more famous even than the ancient battle of Thermopylae.

"The Forlorn: where one battalion held up the Emperor's best for two weeks," van Kampf said in agreement. He waved his hand back at the troops behind him. "The Kashtreya battalion, to be precise."

"Them?" Monet asked in surprise. "They joined the Empire?"

"Naturally," van Kampf said. "Do you recall what happened to their commander?"

Monet shook his head.

"He survived the battle, you know," van Kampf said. "Very much like your General Cowan." He nodded as he saw the growing alarm in the lieutenant's eyes. "He survived, was charged with cowardice, was shot by someone and died in dishonor."

"So the Kashtreya—"

"The Kashtreya accused their government of assassinating the commander," van Kampf cut across him. "Within three months, members of the Kashtreya had proof, the government collapsed and—naturally, the Emperor moved in to restore order."

"The Kashtreya were cowards."

"No, their government was," van Kampf said. "And the Kashtreya proved it." He gave a quick, short smile and continued, "The Emperor makes many of his acquisitions in this manner, you know. Just letting corrupt governments prove their unworthiness, their willingness to sacrifice not only lives but honor for their own ends."

He turned back toward the grieving men of the Star Rangers. "How long, Lieutenant, do you think it will be before I can welcome them as the Emperor's Own Star Rangers?"

Lieutenant Monet made an inarticulate noise, half moan, half gargle.

"Do you think these men will stand by, these men who fought ten divisions to a standstill, do you think these men won't demand justice? And do you honestly think that a government that can coerce a mere lieutenant into murdering their best general will long survive?"

General van Kampf shook his head, enjoying the lieutenant's misery. "Six months. Six months at the most, and then your planet of Rhone will be another Imperial protectorate." He met the lieutenant's eyes squarely, his lips stretched in a vulpine smile. "And *that's* why I let you assassinate him."

Nine Letters Found in a Muddied Case on the Road in Baden, Germany

Xander Briggs

August 6, 1837

Dearest Isabella,

At last we have done it! The beast is dead! After near two months of tracking the cursed thing throughout these bedamnéd woodlands, we were finally able to follow the so-called "Schwarzwälder Wolf" back to its lair. We fell upon it yesterday evening when it emerged to hunt at dusk. I will spare you the grisly details, beloved, but I think Andrew and I both performed admirably in our tasks and, more, proved that this system we have devised works. Not only on this menace, or the Greyshire Beast, or the Balkan Terror, but on any creature of this type. With what we have gathered from this case and those others we have dealt with through the last several years, we can compile a definitive book on the hunting and dispatch of these natural aberrations so commonly called monsters. An encyclopedia of lore and technique so that not only fellow-hunters but local governments and even the general population might see the signs and be able to stop such an outbreak before any others die or otherwise succumb.

The beast did manage to score a strike against me in the midst of our struggle (Andrew lost control of the noose for a moment), but it scarcely broke the skin, and I'm certain that even these inept rural physicians can keep a wound clean until we return to Stuttgart. The only matter of business that remains here is collecting the bounty we were promised by the regional constabulary and bidding farewell to the townsfolk who have harbored us and our strange demands throughout our stay.

Along with the other presents I promised you, we are also bringing back the creature's head. Andrew is insistent that we pickle it so that soft tissue might be intact and we might turn it over to the Royal Society. While I understand his desire to further the cause of Reason and the Understanding of the Monstrous, I fear the so-called Men of Science would simply butcher the thing. It seems to me that such ill treatment would do the brute a great disservice. The beast was truly an impressive creature, a force of terrible beauty in its own right. Perhaps it is some Pagan sentiment that stirs my heart, but I think such a worthy adversary deserves a nobler memorial than mere dissection.

Ah, but Andrew calls. I suppose we are to go and see the magistrate now. Take heart, beloved, for I shall return to England and your arms in a scant few weeks. I will write again when I know the date.

Yours Forever,
Reginald

August 15, 1837

Isabella,

I apologize that this letter is not what you must hope it to be. I promised that I would return soon—and I shall, as soon as I am able—but circumstances beyond my control conspire to delay us here. It is a small matter, but requires my personal attention.

On a brighter note, in light of our delay, Andrew has relented to my wishes for the disposal of the beast's head, and had it taxidermied by one of the local furriers. In fact (if you will pardon your husband the morbid conceit) it is sitting on the desk in front of me, as if its glass eyes might watch me write. It is not as terrifying as it was in life, I think, but now it haunts the mind in an altogether different way. When the monster's muzzle—no, I will speak truly and call it a face—is not animated, it is easier to see the human aspect of the thing. It was human once, however long ago, yet unlike the cruder beasts we had fought before, this one seemed to have somehow mastered its baser instincts and retained enough intelligence to become...something different. A villain to this place. A true threat. Yet, if I am correct and it gained its dominance and power with a shred of human intellect, why turn that intellect against its fellow man? The more I contemplate the puzzle of the werewolf, the fewer answers I seem to have.

Yet I should speak of better things. While we search for solutions to our pressing problem, we have taken the opportunity to delve deeper into the lair to which we tracked the beast. It was rough, but surprisingly well-appointed. Again I am reminded of the theory that it was once human, and suppose that it still retained some desire to live as its human self must have done. Most curiously, however, we discovered that the dwelling-chambers near the surface connected to still-deeper caverns, which were completely navigable even to the surface. If it had only fled deeper, it could have escaped our pursuit. Why did it not? As the thing is dead (and thankfully so! I do not forget that it had slain upwards of fifty locals in its mad marauding), I suppose we shall never know.

Though my return may be delayed, still know that I will be with you as soon as I am able. Keep me in your thoughts and prayers.

Truest love,

Reginald

August 30, 1837

Isabella,

I appreciate your desire to be with me as soon as you are able, and it is with every ounce of my being that I wish I could be in your arms, but your plan is utterly unfeasible. This is no land for a proper woman. It's scarcely a land for a proper man.

Our conclusion of this matter has been complicated, but we are endeavoring to resolve the difficulties as soon as possible so we might return to England, and to you. Please, be patient and bear with me. You are in my thoughts and prayers every day.

Yours,

Reginald

September 2, 1837

Beloved,

My last missive was not entirely sincere, and the weight of what I omitted has weighed so heavily upon me that I feel I must explain. I do not know what will become of me, and I will not carry the burden of dishonesty to the grave with me. Not if it is dishonesty to you. I said that I did not wish you here because it is a difficult land. That is true, but a merest inconvenience, and something I would bid you suffer if that was the only thing that kept us apart. No, beloved, the true reason I bid you stay in London is because I dare not allow you close to me at this time.

I do not know how to even begin to broach this subject, for I fear it will sound as if I have been untruthful, but you must know that if I lied by omission, it was only to protect you and your feelings. In truth, we have not yet returned because the wound I gained from the beast has certain properties. I admit that some of our sources of research had hinted that the beast might be possessed of some form of curse that might be spread like a sinister infection, but the folktales were many. How were we to know which ones were true?

Though the wound has healed and has scarcely even scarred, I have begun to experience queer symptoms. The local priest, who is the best expert in the truth of these matters that we can find in this area, says that it is likely my symptoms may worsen as the full moon draws nearer. Still, we have some time until that date, and we have many remedies yet to try. I am a fit man, and I think my body can tolerate whatever the Devil may throw at me. I only ask that you have patience, and remain in London. If you would do anything to help me right now, Isabella, I bid you pray. Pray as often and as truly as you can, for it seems by the priest's appraisal that this is not so much an ailment of the flesh as a corruption of the soul. Pray my soul is strong enough.

Yours,

Reginald

September 4, 1837

Isabella,

I have found enlightenment. It is a strange thing to say, perhaps, but oh, my love, if you could have felt what I felt! The full moon came as they had said it would, and I awaited it with dread. Andrew insisted I confine myself to a certain willing farmer's shed, so I would not disturb others when the change inevitably came.

So I agreed, and at first, it seemed that nothing was happening, until I seemed to hear a song, a song that came from the wood and the air, and it wasn't only a song, but a smell, as well, green and crisp and cool, and I had the fancy that it was the sound and smell of moonlight, which must be flooding the world outside my dark, putrid shed, and I inhaled the moonlight with every breath, until it coursed through my veins. Ice and fire were one, as the poet might say, and so were man and beast. It was painful, yes, a pain unlike any other, like my entire body was being rent apart around me, but behind the pain flowed joy, a joy I could not suppress.

I broke down the door to the shed, and I was delivered into the moonlight and took my first breaths in my soul's form. I ran as a wolf, Isabella, and I have no words for the beauty of the thing. I was free, free of everything that binds and confines a man. I had no conception of guilt or shame or suffering, knew only the beauty of the moment and of living. Oh, beloved, I cannot explain. If only the bard Blake could know how the mind-forged manacles might be bitten asunder and cast off! I was alive and wild in the forest, and in the moonlight, beloved, I truly think that my soul was alone with God.

Andrew presses me to continue the search for a cure, but there is so much of this newfound flesh that I wish to explore. I admit that there are things that I must learn to temper—the beast's hunger, for instance. No, you need not worry that I have become a monster like the one we slew. I limited my own predations to a single young ewe, but the hunger was not sated until I was restored as a man the next morning and able to gorge myself at breakfast—and even then, my body craved meat and much of it. I think perhaps that it is because it took a great deal of strength to undergo the transformation, and my own flesh was much-depleted. Tomorrow night (for the beast ran three nights of the month when it first appeared) I will try to eat as much as I can before dusk falls, and see if that will at least dull the need.

I apologize again for this delay. I will continue my quest to remove this affliction so that I might return to you, and I am optimistic that we might, especially now that I know that I still retain my mind when the curse is active. I will write again when things develop further, and I thank you ever for your continued devotion.

—Reginald

September 17, 1837

My dear Isabella,

I took the head into the wood with me and returned it to its home. Andrew objected, but I think he has begun to fear me too much to go against my will. I have spent long nights gazing into the creature's face, the face of this being who we had tracked, whose habits we had learned so intimately, who in his death gave me a new life. I could no longer in good conscience treat a piece of that noble corpse as a mere hunting trophy. I buried it outside the caves where the wolf had dwelled, and marked the grave with a cairn of stones. I would have said a prayer, but what God would I address it to? Into whose arms does a werewolf go in his final rest? So I was silent and solemn, and let the birds and beasts of the wood sing the dirges that they know. I think that is what he would have wished.

Do you remember when we met, and all the world was full of hope and the promise of revolution? We vowed we would never let this world oppress our dreams and our God-given faculties, and yet what has become of us? You should have been so much more, and for all my love, sometimes I regret having bound you with the shackles of matrimony. If I die here, will you reach for freedom? You are bright and strong, more powerful a person than I shall ever be. Will you prove that to those who would oppress you because of your sex? A widow might do more than a maid or a married woman. Might have a shred more self in the fool man's eyes.

The town has a stench, these days. Perhaps it is the lingering summer warmth, or perhaps it is my own senses that are made more acute by my transformation. It sickens me to go out on windless days, and yet being trapped in my chamber is nearly as sickening. What if this lingers, even once I am cured? London was already a cesspool even before I had seen through the eyes of a beast. What must it be, now? I fear that it is my mind which has changed, or some essential element of my spirit which now longs to rove free in the world of nature. The forest calls to me, even on moonless nights. I think that if it were not for you, I would never return to the cities and the world of men. You are my anchor, Isabella. Hold tight until this storm has passed. I cannot imagine what I shall be if I should come unmoored.

—Reginald

October 12, 1837

Issi,

This is the last letter I will write to you, for I am leaving the town and will not return. Perhaps I will live as a Pagan beast in the forest, perhaps I will find new caves to shape a dwelling for myself. I do not know, but I do not think the natives will take kindly to me returning to them to post my letters. Know I love you. I love you more now than I ever have, and my soul is torn open with that loving.

I dreamed last night that we ran together as wolves, free of all bonds and constraints, free to be who we were, beings of radiant light. The night was silver and green around us, alive with the music of the spheres that man has forgotten how to hear, and as we spoke without words, I remembered all the power of our first kiss.

It is no wonder the beast, my father, my savior, went mad in his lonely wood and lonely cave, for neither man nor wolf is a solitary creature. Men drove him from civilization because he represented something older and greater than they, and it was long ago that they hunted true wolves near to extinction in these parts. What place is there for a creature who is the best of both?

The moon will be rising near-full tonight, and tomorrow night they say that astronomers predict an eclipse. The locals see it as a dark omen, especially falling upon the 13th of the month, and a Friday. A witches' sign, they say. I have never seen a witch, but I think now I would have much to share with them.

Andrew returns to England without me, and I do not begrudge his decision. The world is alive beneath my paws and in my nostrils, and every leaf and twig is God. Tell them you are widowed, beloved, for I think in many ways you are. The man you loved is dead of his wound, and something far greater was reborn from those ashes. Farewell, my Isabella. I will not forget you.

—Your Love

October 16, 1837

Mrs. Hanson,

I write to you with grim heart and grimmer news. I don't have Reg's skill with words, so I won't mince them. He's gone. He took a wound from the beast we were tracking, and he fought bravely, killed the thing himself, and it was my fault I couldn't hold the thing as well as I thought, so if you need someone to blame, blame me. I never knew a better man and I am honored I was able to work with him. The priest here says he'll do his best for rites, and even though there's still trouble, I'm coming back to London. Maybe I'm a coward, but this one's a job for someone else.

Because it's what Reg asked for, I'm posting you his share of the bounty we got for the beast. I know it's little consolation, but it's what I can do.

Deepest sympathy,

Andrew McCall

November 30, 1837

Mrs. Hanson,

I'm glad to hear your family has taken you in, in this troubling time. I'd hate to think you'd have to suffer this alone. Sadly, the distance and my dealings in London mean I have to post this to you instead of delivering it in person, though you'll have to give my best to your sister Clara, if she still remembers my name.

I still think it's a bit of a grim memento to keep, but I'm a man of my word, and you're right. It does have notes in Reg's hand. So here's the map to the wolf-beast's cave, as promised. I'm not sure what you want with it, and I hope no one else plans to use it, but if it helps you remember him, I hope it brings you comfort.

If there's anything else I can do, don't hesitate to write. Reg would've wanted me to take care of you however I could.

—Andrew McCall

THE ONCE AND NOW-ISH KING

J.M. Frey

THE FIRST THING THAT Arthur Pendragon, the Once and Future (well, *Now-ish*) King, did upon his rebirth into the world at the moment of Albion's greatest need, was to open his shriveled red mouth and squall out: "Oh *hell*, no."

Which startled his mother quite badly, you'll understand, as she had just put him to her breast for his first little feeding. She shook her head and glared balefully at the IV needle in the bend of her elbow, ignored her new son's outburst, and went about her task.

The second thing that Arthur Pendragon, the Once and Now-ish King, did upon his rebirth into the world at the moment of Albion's greatest need, was to consume his body weight in breast milk. After which, he soiled his nappy, burped quite dramatically, and took a wee bit of a nap.

Getting born was hard work, you know.

The next thing that Arthur Pendragon, the Once and Now-ish King, did upon his rebirth was to wake up and ask to where that good for nothing senile git of a wizard had gotten. Nobody else was in the hospital room with Arthur and his new mother, so he had to repeat it a few times to convince her that she was not, in fact, hearing things. "Great ancient sorcerer with the beard?"

"What, Dumbledore?" his mother asked, trying to make her eyes the size of regular eyes again, rather than saucers. She wasn't quite succeeding. "Or, um, Merlin?"

"Yes, Merlin!" Arthur shrilled, then frowned because his voice hadn't been that high since, well, since the last time he was a baby. In a more sedate, and what he hoped was a more kingly tone, he went on to clarify: "Who the hell else would I mean?"

"I, uh, I'm sure I don't know, dearest," his mother said, and started to cry.

Arthur felt quite bad about that, because she seemed a nice lady, especially since she had just put up with him in her womb for nine months. He resolved to be a bit gentler with her thereafter.

Were Guinevere here, she would surely have clipped him round his ears already.

Arthur was quiet on the way home, watching with utter fascination as his new father manhandled the strange metal carriage in which they rode. The motion of the vehicle made him nod off, soothing and quite like being tucked up safe and sound in a caring person's arms. His only grievance with this was that he had hoped to see more of the strange and wonderful world outside of the vehicle's windows. There were tall buildings and everything was covered in glass. Some great king must have been very wealthy to afford to give his subjects a whole city of glass.

The thought caused his tiny tummy to burble with foreboding, because perhaps this wealthy king was the very person he had been brought back to defeat. Shoving thoughts of his destiny aside for now—it was not as if he had Excalibur, or was yet strong enough to even lift her—he let the rocking motion lull him into a doze.

Once they arrived home, Arthur made a point of vocally admiring the shade of green on the walls of his nursery, and complimented his mother on her pretty coming-home dress. He had, after all, promised himself to be nicer.

She started crying again, and Arthur, who had never really been all that good with girls and who probably wouldn't have ever been able to attract a wife had he not had a crown weighing on his forehead, looked at his father and said, "What did I do?" He *really* wished Guinevere were here. His father only plopped down into the rocking chair and stared in horror at his little face.

"What?" Arthur said.

"I...don't think this was in the baby books, hon," his father said, all the blood draining from his face. If the man was going to swoon, Arthur hoped to at least be set down somewhere first. But the man stayed upright. He gulped on the air for a bit, then when his colour had mostly come back, he stood and lay Arthur in the middle of the crib and grabbed his wife's wrist. They left. Arthur heard the footsteps pad across the carpeting, traverse the hallway and then descend the stairs and go out the front door.

Oh, dear.

For a long, long time, Arthur lay still, listening. There was no shouting, no noisy roar of an unhappy lynch mob or of the metal vehicles. There was only Arthur and the inadequate swaddling blanket and the boring white ceiling. There were also five fuzzy white sheep that kept going around and around above his head, hypnotic and really sort of...marvellous.

Right around when his stomach started to cramp with hunger, but after the King of Albion had suffered the indignity of losing control of his own bowels and soiling his nappy, his mother came back.

She hovered in the doorway for a moment, and Arthur gummed his bottom lip and tried to decide if he should say anything. It was, after all, what had gotten him into this mess. Before he could, she darted across the floor like a war charger and scooped him close and pressed his cheek against her neck and said, "I'm sorry, I'm sorry, I'm so sorry. It doesn't matter, it doesn't, you're my son and you're perfect and I love you."

Arthur reached up and patted her cheek gently. "I understand," he said, and sort of thought that he did.

Then his mother offered him a bottle, and he tried not to be disappointed. He wouldn't want to nurse a baby with the thought processes and memories of an adult man either, really, but the bottle meant she was rejecting him, if only a little. Arthur's stomach swooped in fear, and he realized it was because he didn't want to lose those tender, affectionate moments when he was wrapped in his mother's arms, head against her breast and the sound of her heart soothing him. He supposed he couldn't blame her. It had to be weird, having a fully articulate, fully cognizant child latching to your breast.

Arthur was doing his damndest to stay asleep and not let the little hunger cramps or the haunting sense that he wasn't bundled up enough wake him every few hours. It was uncomfortable and odd, but he was determined. He was absolutely capable of letting his parents get a full night's sleep, and perhaps to do the same himself. Having always been a man of strong will, he managed to do just that.

Somewhere in the middle of all of it, Arthur also managed to dream.

He was standing on a battlefield and he knew Mordred was behind him, but he couldn't turn around fast enough. He hadn't been fast enough in real life, either. Then there was Guinevere's big liquid eyes, and Lancelot's guilty frown, and something Merlin whispered in his ear about coming back one day, about the future of the kingdom resting upon his soul, about being called forth again like the pagan gods from their barrows...

And then there was a shrill screaming, the likes of which Arthur hadn't heard since once of his horses had fallen into a pit dug in the road by his enemies and snapped its foreleg. He'd killed the stallion for pity. It wasn't until someone's big warm hands were on his back and he felt himself tucked protectively against his father's soft, sloping chest that he realized he was awake and the shrill, plaintive sounds were coming from him. He, the Once and Now-ish King, was sobbing hysterically.

"Shhhh, buddy," his father said, and jogged him a few times, bumping him closer to wakefulness. "You're safe, you're safe. Daddy's here."

Arthur snuffled closer and let himself cry out the rest of his residual fear, because what his father said was true. He was safe here. At least for now. There were no dragons to slay, no traitors to rout, no scheming and politics to navigate, no affair to untangle. There was only Arthur, and his father's warm assurance, the sound of his mother's soft snores in the other room, and the woolly sheep spinning in a calm, slow circle, blown by the cool breeze of the nighttime air slipping past the gap in the endearingly crooked windowsill.

"Daddy," Arthur said, curling chubby fists into the collar of the man's sleep shirt, and didn't feel ridiculous at all for using such a juvenile term. King Uther would have boxed young Arthur's ears for daring to utter it, but here, now, it felt right. "I'm Arthur," he breathed.

"I know," the man said, and dropped a soft, dry kiss on his son's cheek. "That *is* what we put on the birth certificate."

The open affection of the gesture shocked Arthur into more tears, though these ones were soft, quiet, and grateful.

A few days later, Arthur's father was comfortable enough with his verbosity to hold complete, if distracted, conversations. Which was good, because the nightmare of his death had been subtly shifting each time Arthur fell asleep; he still stood on a field, but instead of being behind him with a sword, Mordred now stood before him on a broad grassy plain, and unlike the battlefield of his memory it was free of blood and the fallen. Instead of being alone on that knoll, he now had the vague impression of being watched on all sides, and of the tension that crackled between him and his traitorous nephew. They both wanted—coveted—something, and Arthur wondered if it was a crown again, or something more vital. Something more dangerous.

He stood and stared at Mordred and Mordred stood and stared at him, hands out as if prepared to grapple, weaponless and ready to strike. Arthur wished he had Excalibur so he could wallop the whelp down before the ungrateful snake could do him in a second time.

But then the dream ended; it always ended before either of them made a move.

Arthur felt that it was perhaps a warning, a vision of the future or the battle to come, and Arthur wanted to be certain he knew what it meant when the time arrived. He needed to understand, and the only way he could do that was to ask questions, to discuss.

But he couldn't do that until his father, so far the only other person besides his mother he trusted enough with this information, understood what was at stake.

"I feel the need to clarify," Arthur said as his father closed the bedroom door behind them. Downstairs were his mother's parents and his father's sister, all of whom had come to coo at the new baby and who, Arthur's father had patiently explained that morning, probably didn't need to know that their shiny new grandson and nephew could speak like a functional adult. Arthur, therefore, had spent the morning making gurgling sounds and being as adorable as he could manage and was really starved for some honest adult interaction.

"Clarify what?" Arthur's father asked, holding Arthur away from his body as if to ensure that the slight smell wouldn't travel through the nappy and into his own clothes.

"My name," Arthur said. "I'm not just any old Arthur—though I am thrilled that the name has gained such popularity. I am Arthur, *King* of the Britons, Uniter and Ruler of the land of Albion. And put me down already, man, you look ridiculous. Honestly, it's not going to *explode*."

Arthur's father chuckled and put Arthur on the change table and began the lengthy process of preparing to change his nappy.

"You *do* know me, don't you?" Arthur asked worriedly, when his father hadn't immediately been shocked, or gone into raptures, or at least made a leg and called him "your majesty." Perhaps he was forgotten.

"Hm, what?" his father asked, rooting around under the table for the wet wipes and dry powder. "Right, yes, King Arthur, quest for the Holy Grail, Sean Connery, myths to make the Welsh feel better about themselves, all that."

Arthur furrowed his chubby brow as best he could. *All* of him was chubby right now and it actually was slightly annoying. It was hard to be taken seriously when one was so damnably *cute*. "Sean who?"

"Actor. Played King Arthur in the films."

The thought that he had passed into history had been certain to Arthur; he had already been a great historical figure while he had lived. That he would pass into legend was a possibility, though he didn't enjoy the idea that he might have been forgotten as a real person. To find that he had become a *myth* hurt in ways that Arthur couldn't directly pinpoint, but he thought that it might have something to do with the idea that all of his bloody and hard work had been reduced to the sphere of an epithet, and all the people he had known and loved had been distilled into archetypes and clichés, ghosts of themselves.

But to find that there had been a *film*...horrifying.

Arthur had already seen two films in his admittedly young life— one that made his mother weep and smile as the man declared his love for the unattractively thin woman with a wide face (arms like toothpicks, she'd never be able to raise a blade to defend herself or her children from invaders), and one filled with great balls of fire and fast chases in those metal vehicles he now knew were called "cars"—and wasn't sure he had any great love for this bastardization of the bardic tale-weaving he had known in his last life. Though, he had to admit, the television was a remarkable invention.

To take his mind off it, he asked, "What exactly is wrong with Albion, anyway?"

"Pardon?" his father asked again, concentrating on his task and perhaps watching Arthur's willy with more apprehension than was strictly polite. After all, Arthur hadn't weed on him on purpose, and he had apologised besides. "What's an Albion?"

"This land. I united it. I ruled the whole island once, you know. Don't tell me somebody let it get all split up into different kingdoms again after all the hard work I did."

"It was for, oh, a thousand or so years," his father said, reaching for the fresh nappies, eyes still on Arthur. "But then Scotland and Wales and part of Ireland got sucked back in, wars for a few centuries about all of that, too, and so it's all mostly united again. The United Kingdom of Great Britain and Northern Ireland. We just say the 'UK' now, son. Oh, but, uh, I guess there's the colonies, too, only they're not colonies any more as we've become a commonwealth state and—"

Arthur coughed and his father trailed off, concentrating on getting the nappy under his son. Not a Kingdom anymore but a whole *Empire*; Arthur felt overwhelming responsibility pressing strangely on his little shoulders. Perhaps it would mean that he would be less prepared when the hour of need came, but right now Arthur wished that he could have had a childhood like the last one: oblivious of his destiny and happy in his innocence.

After a short silence, Arthur prompted: "So, Albion's greatest hour of need?"

The man shrugged. "Rotter in Downing Street? War in the Middle East? Decline of social niceties in direct correlation with the rise of texting and tweens?"

"Maybe it hasn't happened yet," Arthur ventured. Then he sighed, because baby powder? Best. Feeling. Ever.

"You'd be born before the thing that would make you need to be born has happened?" his father said, and finally looked up.

"Magic works in strange ways; besides, Merlin lived his life backwards. He always knew what was going to happen before it did." Arthur wanted to grin, but a wave of melancholy swept over him instead. "It was always frustrating, though, because he never remembered the day before. It was...difficult. Having a friend who never shared the same memories, I mean. Who never...shared anything you loved. Except your friendship." Arthur swallowed. "And the in-jokes never worked. Anyway. He'd know when I had to be born again. So that means whatever it is, it probably hasn't happened yet."

"That's a comfort," his father allowed. "I guess. None of us can choose his destiny."

Arthur frowned. "No; but some of us have it chosen for them." Arthur let this percolate for a bit as his father tamped down the sticky tabs on the side of his new nappy and picked him up. "By the way...surprisingly insightful, old man," Arthur said, snuffling and burrowing close to his father's warmth and the comfortable, safe smell of his neck.

His father smiled. "Thanks, kiddo. You get your brains from me."

Arthur felt that a good gummy yawn was probably agreement enough, and proceeded to put thought into action.

Arthur dreamed again. He dreamt of the great grassy plain, and of thousands of millions pairs of eyes watching him from stands erected all around him, hemming him in. But it was getting more detailed, the more he experienced it; or maybe it was just that he was familiar enough with the skeleton of the dream that he could allow his mind to take in the other, seemingly less important details.

It was a tourney field of some sort, but it was bisected at its narrowest, rather than with a rail across the length. This was not a jousting field, nor did Arthur wear any mail or armour. That it was a place for fighting, he knew, but what kind escaped him.

Mordred just crouched before him, a flapping swatch of white suspended on a metal frame behind his head, smirking and horrible and waiting.

They were both dressed in a ridiculously flimsy pair of uniforms, with thin boots and shin guards. The material was so slight that it would not block any blade, and it was in a colour so bright and garish that they would never be able to hide from their enemies. Perhaps that was the point; to prove that the knight wearing it was firm enough of mettle and strong enough of arm to not require armour.

The people in the stands around him blasted their disproval of his inaction into short, obnoxious trumpets and the sound filled the grounds with the angry buzz of disturbed hornets. They looked at him with such eager *expectation*, and Arthur had no idea how to give them what they wanted. He had always feared not being able to satisfy his subjects, but their now gazes were positively hungry. Arthur wondered what could be at stake should he fail this test that would make them so desperate.

A golden club sat in the middle of the tourney field. It was cup-shaped and large, with a great ball cradled between the carven swaths of its base. Arthur knew it was not the Grail. Beyond that, he had no idea why it might be significant, and his ignorance annoyed him as much as the anxiety in the audience's eyes ate away at his confidence.

A sharp cry woke him and he was chagrined to discover that once more it had come from him. Imagine, King Arthur, the strongest arm at the Round Table and the firmest of grip on the crown, unable to contain his own whimpers. Or bowels, for that matter. He shifted once in the darkness, but no tell-tale dampness announced its presence and he sighed. He was getting better at controlling *tha*t, at least.

When his mother came into the room a few minutes later with his bottle, Arthur peered up at her from his crib and said, "I'm sorry, Mother."

"Babies are like ink cartridges; low capacity and need to be refilled often," his mother said with a strained smile. There were dark smudges under her eyes and Arthur felt so guilty that he couldn't help the involuntary squirm.

"I didn't mean the night feedings, though I appreciate that, too," Arthur admitted, waving his hands happily at the bottle as his mother held it in his direction. She didn't like to pick him up to feed him anymore. Arthur missed the feel of the beat of her heart next to his cheek, the soft warm milk-and-rose-water-smell she had, the gentleness of her long fingers on the back of his neck, but he didn't dare say as much. He felt he was imposing on the poor woman enough. "I meant for...well...everything else."

His mother let him latch onto the plastic nipple of the bottle and stayed silent as he sucked. The formula didn't taste as wonderful as the breast milk had, but the fake bottle also wasn't giving him strangely twisted feelings of both young security and old lasciviousness.

When he was done, his mother rubbed his full belly in gentle circles until the little burp of swallowed air bubbled out of his mouth. Kaye had always outdone him at banquets, but Arthur was becoming increasingly impressed with his own manful belches.

Normally after the bottle, Arthur's mother left his nursery immediately. She was never inattentive or neglectful, not after that first time, but she wasn't comfortable around her son, either. He left himself drift back in the direction of sleep. If she wanted to watch him do so, he was happy enough to oblige.

"Why don't you talk to me as much as your father?"

Arthur blinked his way back towards consciousness and debated what his answer should be, or if indeed he should answer at all. But then, he never had been all that good at keeping his mouth shut when he should have—the sword in his back in the middle of a battlefield from the man who should have been his heir was proof enough of that.

"It seemed to make you happy," Arthur replied softly.

His mother jerked back, then leaned over the rail of the cradle and pressed her lips to his forehead. "I have a son who is healthy and content. I am happy."

"Then why do you look so sad all the time?" Arthur asked as she pulled away. Her eyes were sparkling again, like she was about to cry, ready to prove him right.

"I didn't ask to have a son who is the reborn Rightwise King of All England," his mother said softly.

"I didn't ask to be reborn," Arthur replied softly. "So I guess we both got the short end of that stick."

"I'm scared," she admitted. "I'm scared of what this means for the world. I'm scared that you're going to be hurt. That you're going to die."

Arthur kicked his feet for a few moments, looking up in the darkness at his mother's sad, dark eyes, the halo of woolly sheep that circled her head obliviously.

"What's your name?" Arthur asked.

"Evangeline," she said. "My friends call me Iggy."

Arthur tried to smile, but all he managed was a gummy lip purse. "Iggy," he said. "I'm scared too, Iggy."

She put down the bottle and picked up her son and sat with him in the rocking chair and cuddled him close. "I'll protect you, for as long as I can," she whispered into the faint reddish wisps of his hair. "And I guess you should call me 'Mummy.'"

"Do *you* want me to?"

Iggy pulled Arthur away from her stomach and met his eyes seriously.

"Yes," she said softly, and smiled. It was tentative, but it also felt like a victory, if only a very small one.

"Very well," Arthur sighed, content for the moment. "Mummy."

She pulled him close again and rocked him slightly. She hummed a snatch of a lullaby that Arthur was surprised to realize he remembered from his first childhood. Then she told him a soft, sad story about the Lady of the Lake. Arthur didn't have the heart to point out to her that he already knew this story with a bit more familiarity than he really would have liked, considering how it ended.

Every night for the next few weeks, Arthur dreamt of the tourney grounds and the golden cup and the buzzing, expectant, hungry eyes of his audience. There were other knights with him. Though they, like him, wore new faces, he knew them for Owain, and Cai, Gwalchmai, Peredur, the golden Geraint, the frightened Trystan, bold Bedwyr, Cilhwch, Edeyrn, Cynon, and even that bastard Lancelot. They, like him, wore the flimsy white uniform quartered with red bands, the ineffectual shin armour, and the shoes with spiked bottoms. Opposite them stood other knights in fierce red, Mordred at their head with his customary, bloody smirk. Between them stood the gold cup, the new grail for which Arthur had realized across the course of his nightly dreams they fought on this flat, green battlefield.

"If you can make this kick," Lancelot said behind his shoulder, "it's ours. The whole world."

"No pressure, then," adult Arthur said in his dream. And then he began to run towards Mordred and the strange limp net that hung like a shredded battle flag behind him.

He could feel himself wind up for something, to make some sort of move, felt his focus narrow to a single prick of white and black that lay stark against the lush green grass.

But then he woke.

Again.

He resisted the childish urge to howl in frustration.

"A babysitter?" Arthur said dubiously from his quilt on the living room floor. Those fantastic little woolly sheep were dangling above his head, suspended on a yellow plastic frame patterned with dragons. He loved those sheep – they were so entertaining. He tore his attention away to attempt to raise an eyebrow askance.

"You forget, your majesty," his father said kindly, "you can't even sit up on your own yet."

Arthur, who couldn't exactly prove the statement wrong, said grudgingly, "Okay. I guess. Enjoy your night out, Dad, Mum."

"Thanks, darling," his mother said, and smiled. It was one of those real smiles, one of the ones where she realized that maybe everything was going to be okay and that her life hadn't turned out all strange and terrifying. She was smiling like that more often lately, and Arthur was proud of himself to be part of why that kind of smile was ending up there.

Then the doorbell rang. His mother went to answer and his father gave him the thumbs up. Arthur tried to roll his eyes. Then he tried not to think about what they might be doing out alone tonight. And *then* he tried not to think about what it would be like to have a sibling.

The young girl came in ahead of his mum, blonde and probably about fourteen or so. Arthur wasn't so good at estimating people's ages any more—back in his first life, this girl would have been a woman already, preparing to marry or perhaps with children of her own. In this life, kids this age seemed stuck in a strange limbo between childhood and adulthood, irresponsible and yet filled with a coltish sexuality and raging libido that had no direction, and instead exploded all over the media.

There was something different about this one, though. Something in her that Arthur had never seen in the hundreds that were splashed all over the television that he watched with his father while cuddled on his tummy, or that his mother read about from the tabloids to help Arthur get sleepy enough for his naps. Her eyes looked old. Her bearing was comfortable, as if she completely inhabited her skin, was used to being in there.

It wasn't until his mum had kissed him on the cheek and reminded him quietly that normal babies didn't speak in fully articulate sentences, his parents had left, and the girl had come to sit on the floor beside him and tweaked his toes that Arthur finally clicked.

"*Merlin?*" Arthur squawked.

The girl scowled, a little wrinkle forming between her eyebrows that Arthur knew quite well. "What the hell do you think, your majesty?" she said, and though her voice was high and sweet, the old sorcerer's tone hadn't changed at all in the few thousand years since the last time the king had been chastised by Merlin. It very clearly said: *you are my king and I respect you and love you in a brotherly way, but by all the dragons that once roamed Albion, you are a frigging idiot.* "It's not as if I planned this. The universe and Albion chose, not me. Besides," she said, and took a moment to pop her hideously pink bubble gum with an obnoxious snap. "You should see *Lancelot.*"

"Ugly?"

"Very."

"Awesome," Arthur said, trying out one of the new words that the people around here seemed to like so much. "I hope his vanity is wounded. About time." Arthur, understandably, had little love for a man who poached other people's queens.

Merlin snorted indelicately.

"Well," Arthur conceded, waving his chubby toes in her direction, then put them in his mouth because, well, he could. Around his toes he added: "I guess I don't feel so cheated after all."

Merlin looked at her wristwatch, snapped her gum again, and said, "The football final is on. Mind if we watch?"

"Football?" Arthur asked. "I don't know football. Is it a sport?"

Merlin snorted again, that mannish sound that was so wrong

coming from lips slick with gloss. "It's a religion. This is a nation obsessed, your majesty. Even you won't resist for long."

Merlin propped Arthur up on her lap and Arthur leaned back into the warmth of her stomach and the reassuring patter of her heart. He watched with interest as Merlin explained the rules, and the work and passion the various nations of the world invested in the FIFA tournament.

It wasn't until partway through the second half that Arthur realized that while he had never watched football before, he recognized the pitch and the stadium. And when the game was over and the blokes in orange were declared the tourney winners, Arthur immediately recognized the golden cup being hoisted aloft.

"The saviour of Albion, indeed," he murmured.

Merlin just snapped her gum.

∾

His Last Monster

J. P. Moore

HER GRANDFATHER CHOSE THE lake. He smiled, then noted that there was no island. Brid was only four, but she would remember the sun showers that day. She would remember the crows feet in the corners of his eyes, and the sweat plastering his hair to his forehead.

"No island...yet," her father said.

She stood on the beach, holding a barley rush doll she had made with her grandmother. She watched as men framed boats in green wood and covered them with skins. Then, her father rowed thirty yards into the lake and began the process of dropping stones into the dark water. It took just days for the island to break the surface. Hard clacks of stone against stone replaced the deep, satisfying plopping sounds. The men added dirt, then planted brush.

The island they had made was a sanctuary from thieves. The lake breeze was solace on warm summer days. The water was sweet and, after it dripped through a bin of sand and ash, clear as crystal. She imagined the lake as a giant potion. It might have kept her mother alive, years earlier. It was reassurance when her father left with a war band to rid the world of monsters. But it failed to save her grandparents. Father Murdoch had them buried, and took Brid for his servant.

Raiders and thieves—they claimed the island. They won in the end.

Her father had done nothing to stop them.

She was twelve before he returned.

Father Murdoch was fat. Not in a negligent way, not like her grandfather had become fat. No, Murdoch was fat as if God had designed him to be fat. Murdoch was no ascetic like the Culdee brothers who were bone white with ash clotting in the sunken hollows of their famine. He celebrated excess.

Murdoch's favorite priestly law, Brid suspected, was the one about accepting food. A priest of his order had to respect dietary restrictions, but could not spurn any food given as a gift. So, when the relics of Saint Declan toured the countryside, Murdoch hinted that the cattle and sheep lords who owned this rocky corner of Ireland might touch the pieces by contributing to his larder. The saint's dented, tarnished bell was said to cure pains in the joints, a promise so compelling in the coastal winter clime as to provide Murdoch with enough dried meat and pickled vegetables to last through the whole season.

Brid saw none of it. She ate oat gruel. Sometimes, shriveled bodies of cockles or other shellfish dotted her meal.

"Bridget," Murdoch would say after measuring a handful of oats in the morning. He presented them in his fat hand, a soft pink pillow. "This has to last you the full day. Exercise restraint."

His voice was thick, as if his tongue were too big for the tiny mouth set in the center of his shiny face. Tiny mouth, beady brown eyes, shrew's ears below a tonsure that seemed barely able to contain his broad speckled head—he looked like a rodent. Indeed, Brid enjoyed the fact that more rats than people gathered to hear his sermons.

The cockles in her gruel were always sandy, for she never had time to clean them. As she chewed, Murdoch yelled at her for making too much noise. He was never violent, for that might have been too much effort for his muscles, which she imagined as richly marbled with fat as the meats he relished. But he yelled. He yelled from the pulpit at the nearly-empty pews. He yelled at the rain when it leaked through the thatch of the outhouse roof. He yelled at his larder when he had eaten the last morsel of some favorite food. He yelled, and she worked.

And he stared at her, his lips parting around two large front teeth and his fingertips tapping against his thumbs. She worked, and he stood in shadows watching her. She slept, and he stood over her. She was not sure if his distrust was that pervasive, or if he was trying to arrive at enough courage to enact some lewd plan.

Murdoch used her noisy chewing to demean her father. This required some strategy, for her father was a hero. A great man. But, the hero had sired a worthless daughter and then abandoned her.

"He killed a one-eyed beast that stopped trade in the Byzantine seas," Murdoch said. "He chased a monster from a lake in Scotland. He rescued a Bengalese queen from hell."

Murdoch shifted, leaning over his lavish breakfast as if Brid's father were about take it from him.

"But the hero's daughter cannot even chew her gruel quietly."

Her father also destroyed a murderous swamp demon, and then went after its mother. He slew dragons of all types, in all lands. He ran at great speeds, and lifted things too heavy for any man to budge. He subdued a giant with nothing more than a sling and a stone. It was all wonderful news, the only news she ever had of her father. She looked forward to the priest's rants.

But Brid appeared at the end of every tale. A letdown of immense proportions. The beast from which her father had run. Chewing loudly. Failing to pick up after herself. Tracking mud through the chapel that she had just mopped. Leaving spots of polish on the chalice.

She would look at herself in that chalice. Curling brown hair, green eyes, a crooked smile—she might have been pretty, she sometimes thought. Certainly, the monsters were terrible, unimaginable beasts.

Murdoch always preached about signs, but there were none that day. Or, she had missed them, like a shepherd wandering the desert beneath the huge star but never looking at the sky.

Murdoch had risen very early, so she had little time to prepare her own meal before tending to his needs. As he finished his breakfast, she was still stirring her gruel in the heavy pot over the fire, worried that she would not get to eat at all. But he was on a tear, wasting a lot of time spouting insults through the last mouthfuls.

Then, he paused and took a breath before speaking to his plate.

"He's come back, you know."

She did not hear it at first. The words somehow got under her skin. She blinked and turned.

"What did you say?"

"He's chased the thieves from that island of yours. We've made a deal. He attends to a monster in the Bricklieves and arranges for a large donation from the landowner. In return, I'm to let you go with him. Now, in fact, to help him prepare."

Brid stared at him, unsure of what to say. She gripped the wooden spoon so tightly that her nails dug into her palms.

"He'll treat you worse than I did," Murdoch said. "And I'll get on fine without you."

She turned back to the gruel, to the thick bubbles that made craters in its skin. She kicked a clump of peat into the fire and stirred, her jaw still agape and her eyes still wide.

"Or, he'll die. And you'll be back. Either way, you'll wish he'd stayed away."

Her grandfather's island had settled into disuse. There were no signs of thieves, of any recent habitation. Brid had imagined a valiant fight against a brigand stronghold. But this was a ruin. The thatch roofs of the three structures—a home, a pen, and a storage hut—had all fallen. The straw was dry and white. Thorny wild weeds grew in waist-high patches, higher in some corners so that they were almost taller than trees, reaching over the planks of the barricade that surrounded the whole island. Swirling worm-trails like the glyphs of some ancient writing etched the planks. Even the lake was unhealthy. The water was cloudy with black muck.

The bridge was gone. Brid's father paddled a leather boat from the shore to the island.

Her memories of the place, of the men building it, were of a day like this. Bright sun in a blue sky, spring. The air was warm, but a cool breeze moved over the surface of the lake. There was a hint of rain, but only from rebellious black clouds that puffed into existence for a moment or two before dissolving.

He stepped from the boat without a word. He had not spoken much, and seemed to avoid looking at her. She did not feel free to speak, as she was interested only in asking questions that he did not seem ready to answer.

"Bridget," he had said.

She had looked at herself in the chalice, as if to make sure.

"Come with me," her father ordered.

Now, he unsheathed his sword and cleared the weeds, swath after swath, making a green and fragrant carpet of their stalks and leaves. Soon, much of the island was clear. Tiny insects, their bodies dashing from those weeds into tight clouds of panic, hovered over the lake.

Her father was not at all what she had imagined. He was tall, just as she remembered. But, for a hero, he was somewhat slight. He had a narrow head with sunken cheeks. His arms were not shining, bulging sacks of muscle. They were hairy and oddly proportioned, his forearms thicker than seemed normal. His hands were massive. And they looked old, with thick veins beneath loose skin. The hair on his arms and on his fingers was coarse and gray. The hair on his head was close-cropped, silver, thinning at the top. There were countless tiny freckles there, coaxed from suns of many different lands. The skin about his eyes sagged, but the pupils were sharp and dark.

She had imagined glorious, glittering armor studded with jewels and lined in silver or gold. His leather tunic was plain but for the salt stains of sweat in the pits of his arms. Nicks and scratches marred the surface. Toil and wear had polished the armor in places—where his scabbard rubbed against the skirt, or a strap from some heavy pack had fallen on the left shoulder.

He looked more like a brigand than a hero.

When he moved, when he struck at those weeds—looking in one direction, walking in another, swinging his sword in a third, all the while seeming to give the weeds as much respect as any dragon or swamp monster—she saw the formidable truth of him.

And this while he favored his sword arm, which seemed unable to rise above his waist.

When he had finished, he stood in the center of the island, flexing his fingers around the hilt of his sword. He cracked the joints of his neck. The sound of it skipped across the lake like flat stones.

"All right," he said. "Bring our things."

Brid stepped from the boat and pulled it higher onto the island. She began to lift a pack of her meager possessions—some clothing and little else. She saw him from the corner of her eye. A flash of movement, there. She turned to her father. He had fallen to his knees. His skin was pale. His eyes were closed, their lids fluttering. His mouth was open. The sword dropped from his fingers. His head lolled and he crumpled into a heap.

Brid's father was still breathing. He was still alive. She kicked the door to the home. The one room, round with a pit for a fire in the center, was bare but for the fallen thatch. She piled some of this into a bed. Brid dragged her father by his brown leather boots. His tunic scraped against the ground, against the rocks jutting through the fallen weeds, as he crossed a threshold he had not crossed in many years.

She unlaced his tunic and pried it from his torso. The smell made her gag. Rags, wet and slick with pus and blood, clotted to his right side, from the pit of his arm all the way to his hip. She reached for the rags but paused, unsure of what to do. He had several sacks in the boat, but she knew nothing of their contents. She went to her sack and spilled her clothing to the ground. She began tearing a robe to shreds, then soaked the strips in the evil water of the lake. The tan cloth went muddy gray. Brid twisted these shreds until they were just damp, then returned to her father's side.

She pulled the soiled bandages from his skin. The cut was swollen and angry red, shallow at the ribs but much deeper in the soft side of his stomach. A black mixture of herbs and dirt filled the slice. Medicine, perhaps. As she watched, beads of fluid gathered on the edges of the wound. She placed the damp strips of her clothing over the gash. He flinched at this, but it seemed to bring relief. Sweat covered his brow and dripped down his temples, catching in the hair that tufted from his ears.

Why had he not told her?

He screamed as he lay near death in the night. He screamed so long and loud that she worried about his monsters converging on the lake, standing where the black water lapped against the edge of the forest. She wondered if the lake monster, the swamp demon, and countless other beasts were just waiting for her to go to sleep. What power did she have to keep them at bay?

They did not come. The next morning, Brid dragged his packs into the home to save them from rain. She discovered a number of weapons—swords, axes, and a small knife. She also found a waxed cloth bag full of dried meat. Perhaps several days' worth of food, she thought, for herself and for her father. She chewed the meat and then pried open his mouth, dropping the small gobs into his throat. Sometimes, he swallowed.

She was very proud of herself for thinking to set his helmet outside to catch the rain. There was now fresh water to dribble into his mouth, and for her to drink as well. She wondered about constructing a basin with sand and ash to filter the lake water. She remembered her grandfather doing that. She doubted the water could ever be potable now. She was thankful, then, when the rain came so hard on the end of the third day to not only fill the helmet, but to leave a large puddle in the bottom of the boat. The home, however, had become a mud pit. Flies gathered in this swamp, feasting on her father's wound.

Still, the wound calmed, going from red to pink. Its smell was less diseased, less dead. The water helped to keep it clean, to wash away the rotting remnants of whatever salve some far-off physic had applied. Now, she saw the crossing stitches of gut or some plant. They were like the laces of a boot, closing him tight.

She did not want to hope. She started to wonder what she would do if she woke one morning to find him dead. It was not so much a question about where she would go, or how she would survive. Rather, it was a question about what she would do with him. She might set him adrift in the boat, but he would just end up in the reeds at the northern shore, food for insects and crows. She could bury him. Certainly, one of his weapons would serve as a shovel in the soft dirt of the beach. As she worked his tinderbox to set a pile of straw alight, its dampness rising as a billow of steam from a weak flame, she realized that she could build a pyre. That, she decided, was the answer.

On the fourth morning, she shivered by the boat and watched the water. She jumped at a clatter behind her. Brid turned to see swords and axes. They lay before two boots, her father's boots. She looked up and saw him. He was a silhouette against the rising sun. Brid's father then crouched beside her, groaning as he did so. He was still pale, though some color bloomed in his cheeks. His hair was wild. He had already shaved, cutting himself on the neck in the process.

He seemed to be smiling, though she could not be sure. His lips were tight, and their corners drew straight back into his cheeks. There was a glint in his eyes, though—relief or happiness, perhaps. The glint made her imagine the feasts, the celebrations, poets' songs describing his feats.

He groaned again as he reached for one of the swords, which he put across his lap.

"A sharp blade requires constant attention," he said. "The weeds have dulled this one."

Then, oiling a rectangular stone and dragging it across the blade, he showed her how to sharpen the weapon. He stood, gesturing at the others. Brid understood. After years of Murdoch, recognizing opportunities for work was second nature. She took up the stone and one of the swords and enjoyed the gritty sound of the job. Brid's father nodded. He turned, again a silhouette in the sun, and then paused. Brid squinted. He reached and tousled her hair.

She had no qualms working for him, helping him to prepare to fight the monster in the mountains of the Bricklieves. She sharpened all of his weapons. He began practicing with them, growing stronger as the hours passed and his wound healed. As the sun rose and set, and his screams dwindled to thrashing and then just twitching at the demons in his nightmares, he swung those weapons in ever more beautiful arcs. Brid brought him water. She encouraged him, dragging him from the straw in the morning. This became a routine, like one of Murdoch's routines. She would set his breakfast, shake his knee, even pull on the arm of his good side to get him to sit up from sleep. He would protest at first, even bat at her as if he swatted at a stubborn fly. Then he would see her, smile, and tousle her hair. He ate his breakfast—typically fish that he had caught the night before. He was saving the dried meat. After devouring the fish, he was out to train against a man-shaped arrangement of debris he had built and to which he had attached a shield and a sword.

She asked him once about the stories that Murdoch had told. Swamp monsters. Dragons. One-eyed demons on islands far away. He shook his head.

"Poets sing songs," he said. "My memories are not as interesting as theirs. Listen to them."

She wondered if it were humility, or if the memories were sharp. He had seen nightmares, things that she could not even imagine. And he had beaten them all.

Waking. His wound. A dummy. These were his monsters now.

Brid woke. Her father was shaking her.

"What is it?" she asked.

"It's time to go."

Outside, he had loaded the boat with several of his packs. He motioned Brid to board as he prepared to push the boat into the water.

"We're leaving?" she asked.

He nodded, the muscles in his forearms hardening as he lifted the back of the boat.

"We go to fight the monster," she said.

"We do. I'm ready."

"Wait," she said.

With this, she ran back into the home. Brid looked about the straw, the mud, the spaces that they had cleared to support a semblance of a life on the island. She took up one change of clothing. Then, as she turned back toward the door, she noticed his weapons. The swords, the axes—they were all still there. He had packed none of them. Brid was not sure what this meant. She took the small knife and a scabbard she had fashioned from scraps of leather and fallen thatch, and joined him back at the launch.

"You're going to fight with your bare hands?"

He flexed his hands. Then, he looked at them, as if reconsidering his strategy. As he looked at those massive palms, he smirked and nodded. Brid was not sure what it was all about, if he wanted to prove something or if he felt it unfair to be armed against the monster. Or, he was jaded, thinking that there was nothing left to do. She had spent a lot of time sharpening those blades. And he had practiced with them, becoming so perfect in his swing that they looked to be a part of him.

"Why?" she asked.

"Just get in the boat." His face hardened as he barked the order. Anger pulsed up her spine, but she climbed in.

She felt the ground scraping against the leather of the hull as he pushed her into lake. He hopped in behind her, working the paddle.

Mist clouded over the water. The fog was cool on her face. The droplets gathered in her curls, which she smoothed with her hands. She was still very tired.

Murdoch stood on the beach. He held the reins of a small gray horse. The priest barely looked at Brid, except to regard her with disgust before turning to her father. She then realized how unkempt and dirty she was—covered in ash after days of tending the fire, splotched with mud, her robe torn. She guessed that even she would be horrified by her reflection in the chapel's silver chalice.

The horse must have been part of the deal. Brid's father offered only a nod as payment. Murdoch waved a short blessing at them, vague movements and mumbles. Perhaps he had forgotten the proper form.

Father Murdoch gave a glance to Brid as he left. He looked as if he might say something. Whatever it was, the priest swallowed it.

Brid and her father traveled the whole day. He led the horse, which carried his packs. She walked beside him. Brid drank when he drank. She ate when he ate. He would reach into one of the packs and produce dried meat. He made quick work of the stuff, but it took her some time to chew.

Night had almost fallen when they reached the mountains. They stopped at the door of a tenant shepherd. He refused to let them into his home, but was happy to allow them to camp on his lord's land.

"Where is the beast?" her father asked.

The shepherd, a short and thick man whom Brid had never seen in Murdoch's chapel, pointed up the slope that rose just a short walk from his home. Several sheep and a big brown ram with enormous horns, a formidable animal, stood between them and the bottom of the slope. It was some monster that could swallow these creatures whole, that the ram could not barrel into submission.

"The monster drank from a faerie pool," the shepherd said. "Now it's stuck in our world. Those are the only sheep I have left. Not nearly enough wool to pay my rent."

The shepherd looked past them, to the horse.

"You can leave that here," he said.

Brid wondered if the man was interested in the packs or the horse. He licked his lips. He was hungry. Brid's father shook his head.

"We take the horse with us," Brid said, trying to sound brave, trying to act the able companion to her father.

"The monster will eat it."

Brid looked between the shepherd and her father, then realized what her father had intended. The horse was bait.

"That's the plan," her father said.

Brid's father set up a lean-to at the foot of the slope. The sun had set, and Brid could see nothing at the top of the hill. They heard no monster. Her father did not seem concerned. She guessed that there was nothing he could learn from a desperate shepherd.

There were no stars or moon, just mist and the threat of rain.

Brid's father stamped and made guttural noises at the ram, which postured once but then seemed to decide that it could tolerate these invaders. It stayed close, and stood always between them and the other sheep, a female and three ewe.

Brid fell asleep without any trouble.

He woke her again and, leaving the camp behind, led her and the horse up the slope. The ground was thick with bracken, which hid loose rocks. The horse had trouble picking its way. Brid's father pulled. He groaned, for pulling the reins strained his wound. The horse must have figured that it had no choice, and so resigned to climbing.

The slope leveled into a field of burial mounds, a plain of the dead that stretched into fog. Some of the mounds wore a blanket of thick moss. Brid could see nothing of their stones. Others were bare, in various states of collapse. Brid did not sense the monster, but felt some energy, some rhythm that frightened her. It had an effect on her father, as well. He moved with more nervousness. His eyes darted at every sound. Each had an explanation—breeze whistling through the bracken, a badger picking through the stones, a crow crying overhead. The spirit of the place sharpened the edges of each of these sounds.

Brid's father stopped at a sheep's carcass. It was a mangled thing of bones and blood-stained wool. Dried skin and muscle stretched over the skull. He regarded it for some time before looking at Brid. Handing her the reins, he pointed at a thin pillar that rose near the mouth of one of the tombs. She could barely see it through the mist.

"Tie the horse there," he said.

She led the horse to the stone and tied the animal. She turned and shuddered, for she was unable to see her father. The mist had grown thick. Brid stepped, thinking that she headed in the right direction. Her heart beat faster with each second. The horse whinnied. She heard nothing more. She tripped, and scrambled forward in a panic.

Hands on her shoulders, then. The monster. She could hear it grunting. She reached for the knife strapped to her leg.

Her father. He lifted her and smiled. A real smile. He led her to one of the mounds and directed her to sit. The two paused there. He stared toward the horse, but Brid doubted that he could see it. Perhaps there was no monster. Perhaps the sun would rise and burn away the mist, and there would be nothing to do here.

Then, the horse screamed. Its voice rose, louder and louder. She imagined it pulling at the reins, unable to escape.

Brid's father gestured her to stay. Then, he disappeared into the mist. She flattened herself against the tomb, hoping to sink through the moss and stones and join the dead in safety.

She wondered why he had brought her.

Brid heard the monster, then. Grunting. Snarling. She could not see the beast or her father. The horse's voice reached heights of fear that she would not have thought possible. The monster's snarls were now a frenzy of hunger, of murder. A second of silence, and then a sickening crunch sounded across the plain. The horse made no more noise. She heard the monster, ravenous, sloppy, feasting on the horse's hot blood.

Her father let out a full, loud shout. He had waited, and now launched upon the beast. She imagined him on its back. The monster was a tall thing with scales or thick, leathery hide. It would have long arms and claws. Two eyes, useless in the mist, above fangs. Wild hair that resembled the bracken.

The fight went on for several minutes. Her father shouted. The monster snapped and yipped. Then, there was screaming.

Her father—the outburst was sharp and pained, and died as it reached high tones that were beyond his throat.

Silence, then a rushing of heavy feet.

Brid clambered to the top of the mound, seeing nothing but the other gray mounds in the fog.

One of these mounds unfolded. It was the monster. It smelled her and shot toward her. Panicked, she rolled. It was on top of the mound. It was not what she had imagined. It ran on four legs and was larger than a horse. Tusks twisted through the fog. It probed with these, and with quick snotty breaths through a snout that was much like a boar's. Red eyes, haunted by some hellish fire, caught her. Brid saw the spirits of the tombs behind those flames. This beast, whatever it was, had prowled this plain too long. Now, it belonged to the dead. They feasted and murdered through it.

The monster was upon her, its breath beating her. She covered her face, as if it would do any good. What would her father have done? His instincts, his bravery, must be in her. The monster snapped at her, ripped the cloth of her robes. She struggled to free the knife and then stabbed and swiped. Hot liquid fell upon her face and arms, into her mouth. Salty metal froth. The monster squealed, a pig's squeal, but kept on her.

Her father leaped onto the monster's back with such force that the thing fell from Brid. She rose as the two landed beside her. The beast was smaller. Or, her father had grown. She was not sure. She took slow steps toward them, feeling dead, feeling like a ghost of the plain. She looked at her hands. Her robe was stuck to her skin. She combed blood and gore from her hair with her fingers.

Her father had the monster by the neck, squeezing, reaching into the wound that she had made. He pulled and broke whatever he found within. The monster's red eyes showed panic. The beast's tongue lolled. With a whimper, a weak whine, it went still.

Brid's father collapsed upon its ribs. The thing had gored him, reopened his wound. His blood mixed with the beast's.

He motioned to her and tried to speak. She went, kneeling beside him. He reached for her, gathering her into him and holding her.

There, in the field of dead kings and warriors, the hero died upon his last monster.

Fat Father Murdoch leaned over his plate, wrapping his arms around it. When he realized who stood at his door, however, he loosened—not entirely, but a bit. He squinted his tiny eyes even smaller and rose in his chair. Dabbing at the corners of his mouth with a cloth, he smiled.

"You're back," he said.

Brid made no reply.

"Your father has died. Let's get to work."

He stood, seemingly ready to recite a list of chores.

"He is dead," she said. "But he killed the monster."

Brid stepped into the room. Murdoch looked her up and down and stepped away. One of her father's packs lay against her side. She did not wear a robe, but a traveler's tunic and leggings that the tenant shepherd had given her.

"Prove it," Murdoch said.

Brid reached into the pack and gripped the smooth bone of the tusk. She tossed it to Murdoch's plate, sending food in all directions and spilling his drink. Ale—she heard its thick frothy body slapping on the floor.

Murdoch stared at the tusk. Scraps of pink flesh still clung to its root. She had cut it from the monster's face.

"The shepherd has sent word to his landlord," Brid said. "You'll have your donation soon."

Disappointment fell across Murdoch's face. Whether because she was free or his dinner ruined, Brid did not know. She thought about stabbing him. Her father had made a bargain. He would not have approved.

Brid left Murdoch's quarters and walked across the grounds of the chapel, feeling his stare on her back. She ran her fingers through her hair to work the knots out of her curls. The smoke of her father's pyre still clung to her clothes, her hair, her fingers.

He was in the world, in poets' songs. She had much to learn of him.

Dark Helm Returns

Ed Greenwood

THE SENTINELS ON THE Dawn Tower battlements saw him first.

A lone rider out of the tattered mists of sunrise, hunched low in pain on a falteringly-weary horse.

His armor was blackened by fire, and abundantly scarred by the deep scorings of hard-swung blades or the talons of some monster that must have been as large as a donjon keep. His visor was down.

Yet they knew him by the banner hanging from the lance in his hand, and raised a cheer, ere sounding the warhorns in deep, thunderous salute.

At that din, Thalon Dark Helm raised his head, squared his shoulders, and lifted his lance on high in brief, wordless acknowledgement. For a breath or two the crossed wing and sword of his bright blazon fluttered for all to see, ere he sank down as before and came on, his mount's gait slow and dogged.

And as he rode that last little way, across the meadows kept open for the stretch of a bowshot from the high walls of Dantoryn, the greatest knight of the realm plucked out his weather-cloak from where it was rolled on the high saddle behind him, and wound it around himself as if he was cold, or ashamed.

The deep shout of the warhorns had made many a head peer to see why, and word of Dark Helm's return spread through the city like a racing wind, as goodman called excitedly to goodwife, and goodwife to neighbour.

And when at last he gained the gates, the guards of those portals had them open for him, with drawn swords raised in greeting.

"Dark Helm!" they cried joyously. "Victory! All hail Prince Thalon! Dantoryn forever!"

The rider surrendered his lance to eager hands, swaying in his saddle exhausted, then flung up his visor with a weary swing of one arm.

And the shouts of the guards faltered, for Sir Thalon Dark Helm stared back at them unsmiling out of his one remaining eye, his handsome visage marred by deep, ill-healed clefts that made such a ruin of his nose and the right side of his face that onlookers were glad of the eyepatch he now wore.

Despite its fresh and unfamiliar ruin, it was a face they knew well. Thalon Dark Helm was home, returning as he'd vowed to do—which meant the traitor Baron Grauth was dead, his foul rebellion shattered, and the Dolphin Throne was safe once more.

Dark Helm had gone forth months ago, at the head of a bright-mailed army of thousands, but was returning alone. Yet his unbroken lance could only mean victory, not defeat.

His horse was shivering as if from cold or fever, and had slowed now to a plodding, sagging walk. In sudden silence the guards melted away before him, letting him ride on, up the broad cobbled way, toward the distant height of Dolphingard.

Where Dark Helm's prize, the hand of the fair Princess Aerele—and the Dolphin Crown, in time, when the gods willed it that old King Briard should breathe his last—awaited him.

As he rode, Dark Helm clutched his cloak close about himself with his great war gauntlets, and the watching crowd marked that it was not his sky-blue cloak they remembered, but a mantle the maroon of Malaeran wine, or of blood.

And as the tired warhorse went on up the street, something fell in its wake. An armored boot, with the metal greaves and kneel-sheaths that shielded a warrior's leg above still strapped to it. It was empty of all but blood, and the knight rode on uncaring, his armor gone below the knee—and nothing of himself laid bare by that lack.

It was several streets later, on the long climb to towering Dolphingard, ere they noticed that the bottom edge of Dark Helm's cloak was copiously dripping.

And that the dark liquid it left behind on the cobbles was blood.

The horrified shrieks of the princess, as she fled wildly from the audience chamber, came as a surprise to no one.

Not that many were there to hear them. The king, the four everpresent knights of his royal guard—two small, swift, and agile, and two great armored mountains able to block wide doorways by themselves—two scribes, and the seneschal.

Who all faced the returned and victorious Sir Thalon Dark Helm, and the two chamberlains who'd helped to remove his battered armor.

All of them wore expressions of similar grimness, for Sir Thalon was as much loved at Court as he was in the city below. Not a man there envied the Dark Helm with more than passing wistfulness, or wished him ill.

The royal vow had been as clear as the knight's own, and had been welcomed by all as a popular choice for Dantoryn's future. Queen Naedranna was long dead, and King Briard had vowed on the altar of the gods to take no other wife. Which left the Princess Aerele to become Queen, in time—so long as, the priests' laws insisted, she married and bore royal heirs. Dark Helm was the most valorous and handsome knight of all at Court, and the king loved him as a son, and so had made the second vow of his reign.

He who slew the rebel Grauth and returned to pledge loyalty anew to the Dolphin Throne should have the hand of the princess, be styled "Prince" henceforth, and wear the Dolphin Crown, ruling jointly with his bride.

And here before them was the victorious knight, surrendering a small bundle from within one gauntlet: Grauth's heart and eyes and tongue, all wrapped around the baron's signet ring, as proof of that slaying.

Yet not a man there—Sir Thalon among the rest—blamed the princess for her horror and flight.

For what had emerged from that torn armor, formerly the

brightest, grandest coat-of-plate in all the realm, was something less than a man.

"Grauth," he explained tersely, "had a dragon."

They'd fetched a stool in some haste, for Thalon had only one leg left to him, and the blood-drenched clout he wore could not conceal the loss of not only that leg and hip, but of what made him a man. Above that ruin, his side was scored by deep gouges, bared bone gleaming through the deepest of those raw furrows. From them, the foul smell of gore and oozing corruption flooded strong across the room, making even the stout knights of the guard wince.

After that, the missing eye and the furrow that almost divided Thalon's face in two were mere ugly details.

"A wyrm?" the seneschal snapped in apprehension. "Should we—"

"*Had* a dragon," Dark Helm repeated firmly.

"Summon the healers!" the king ordered, his voice almost a sob. "*All* of them, right now, no matter what other work or excuse!"

The chamberlains ran.

Leaving the king looking stricken. "Thalon," he began haltingly, his damp eyes pleading, "I will not be foresworn before the gods, but a man who..."

He fought to find the right words, until his loyal knight took pity on him.

"Has been unmanned," he supplied gently, and fell silent again, waiting.

King Briard nodded almost gratefully.

"Has been unmanned, *cannot* father the heirs Dantoryn needs. So..."

On the verge of tears, the wearer of the Dolphin Crown ran out of words again, but his meaning was clear, even if the royal guards hadn't stepped sternly forward in menacing unison.

If the victorious Sir Thalon chose to press his claim, he would regrettably succumb to his grievous wounds in this audience chamber, here and now.

"Your Majesty," the maimed knight said quietly, ignoring the looming knights, "I cannot fulfill the needs of the realm, just as you say. Wherefore your vow cannot stand. The gods themselves would see as much." He smiled a bitter smile. "And so do I."

Then he raised his voice a little, and went on slowly and firmly, ensuring all could hear. "I did not ride forth to win the Dolphin Throne, but out of loyal service to my king who sits upon it. I gladly renounce all claim to it."

A shared sigh of relief arose in the chamber, and the royal knights visibly relaxed. The ruined man sitting on the stool amid his own spreading blood and the gathering flies was scarcely a formidable foe, but they were loath to draw steel on one so beloved.

"However," Sir Thalon added, setting forth words that brought down tense stillness again, as carefully as a royal jeweler setting forth polished gems on the glass-topped table for the Princess Aerele to choose from, "I do not renounce my claim to the hand of the Princess Aerele. Her I yet desire, and cherish above all else, and *would have*."

And he stared into the astonished eyes of his king in calm, unflinching challenge.

Swallowing, visibly dismayed, King Briard stared back.

"But...but, Thalon," he muttered, shaking his head. "I would stand by this as your right if she agreed, however reluctantly. She is the sole Princess of Dantoryn, and of my blood and rearing, and knows her duty. Yet she ran from you, cannot even stand revolted at what you have become. How can I—how can any man, if he is a man—work such cruelty on my daughter? I ask you: how?"

"Your Majesty," the knight he loved made answer, "leave this with me. I shall woo her as anyone should woo a mate, and return to you for your blessing when she willingly accepts me. Willingly. There shall be no unwilling obedience, no coercion—and no cozening by magic. This I *swear*."

"All the healers in six kingdoms can't make him a lion again," Roregard muttered. "Or give him back his missing leg. They work magic, aye, but—"

"But not miracles," Sunder agreed, in his usual cautious murmur. Chamberlains in any Court gained much practice in guarded speech. "Think you he'll throw himself on the altars and plead with the gods?"

"Huh," Roregard grunted. "The gods decree and forbid. I've not seen them tossing miracles at sword-swingers. Dantoryn's desires are not theirs, nor those of kings. Or princesses, for that matter."

"*That's* true. Otherwise, Princess Aerele—the gods keep her safe—would have been struck down by lightning months back."

"Earlier," Roregard replied. "The gods see all. Who knows how long she'd been lying with the Lady Thornwood? Or her own maids? They were...found all easy abed, like old friends, not with hurled-aside garments or—or any signs of the haste and fire of first passion. All the city—huh; save Sir Thalon—must know she prefers the company of women, a month ago or more. The priests would do more than just shun her, if she was less than the Princess of Dantoryn."

Nodding, Sunder let out a sad sigh. "The maiming of Thalon is the best that could have happened, for her. She'll not have to endure his embraces, now."

Roregard gave his fellow chamberlain a look. "You were hoping to endure them, someday, aye?"

"I was," the other chamberlain admitted sadly. "Not much left of him to warm me, now."

"Think you he'll turn to dark magic?"

Roregard blinked. "And pay for it with what? He's a knight of the Court, remember? The king even owns his *horse*."

"Mmmm," Sunder said dreamily. "His horse..."

Roregard's sigh was a gust of exasperation, not sadness.

"You," he snapped, "should hie yourself down to Smallstreets and hire a bedmate for the night." He snorted. "Or take a piece of Dark Helm's armor with you and wave it about, and take your pick of those who'll hurl themselves on you for free."

Sunder whirled, eyes alight. "Yes! *Bright* wisdom, Rory, bright wisdom!"

His arms were almost around the older chamberlain before Roregard backed away with a louder snort than his first.

"*Don't* be kissing me, now," he growled. "I prefer wenches, remember?"

Sunder's fond chuckle drowned out a faint sound in the passage outside the room they'd been whispering in.

It was the scrape of a crutch whose user hadn't quite mastered it yet.

The voice from the other side of the door was cold and suspicious. "Are you alone?"

"I am."

"Unarmed?"

"No. I'm a maimed man, not a fool."

"A crutch is an easy disguise."

"A missing leg is a harder one."

"I *know* that voice. Who are you?"

"Thalon. Sir Thalon. Dark Helm. Or was."

"And just why do you think *I'd* be enough of a fool to open my door to the king's favourite? He sends his knights to put their swords through wizards who won't wear Court livery."

"I don't have a sword with me. Or a dagger. I do have a need, and am willing and able to pay well for a remedy."

"Oh? What'd you steal from Dolphingard?"

"Nothing. What I offer is my own."

"Well, what is it?"

"Something I won't name, out here in the street. Not when I can go another two streets over, and knock on the door of Ondrar Manyspells."

"*That* ox-vomit? You—"

There came the rattle of door-chains, and the thud of a heavy door-bar being set aside and grounded.

"Push open the door and come in. Alone. If there are bowmen, or anyone tries to rush in with you, I'll blast all of you straight to Ondrar!"

Dark Helm leaned against the filthy stone wall and swung his crutch. The heavy old door groaned open.

The old and long-nosed man standing at the end of the hall with a glowing-tipped wand aimed and ready in his hand snapped, "Come in and shoot those bolts across! Quickly!"

Dark Helm obeyed, falling against another wall with his shoulder so as to act in haste.

When he turned around again, Lorn Mrallor, the most feared mage in the realm, was standing much closer, peering at his face.

"You *are* Thalon," he murmured. "What happened to you?"

"A dragon," the knight said flatly. "Can you make me whole again?"

Mrallor gave him a long look. "That would depend on what you've lost. And what you can pay."

"And if you'll swear to keep your end of the bargain on a consecrated altar," the maimed knight added, in the same tone as the wizard had used.

Mrallor almost smiled.

"I'll so swear readily, if I like the bargain. Having a grateful knight at Court—the *greatest* knight at Court—could be very useful."

His wand waved about for a moment, then aimed at Thalon again.

"So what can you pay?"

Dark Helm smiled. "What is the prize wizards hunger most for?"

Mrallor looked contemptuous. "No, we have no use for princesses or castles full of gold, man, nor..."

His face changed.

"You didn't..." he gasped.

"I did," Sir Thalon Dark Helm replied, and drew something forth from his under his robes that glowed, even through its bloodstained swaddling. He held it up.

"The heart of a dragon," he said softly. "More power than any mage alive has, or will have for years to come. It was a mighty dragon."

Mrallor was staring with awed hunger at what was more than filling Thalon's hand. "I can see that, man," he whispered. "For that, you can have my spells for two summers, if need be, and the winter between."

Thalon winced. "Let's get started, then. I don't want to wait that long."

"Daughter," King Briard said softly, "so long as you wed a man for long enough to give Dantoryn an heir—lad or lass—that my barons cannot dismiss as illegitimate, I care not if ye prefer ladies. I know what you see in them; I preferred ladies, too. Until I met your mother, and knew I'd found the one the gods had meant for me."

The Princess Aerele had sent all her servants away, and her father had banished his bodyguards beyond the doors, too. She was now glad of that, for despite her resolve, tears were brimming in her eyes. "I—I have not found *my* true mate, Father. Sir Thalon, had he been a woman..."

"Yet he is not, Aera," the king said gently. "We are but royalty; we cannot make the gods dance as we desire. I hope you will kiss and embrace Sir Thalon as if he was not disfigured, when next you see him, and that we can both enjoy his loyal friendship for many years to come. Yet he cannot sire your children, nor—"

There arose a sound, then, in the air between them. It was the discreet rapping of a man's knuckles upon a door. Where there was no door.

"What magic—?" the king growled, reaching for the knife at his belt with a frown, and waving at his daughter to back away.

A line of light occurred, in the empty air whence the knocking sound had come, and out of it an unfamiliar man's voice said gruffly, "A staunchly loyal subject desires to apologize for intruding, and craves immediate audience with the Princess Aerele."

"Who are you?" King Briard demanded, blade out. He dared not flee and leave his daughter imperiled, yet flee he must if the guards were to be summoned. Frantically he waved at her to go around the walls of the room and past him, out to the distant doors where the guards waited.

"I was Sir Thalon Dark Helm," came a different voice, from the widening line of light that was now the outline of a door. "I mean no menace, Your Majesty, to you or to your daughter. This I swear."

"T-Thalon?" King Briard had always hated and feared magic, and it was not in his heart to change his regard for it now.

The door opened, and out of it stepped a slender woman with a face he'd thought never to see whole again. A face subtly changed.

It was Thalon, yet it was not. His tall, broad-shouldered knight had become a shorter, sleeker woman—with two legs. She was barefoot. The king beheld a long fall of lustrous black hair, a pleasingly-shaped body beneath it, and...eyes he knew.

It was Thalon, and she wore a simple robe and a smile as bright and broad as he'd ever seen. She knelt to him as all subjects did, then spun up and away to face his daughter.

"Aerele," she said gently, "will you have me?"

The princess thrust both of her hands into her mouth long enough to bite them hard and quell a scream. Then she raced forward and flung her arms around Thalon.

"But—but—" The king found a chair and sank thankfully into it. "How can this be? Magic, of course, but who—?"

"Ah," came the gruff voice that had first hailed them, out of the light that was the doorway. "That would be my doing." With each word the voice dwindled, and the light with it, until both were gone.

King Briard frowned, then looked sharply at Thalon. "Was that—?"

"Lorn Mrallor. His spells reshaped me, Majesty, and he gave me a potion that will enable the princess to, ah, provide a royal heir, of my blood, when she chooses. He has also stated his willingness to work a bloodbond spell with your Court wizards, Your Majesty, to ensure his loyalty to you, your daughter, and the Throne."

The king gaped at Thalon, who was nestled in the arms of the princess as if she belonged there. He knew not whether to rush and call on his wizards and knights to hunt down Lorn Mrallor, or to trust in what he'd just been told, and rejoice.

Helplessly, he looked to his daughter.

Who promptly laughed in delight.

∾

Mirror, Mirror

Phil Rossi

DEATH SHOULDN'T HURT THIS *much*.

But hurt was all he felt.

Every nerve ending in his body was on fire. Neurotransmitters flooded his brain and his systems could barely mitigate the flow. The result, pain everywhere yet coming from nowhere—a phantom agony folding him up in its scathing embrace.

Not death. But most certainly the end.

The abrupt pain and heavy darkness, of which he was only just becoming aware, could mean only one thing.

The Hell Rain device had been deployed.

Hell Rain—it was all he could remember. Not anything that had come before, not even his own name. Fingers flying over a shimmering, projected keyboard, a final message home, and then

execute

Erase.

End of statement.

The pain receded and after a time, he could move, and think. He became self aware.

I have a name.

Romo.

He was buried to his shoulders, mired in a pile of his own destruction and hydraulic fluid. When Hell Rain had discharged,

Romo had been flung through two concrete walls. Alive but interred in enemy territory, his constitution had come in handy, but it was his strong mind that would get him...where?

I can't remember

home.

The battles—there had been so many—had widened the chasm between himself and his world before the war. Each life he ended seemed to destroy another memory and smudge another detail. Even still, he had the will to keep going where his brothers had fallen before him. Romo was the only one who could have activated Hell Rain.

Should I be proud?

He would consider that when he was free of his living tomb.

Romo displaced jagged slabs of concrete a single piece at a time, his malfunctioning body armor threatening to fail on him. He was a few short circuits away from dying in a shower of sparks and a piss of caustic and poisonous chemicals. Maybe that really would be the end.

Not yet.

Free of the rubble, Romo trudged across the debris and toward man-sized hole in the wall. Searing pain had been replaced with familiar discomfort—a background throb that made him feel like his brain was trying to be in two places at once. Romo held his breath and inspected the damage his dramatic entry had delivered to the structure. The wall was thicker than he would have ever imagined. Curling his hand around a piece of exposed rebar, he gave it a tug. It was strong and so real. In the room beyond, sunlight forced itself in through cracks in the high ceiling. The air should have been cloudy with dust, but it was clear and still.

Cold.

How could he get used to any other reality than war ever again? Maybe he should just stay put and wait for Mr. Death to come and ferry him away.

I'm a soldier and I still have orders. I have to return to base. To...

Home.

It wasn't enough.

A name.

Sophia.

Purpose.

"Radio," he commanded and heard a weak and distorted chime from his suit's communications link. "Soldier 819 to base." He waited for a response, but his patience was only rewarded with silence.

"Suit," he said. "Are we transmitting?"

"Communications link is open and sending data. No data received."

"When was the last communication received?"

"Five hundred years, forty-seven days, thirty-six minutes, and two seconds ago," the suit replied and Romo laughed, the sound surprising and foreign to his ears.

"Suit, what are your damage levels?"

"CPU at 100%. Structural integrity at 12%. Batteries on reserve power."

"Right," he said. "If you can't tell time, are you still able to get me out of here?"

The layout of the facility materialized before his eyes. The head's up display, once high-resolution, now trembled in a struggle to maintain focus. Faint lines representing the facility's layout flickered, promising that Romo would soon be cross-eyed. A fuzzy red line traced his original path of entry, but Romo could see multiple spots where the corridors were now impassable. He commanded the system to provide him with alternate routes and chose the one that appeared safest.

The path soon brought Romo into complete blackness. The suit's IR filter was inoperable, stealing Romo's ability to see in the dark. Were it not for the HUD map, he would have been lost forever. Time was not on his side. His batteries were almost dead.

Fucking rules. He should be able to fly. He should be able to rise out of the earth like a fucking phoenix and instead he was...*I don't even know what that means...*

Working to comprehend his own fractured thoughts, Romo caught his foot on the uneven floor and crashed to his knees, the impact causing the HUD to wink out. Several bowel-constricting seconds later, the facility layout rematerialized.

And now I crawl.

Progress was slow on all fours, but the path was unobstructed. Even still, Romo would have given his left thumb for a little light.

A voice.

Romo stopped the instant he heard it and listened with his eyes closed, suit-enhanced hearing reaching out into the darkness. At first, there were no other sounds than that of his breath and heart beat, but then he heard the voice again. Right near his head yet impossibly distant. A low, guttural whisper spoke words that were insistent, but beyond understanding. Romo shivered and remained with his hands and knees planted to the cold floor. More voices joined the first, the sounds closing in around him, growing in volume between each hitching breath he took.

They'll keep me if I stop breathing—that's how they'll get inside my head.

That was how they would get their revenge.

Like with silt on a riverbed, Romo had stirred lost souls with his trespassing. All around him, the dead were rising to punish his ears with the chorus of an army and nation destroyed in one merciless swoop. *Guilty.* Hearing the voices until the day he died would be his torment—a fitting sentence. But no sooner than it had started, the chatter pulled away, replaced by a heavy silence that was just as terrible.

Romo crawled on through the darkness, hours bleeding away while the facility map grew dimmer. He was near to the exit now and sunlight came in through a fractured ceiling above him. In the meager light, Romo found comfort and he stopped to gather his courage before crossing a metal catwalk that extended over a black void.

A voice spoke into Romo's ear, sounding terrified and confused. "Stop it!" Romo yelled. "I had no choice. I had to do it."

There's always a choice.

Silence.

Romo crossed the catwalk, trying to radio into base again with no success.

Romo gave the door a push.

It came loose from its hinges, falling outward and landing on the earth with a crunch. Beyond was the outside world and the true extent of Romo's destruction. The entire capital city had been leveled. Stepping through the opening, his senses were assaulted by psychic fallout. Like a wave, sadness, fear, and bewilderment staggered him.

How far does this terrible feeling reach?

Red sunlight fringed a black horizon, the sun hiding in anticipation of nightfall. Shadows pooled around rubble piles that had once been buildings in a growing sea of night and Romo imagined all of the structures coming down at once. A rain of concrete and glass, a thunder of screams, and the impossible sound of minds and souls being ripped from this bastardized mortal coil to be cast into the void.

It made him want to crawl back into the darkness. For surely, that's where he belonged.

You will be a hero.

Hadn't he known what that meant all along?

I couldn't have known.

I would have never...

...but you don't know who you really are.

Heading spinning, Romo went down, already unconscious before he hit the debris-strewn earth.

Static filled his skull. Whispers and hums.

Clicks.

The silence of time passing.

Romo traversed an unknown distance of cracked country highway. He couldn't remember coming to after fainting and he didn't remember falling into motion. Yet, there he was, farmlands stretching out around him for miles, desolate fields and collapsing barns the only signs that the area had been capable of producing.

Producing what?

It is all an illusion.

He paused in the shadow of a massive robot chassis anchored waist deep in the solid earth, its limbs destroyed with rust and and petrified dirt. Everywhere there was silence and Romo wondered at how he could be the only one out there. Surely, his fellow soldiers should be marching toward base.

Home.

I won't ignore my desire. It is all that will get me back.

His suit was gone, he realized, replaced by dark boots, a colorless pair of paints and a heavy wool shirt. He raised his hand to his ear, finding his personal transmitter still in place. If he didn't remember removing his suit, what hope did he have of finding his way back?

Countryside gave way to forest, the road disappearing into a shadow-filled cathedral of thick trunked, ancient trees. Seeing green for the first time since Romo had left the destroyed city made his heart surge. There was peace inside the forest. Birds called out and unseen creatures moved in the underbrush, stirring dead leaves and snapping twigs. I like it here. If Romo could not find his way home, he would make a new home in the forest.

Dawn in the trees seemed eternal, the light never fading. Though Romo knew better—night would inevitably fall and likely with little warning. He had hoped to be out of the trees by sundown but had no way of knowing how large the forest was. The sound of rushing water caught his ear and he followed it off the road, fighting his way through a thicket of nettles and vines.

"Damn it," he cried, a thorn tearing into his exposed forearm.

He came through the brush and found a deep stream. The water was deliciously clear. He could count the individual stones on stream floor, some as polished as marbles. Romo's reflection was a dark silhouette on the surface, defying detail as he bent forward to drink. On the opposite bank, the sun blazed through the trees, the light a deep orange that made the world seem like it was on fire.

Was this like the final moment for the people he had murdered? Had a beautiful fire filled their eyes, a final vision of glory before heaven's gates were revealed. Or had it been a terrifying blaze? A cold inferno. Ice before the black of nonexistence. He shivered despite the warmth and dropped his eyes to the pebble-strewn bank.

I do not deserve to go home.

Instead of taking a drink, Romo considered drowning himself in the river. A crash from the tree line on the opposite bank brought his eyes up. Something large was moving through the forest, right toward him. Before Romo could react, the beast appeared, its mass difficult to discern through the glare of sunlight. Romo saw a glittering horn, sleek white fur, and a muscular body before the creature disappeared into the trees.

Heart pounding, Romo waited by stream for the animal to return, but it did not.

Back on the leaf-strewn old road, he walked on until the light finally began wane. Though he wasn't tired, Romo thought it wise to make a camp for the night. He collected pine boughs until his arms were full and laid them down on the roadside. He tested the makeshift bed with his hand, and satisfied that it would provide some comfort, he reclined, curling his arms beneath his head. The smell of pine and dead leaves enveloped him, and staring across to the other side of the road, he waited for his eyelids to grow heavy. Night never seemed to completely fall, a meager amount of light persisting well after it should have been dark.

It is a strange world I've come back to.

And like the dark of night, sleep never came to Romo, though he lay on his makeshift bed for hours, his mind blank and his breathing metered.

The forest pulled away from the highway and though Romo looked for it, he couldn't see the beast again. But there was a new sight to occupy his mind: High atop a tall hill stood dark a castle, crowned by six crooked spires, all of differing lengths. None of the building's lines were straight.

I've seen this place, he knew, but the recollection was like an ancient sculpture. Familiar contours and shape remained, but weather and abuse had worn away all distinguishing details. Was this his home? The castle, much like the beast in the forest, was tied to a deep part of Romo—a well where old memories stirred. Would they ever surface?

Sophia.

Her delicate hands curled into his own. Her lips, pale, soft, always tasted of something sweet. Her memory was too vivid. Was his mind playing tricks on him? Had his imagination fabricated her to keep him alive?

Romo would not entertain the possibility. His mind was strong and capable, but he needed the memory. Sophia would get him home.

The road brought him only so close to the strange castle. He'd have to leave the path if he wanted to reach the building, but the hill atop which the castle sat was covered in huge slabs of broken stone and would be impossible to traverse without ending up wounded or dead. But being close to the building made his skin prickle and his heart race.

Remember, he told himself.

"I can't," Romo said aloud and the sheer act of trying made him ill with sadness.

Another long day and short night of travel brought Romo to a village by the sea. A dozen dwellings lined a sand and dirt road that ran down a rocky shore where a single pier jutted into calm, blue water. At the center of the village stood an obelisk. Massive, golden, and stabbing at the sky, the monument dwarfed every other manmade structure in sight and stole any chance the village might have had at being called quaint. Romo descended into the village, not ready to acknowledge the strange structure, but instead, choosing to focus on the ocean breeze and the taste of salt on his lips. He went to sea line where he found a lone pier, its thick planks weathered but strong looking. A boat was docked there, the sails tied tight. The halyard clanked against the mast, the sound underscored by the gentle lap of waves against the vessel's hull. The name painted across the aft of the boat read *Sophia Ann.*

Sophia.

Closing his eyes, he listened and heard her laughter, melodic and feminine.

Romo stayed with the boat for a long time but didn't board. Finally, he uprooted his feet and walked toward the town's modest dwellings. As he neared, he saw the houses were all the same, clones with well-manicured lawns and azalea and rose bushes in full blossom. Climbing the front walk of one of the houses, Romo paused for only a instant before knocking on the front door. Nothing moved and he peered into a window beside the door. The world beyond the glass was peaceful and still.

I am a ghost, Romo thought. *I can't see the living and the living cannot see me.* Romo left the house and went to the obelisk.

Standing in the behemoth's shadow, he studied its mottled black and gold surface. Names and dates were carved into to the stone, the letters and numbers shining with an internal glow. Were these the names of his comrades or his victims?

What if they are one and the same? The thought chilled him. There were enough names on the obelisk to fill ten thousand of these villages.

All of the names showed the same date.

A bell rang out, each chime hanging in the brackish air. The sound was close and Romo headed toward it, moving into the full light of day. He found the bell swinging above the doorway to a red school. Small and made of brass, the bell ceased moving when Romo fixed his eyes upon it.

The school house was dark and cool inside. Heavy curtains were drawn, hiding the windows, but a modest light amount of light managed to sneak in, illuminating a classroom that was that was immaculate. Books were arranged in tidy rows on shelves along the walls. Art supplies—paint brushes, water colors, and crayons—were neatly placed in plastic bins. Twenty-four desks were lined up in six neat, soldierly rows and Romo trailed his finger across the surface of the desk closest to him. There was not a single mote of dust on the thing. Atop the front and center-most desk sat a rectangle of paper and Romo went to it.

The drawing of a jack-o-lantern grinned up at him, hearts for eyes and nose. The artwork recalled the castle that Romo had seen on his journey, the lines and curves crude and filled with joy. Looking at the picture made his heart lurch and he began to weep.

"I want to go home." But the fact that he could not remember home only made him cry harder.

Static.

The tears stopped and Romo took control of his breathing. Of all times for his communications system to finally activate.

"Base, this is First Lt. Romo, call sign...Prometheus. Do you read me?"

The static increased in volume and though Romo did not want to leave the school house—he was close to something important—the signal would be stronger outside. Clutching the child's drawing in both hands, he waded through the ranks of tiny desks and pushed out through the front door.

The village was gone.

The hills were gone.

The road—*his road*—was gone. Even the scent of the ocean had left the air.

The school house hovered in a black void. The substantial darkness pressed down on him and Romo was shocked by the oppressive weight of the nothingness.

Vertigo squeezed his innards and he spun around, lunging back toward the open school house door—but they were gone, too. He opened his mouth to scream and the emptiness flowed into him, numbing his chest and erasing him from the inside out. His thoughts unraveled. Was this the end—taken down by the

fallout of his own making? Some other lingering biological agent?
It didn't matter now.

Nothing mattered.

There is still something.

He wanted to call the name out, but could not remember it.

This is important, damn you.

All he could remember was....

The beast in the trees.

She loved

Unicorns.

Even as an adult.

The castle—he *made* it.

who?

Son.

A safe place for the family.

She could keep her unicorns there.

The empty sea was pulling him out.

The sailboat.

The craft was a gift to each other—their
mutual   *Escape.*

Romo had insisted on using her name. She was his

escape.

I left

Jack-o-lantern

the real world on Halloween.

I left

Sign posts. I put them here to lead me back.

Password. To get back to get back.

home.

Sophia.

Someone was in trouble.

Cries desperate and pitched high with terror made Romo's heart stop. He wanted to help whoever was yelling, but he couldn't move and couldn't speak. His throat was on fire.

I'm the one screaming.

But even as the realization dawned, he was unable to stop.

Romo opened his eyes and saw that the void had been replaced by a streaking blue light.

Stop thrashing. Stop fighting. Get it together, soldier.

Romo stopped moving, clenching his jaw tight against more screaming.

The blue light went still, resolving itself into a rectangle. A window? Deep cold penetrated Romo's every pore, making it hard to comprehend this new confinement that had so abruptly replaced the vast, empty space. Restraints bound him at the wrists, waist, and ankles. He had been captured by the enemy.

A deserved fate. Romo was almost eager for the torture to begin.

A hissing filled his ears, the sound of gases venting. Three heavy clanks startled him and then there was a hydraulic whine. Romo's world began to vibrate and the blue square slowly rose away from his face, along with the thick, metal door in which it was set. Beyond the open door lay a big room, but the light was poor and Romo's eyes refused to focus for long enough to discern anything more than shapes.

The hydraulics whimpered as Romo was lowered, feet coming into contact with the cold floor and the restraints that bound his wrists, chest, and waist flinging open. Romo collapsed to the floor and remained motionless for an elastic span of time. He was too exhausted to even lift his head and had to rely on poorly functioning eyes to make a survey of the surroundings. The room was not large and much of the space was taken up by dark, hulking structures. Cursing his vision, Romo closed his eyes.

He stayed on the floor, each respiration slow and metered while he turned his mind inward, focusing his energies on the restorative processes. Meditation carried him away from the cold, confusing shadows and into a world of warm healing light.

A squeaking sound approached, drawing Romo from his trance and making him rise up to his knees in a protective crouch. He felt stronger, but unsteady. A featureless cylinder, propelled by treads and pulleys rolled up to Romo and emitted a series of melodic chimes that almost sounded like a fanfare. A single row of green LEDs encircled the top of the machine and cycled on and off for several seconds.

"Welcome back, soldier," the robot said in warbling feminine voice. "Are you able to move on your own? Perhaps you require some meditative assistance. Music? Incense?"

"No. I'm fine," Romo said. "I'm going to try to stand now." Romo got up slowly, his muscles stiff and burning with the movement, but his legs were able to support him and for that he was grateful. "Where am I?"

With eyes that still refused to focus, he gazed through the murk, studying the walls, ceiling, and floor. Black cables like serpents stretched everywhere, their thickness twined through twenty-four oversized, metal beehives that occupied most of the floor space.

"What is this place?" he asked. "Where am I?"

"You are in tactical squadron room 19," the robot said. "Do not be alarmed, temporary memory loss is common for extended stays in the Cloud."

The Cloud.

Click.

Romo's neurons blossomed to life like a crackling neon mushroom cloud. He watched the memory of himself stepping into the beehive, wires attached to his torso and head. The door sealed and restraints clanked into place. Eyes closed, Romo remembered how a soldier's lids fluttered reflexively as his consciousness was uploaded into the system—the metal beehives—his body alive so that his mind could fight a war incorporeal. A war of information—data wiping, network infection. Digital tools of mass destruction that could bring the outside world to a grinding halt.

Romo placed his hand on the beehive, feeling its smoothness

beneath his palm. He turned to the robot.

"Where is everybody?" Romo asked, clenching his jaw against the shivers that seized his body.

"You are the first to return."

The simulacra—the countryside had been devoid of any other projected consciousnesses. If Romo had truly been the first to return, he would have met others on the way.

You did meet others along the way.

"What is the current mission time?" he asked the machine.

"Mission clock stopped when Hell Rain was activated. Five hundred years 46 days 3 hours 24 seconds."

"That can't be right," Romo stammered, his teeth clacking together. "I want to speak to...the CO." The robot grew in height, its cylindrical body telescoping until it matched Romo's six-foot-two frame. The machine's hull slid open and a slender, articulated limb extended outward holding a robe in a pincer-like hand. Romo took the garment, finding it warm and smelling fresh.

"The CO is no longer in the facility."

"There has to be a CO here," Romo said, glancing around the chamber. "My memory is still fragmented, but I know this is a top level facility. CO's do not just leave for the day."

"There is no CO present."

"Take me to someone who can debrief me," he said.

"I am someone," the robot said.

"Someone human," Romo said, and were he not exhausted he might have been angry with the machine.

"You are the only human here."

Malfunctioning.

Romo should have realized it sooner, but his thoughts were sluggish—there was too much about the outside that he was trying to recall at once. *I should start with simple recollections. Like how to get out of the room.* He turned and looked back to metal womb that had kept him alive for the past...

Three years. My tour of duty was to be three years.

Romo brought his fingertips to his scalp, which was hairless, and he wondered how much collateral damage his brain had suffered during the war.

"The other units," he looked at the robot.

"Soldiers still occupy Beehive Units one through fifteen; seventeen through twenty."

"I'd like to leave now. Take me to the lockers."

The robot chimed and rolled toward the exit. Romo followed the machine past the beehives, through a hexagonal hatch, and into a ready room. Romo went to locker sixteen and placed his palm on a hand plate which grew warm beneath his touch. There was a hum and then a click, and the locker door popped open, revealing a single, gray jump suit hanging from a hook. Photographs and artwork were taped to the door's inside surface. Romo removed the first picture and brought it close to his eyes. A woman with long blonde hair held two children in her slender arms. Romo traced her face with his fingertip.

Sophia.

He traced the children's faces, his children. A boy and a girl— the girl held a stuffed unicorn. It didn't belong to her, it belonged to her mother.

Security encryption on the personal level.

You have to find your way back on your own.

Romo removed another image from the door—a child's drawing of a giant castle, unbalanced with too many spires. He laughed and placed his hand on the drawing, feeling the energy of his child's hand there.

"I am requesting immediate debrief," Romo said, his eyes brimming with tears. He had to get out. He was so close to finding himself. The robot remained rooted to the floor beside him, green lights winking on and off. "Take me to someone that can debrief me." Romo commanded.

"I will do your debriefing," the robot said.

"That won't do," Romo replied and returned to the immersion suite.

"They will be coming back soon," Romo said aloud. "So let's find another robot that is functioning a little better."

"They will not be coming back, Soldier." The robot said. "They are all dead. Only you came back."

"That can't be true."

"I am incapable of lying," the robot said.

"Then you are malfunctioning."

"I assure you. My systems are functioning normally."

"How can they all be dead?"

"Hell Rain," the robot said. "Severed the entire network when it was detonated. Everyone connected to the network perished instantly."

"Impossible," Romo said. "Hell Rain was coded for the enemy's network architecture only. Not ours."

"The engineers were wrong," the robot said. "Or they lied."

Dead? Everyone was dead? How could that even be possible.

"Wait a god-damned minute. How am I still alive? How did my consciousness not get severed?"

"I do not know."

"Then maybe I am dead."

Thick shadows and even thicker dust blanketed the still corridors of the abandoned school. Romo's boots crunched over debris that buried the floor tiles. The institution had been a shield, an illusion of protection for the military vault buried miles beneath. *The students, the teachers, the parents—they never knew. Did my children come here?* Romo was repulsed, but wondered if he had had felt the same gut twisting sickness when he'd first reported for duty there. Rusted lockers clung to crumbling walls and the ceiling above was marked with gaping holes. The place had been abandoned for a long time. For five hundred years? Anything was possible. He pushed through the school's creaking front doors and out into the gray light of the end of the world.

The town he had once called home had been erased almost entirely. Roads were phantom tracings, running through an ocean of reeds and an archipelago sand dunes. Romo stumbled forward on legs that were of water, hope draining out of him and taking his strength with it. Falling to his knees, he curled his fingers into the sand and they became fists. Romo let out a long, mournful wail.

I did this. Omega is my monument.

He descended from the brooding mountain of sand that buried most of the gothic school campus and then climbed a neighboring dune. When Romo reached the top, he saw more echoes of his seaside village. Some buildings still stood, jutting up out of the sand like crooked and broken teeth. The lower roads had vanished, most of the town's grid wiped away by the nearby sea, which he could smell and hear on the fierce wind that flicked sand into his face. The ocean scent was powerful and analgesic. He closed his eyes and did not open them again until his breathing was slow, metered, and under his full control.

Scanning the horizon, he spotted the final echo of an old memory.

A curving stone pathway rose toward the remains of a lighthouse. Much of the tower lay scattered on the hill. The black and white paint on the bricks was faded but not so entirely that the spiral pattern wasn't visible. In the shadow of the falling structure, there stood a stone house.

My home. Romo blinked furiously, but the single-story building did not disappear.

Sophia had hated the house, he remembered.

It's a shoe box! she had said, and the recollection made Romo smile. Sophia couldn't deny the beauty of the nearby ocean, the bliss of falling asleep in each other's arms to the sound of the waves. Pain blossomed in his chest and brought his hand up, massaging his sternum.

My heart is breaking.

Approaching what little of the house that had survived the ravages of time, Romo stepped through a front door that was nothing more than a hole. The interior walls had crumbled away, revealing the building's skeleton and snakes of old, rusting wires that had once brought light, water, and heat. The dwelling was a shell and all that had distinguished it as his home was gone. But it wasn't the material—the art, the toys, the furniture.

It was his family. Their laughter. Their tears. Their music.

All gone.

He closed his eyes and the sound of the breakers filled his ears. He wanted to fade into the white noise and become part of the background. He wanted to blend into the white noise of history just as the rest of the world had.

Music.

He heard it clearly. A simple, ascending melody looping over and over. The sound came from directly below his feet. He got to his hands and knees, frantically removing rubble and debris until four straight lines revealed themselves—a door. The release was nearly frozen in place, but Romo got the handle to give by sheer force of will alone. Haltingly, the door ground open, revealing a ladder descending into the shadows below. With the hatch open, the melody was loud and very much real.

Romo knew the sound. It reminded him of being rushed out the front door, lunch bag in one hand, his wife's hand in the other.

Romo descended the ladder and the smell of sand and minerals nearly overwhelmed him. He reached the bottom, gripping the ladder and pressing his head against the cool metal rungs. By smell alone, he knew he had entered a tomb.

Light from above pooled around his feet on a floor that was hidden in a thin layer of sand, because not even a bomb shelter could keep the sand out.

Romo found Sophia on a small bed.

A nightgown and a dusting of sand particles covered her desiccated remains. A lamp hung above the bed, the amber diode pulsing with the dying heartbeat of the shelter's small nuclear generator. Romo went to her, knelt beside the bed, and switched off the clock, silencing the melody. He reached above his wife's head and turned off the lamp, preferring the meager light from the open hatch.

The stars were chips of glass, glittering in the darkness above Romo. The meager warmth of the day had gone out of the air, but Romo was in a full sweat as he knelt above the three-foot hole in the sand that had been dug with his bare hands. He lowered Sophia's body into the grave.

"I don't remember you," Romo said. "But I still feel you. I still feel our family. My body hasn't forgotten what my mind was too weak to hold onto. I don't know how long you have been waiting for me. But I will be with you when my time comes. I will remember."

He covered Sophia, filling in the hole a handful of sand at a time.

Romo walked down to the sea and saw it right away—lights bobbing on the horizon.

Boats.

I am not alone. But can I start all over?

He already had.

∾

KNIGHTS AND BEANS

Julie Kagawa

"TEA?" ASKED THE DRAGON, holding up a pink kettle in two very long talons.

Sir Roger sighed and settled noisily on a rock, armor clanking. "If it pleases thee, yes."

"Scone? Oh wait, the mice got those. Muffin?"

"I thank thee, but no."

"So, let me get this straight." The dragon set the pot on a wood-burning stove, lit it with a blast of flame, and turned back to the knight. "You went off to slay the evil warlock and his army of minions, rescue the fair princess, and basically save the world, and no one recognized you when you went home?"

"That is the trouble with starting out as a humble farmboy." Sir Roger sighed and removed his helmet, shaking out his pale, straw colored hair. "Thou art surrounded by humble farmers, who care not about evil wizards and minion armies until they are marching through their bean fields."

"Farmers can be quite shortsighted." The dragon nodded sagely. "You can have a lair in the hills right above their silly farms, and not hear a peep out of them for years. But the second you eat one of their cows or daughters, ohhhh, then it's mobs and pitchforks and hired dragonslayers and…" It stopped, seeing the look on Sir Roger's face. "Er, sorry. But this is your story, isn't it? So, what happened? When you went home, I mean?"

Sir Roger sighed again, raking a gauntlet through his hair. "I

245

am sure thou really dost not want to hear my sorrowful tale," he muttered.

"We have time," said the dragon, glancing at the stove. "The tea won't be done for a few minutes, and I'm curious as how the "Great and Noble Sir Roger," the "Hero of Avatonia," wound up covered in mud, wielding a bent sword and smelling faintly of manure, on his way to fight the dragon."

Sir Roger glared at the dragon, now trying to stifle its laughter, smoke trickling out its nose and the sides of its mouth. "Dost thou want me to tell this tale or not?"

"Sorry." The dragon made a visible effort to compose itself, curling its tail around its clawed forepaws. "I'm listening. Please, go on."

"Very well." Sir Roger settled back and brooded at his once-shiny boots, seeing his distorted reflection on the surface. What he wouldn't give for a decent squire, or even a star-struck peasant boy. "Twas a fine spring morning, the perfect day for a hero to come home…"

"Whoa, there, Thunderclap." Sir Roger pulled his big dappled warhorse to a stop and gazed down the dusty road. To his left, bean fields stretched out to the edge of the forest, waving gently in the breeze. To his right, a faded wooden sign perched crookedly on a post, pointing the way to "Beandale, pop. 34, 33, 31." He sighed nostalgically, causing Thunderclap to twitch his ears back, eying him strangely. Sir Roger patted the horse's thick neck.

"Beandale. Tis my old home," he explained, gesturing toward the sign. "Twas where I was born and raised: a simple farming village with simple farmers." Sir Roger sighed again, this time without the nostalgia. "My honored mother and father did nary understand why I wished to leave home and join the army; they thought I would stay home and raise beans just like every other farmer in the village. They did not understand: I was born to be a hero."

Thunderclap shook his mane and yawned, making the bridle jingle. Sir Roger sniffed, taking up the reins again. "Thou wilt keep thine own opinions to thyself, beast," he scolded half-heartedly, and the horse snorted. "Let us away, then. I admit, I am most anxious to see what everyone will say, now that their lost waif hast returned a hero."

The dusty path continued, until it ended at a collection of simple wood and thatch huts. Ruddy, sun-tanned farmers in simple clothes stared at him with wide eyes as he rode up on his impressive warhorse, his armor gleaming in the sun. Sir Roger smiled at them and sat tall in the saddle.

"Farmers of Beandale, you may rejoice! Your lost son hast returned!"

They gaped at him. Sir Roger held his smile and dramatic pose until they started muttering among themselves. Sir Roger felt his smile fade, and he swung himself off his steed, dropping to the ground with a poof of dust.

"Dost thou not recognize me?" he asked the nearest farmer, who squinted in confusion. "I am Roger, son of Roger the Beangrinder. I used to live in the shack by the mill with my devoted parents." The farmer was still giving him a blank stare, and he sighed. "I accidentally set the barn on fire looking for goblins in the hay."

"Roger?" the old farmer finally burst out. "Roger, son of Roger?" His eyes widened, and he broke into a toothless grin. "Woohee, lookit you! Broader then the broad side of a steer, you are. I remember you, now. Runnin' around here with your head full o' dreams and cotton. Never did figure out how to work a hoe properly. Ha!"

"Yes, well." Sir Roger shuffled his feet, then drew himself up so he towered over the farmer. "As you can see, I am no longer the skinny farmer boy I once was. Where are my devoted parents? I want them to see what their wayward son has become."

"Oh, they're still livin' out by the old mill," the farmer said, gesturing vaguely. "Gettin' on in years, but ol' Roger still can grind a bean with the best of 'em."

"I thank thee," Roger muttered, and turned his steps in the familiar direction of the old mill.

He received many strange, curious looks from the farmer folk around him, but none of the surprise or awe he'd been expecting. More like vague curiosity, suspicion, even amusement. He smiled and nodded to a few bent figures he thought he recognized from his boyhood days, but they watched him blankly as he passed and turned away, muttering amongst themselves.

"Roger?" a feminine voice said behind him. "Roger son of Roger? It is you, isn't it?"

The voice made his heart stand still. He had to remind himself that he was Sir Roger now, accomplished knight and slayer of evil warlocks. He was not a skinny, mop-headed boy whose knees gave out every time Alice Fairfleur walked by.

In his most secret fantasy, the one he did not even admit to himself, Sir Roger would ride into the village on his mighty steed, sweep Alice Fairfleur off her feet, and ride off into the sunset in a proper happily ever after. She had been so far out of his league when he left home, a gangly farmer boy with stringy arms and love-struck puppy dog eyes; of course she never looked at him twice. But now…now he was a knight. With knightly muscles and knightly armor, and a knightly chin you could chop wood on. Ladies swooned over his chin now, not to mention his face and muscles and charming, boyish smile. He had a whole saddlebag full of favors: colorful silks and delicate, perfumed kerchiefs he'd accepted from the gentler sex.

But he always imagined what Alice would say to him when he returned. He threw out his chest and raised his chin.

"Lady," he began, turning with his most charming smile.

And stopped.

She was still beautiful, in a worn, simple way. Her flaxen hair was still long and lovely, though it was piled atop her head and tied with a shawl. Her face still bore the dazzling smile and the full lips of her youth, but there were definitely lines now, crinkles around her eyes and mouth. Not so much from age, but from a lifetime of hard, honest work. She was still gorgeous, there was no mistaking it. But she looked less the coy, flirty, unobtainable farm girl and more like someone's wife.

And the child on her hip only solidified that suspicion.

"Gaaah," Sir Roger stammered, unable to take his eyes away from the child, who stared back at him with wide, curious eyes and sucked a thumb. "Lady, I…er…hope thou hast been…well."

Alice Fairfleur laughed. "Still the bashful little boy, peeking at me from behind the haystacks, aren't you, Roger? You haven't changed a bit."

"I…no!" Roger protested, tearing his eyes away from the child. "I…I am a knight now, slayer of terrible…evils. I have a sword…a mighty steed…" He trailed off miserably. Alice laughed again.

"You were always a sweet boy, Roger," she said, hefting the child on her hip. "It is good you came back; your parents will be so pleased to see you. But, you'll have to forgive me; with six mouths to feed, I must hurry home to get supper ready."

"Oh…er…of, course, lady," Roger stammered, feeling the situation had slipped very far out of his control. "Thou must… get supper…ready…*six* mouths?"

But Alice had already slipped past him, and was striding purposefully away, the child bobbing on her hip. "Goodbye, Roger," she called back, smiling. "It was so nice to see you again!"

And Roger stood there for a few moments, wondering what had happened. That had certainly not gone the way he'd hoped. He'd imagined a lot of swooning and stammering, just on the other end of the conversation. But he could not get the image of the child, bobbing up and down on Alice's hip, out of his mind.

"Pull thyself together," he muttered at last. "Thou art Sir Roger, accomplished knight and slayer of evil warlocks. Thou art a hero. Thou wilt always be a hero."

That made him feel a little better, so he continued up the winding path toward the old mill.

"Mother!" he announced, sweeping through the doorway of the old shack, into the little room that felt even smaller than he remembered. "Father! It is I, Roger! Your lost son hast returned!"

"Junior?" came a reedy voice from the back, and a moment later his mother appeared, blinking owlishly through her thick spectacles. She looked very much the same, a tiny plump woman with her hair in a neat bun—except the bun was a bit whiter then he remembered, and her back was a little more bent. "Junior?" she exclaimed again, peering at him more closely. "It *is* you! Oh, you're back! Come here and give your mother a hug!"

He obeyed, as he had all those years ago when he was a boy, though he had to stoop down a great deal now. Her arms couldn't even reach around his chest, but she beamed and patted his cheek like she did all those years ago, and abruptly Sir Roger felt like he was eight years old again.

"I'm so glad you've come home, Junior. I kept telling your father, Junior will come home eventually. Junior will visit soon."

"Actually, tis Sir Roger now, Mother." She blinked at him, and he stood taller, puffing out his chest. "I was knighted by the prince of Graystone himself, for defeating yon evil warlock and his army of minions. I slew the demon the warlock summoned from the pits of hell, rescued yon fair princess, and freed the oppressed masses slaving under him. When I returned, Prince Graystone declared me a hero and knighted me on the spot."

His mother beamed at him. "And you did all that by yourself?" she asked in the same overly-proud tone she'd used when he showed her a sketch he did as a toddler. "You should be very proud of yourself, Junior."

"I...I am. They named a holiday after me, Mother."

"Will you help me with cutting these potatoes, dear? My hands aren't as sure as they used to be."

Sir Roger sighed and took the knife she handed him, walking to the table to skin and cut potatoes.

A few minutes later, his father walked in.

"There's this bloody huge gray horse outside," he announced as he flung the door open, letting it bang against the wall. "It's in the fields trampling the beans! Do you know anything about that, Marge—?" He stopped when he saw Sir Roger, standing at the table with knife and potato in hand.

"Ah, that is...my horse," Sir Roger said, putting down the potato and hastily wiping his hands. "Hello, Father."

His father blinked at him, then snorted through his moustache.

"Junior!" he exclaimed, though he didn't smile. "So, you've finally decided to come home, eh? Playing knight finally got old, did it? All those silly fantasies about having adventures and fighting evil, pah! Waste of time, like I told you, boy. All a man needs is a hoe in hand and a day of good, honest work. None of this nonsense about righting wrongs and saving the world." He snorted again, and eyed Sir Roger critically. "What in tarnation are you wearing, boy?"

Sir Roger drew himself up, towering over the farmer. "My armor," he stated regally. "I am a knight now, Father. I defeated yon evil warlock and his army of minions, I slew yon great demon from the pits of hell, I rescued yon fair princess from—"

"Oh, for Pete's bloody sake." His father stalked past him, shaking his head. "You're the same bloody fool as you were when you left. Marge, do you hear what your boy is spouting?"

His mother waddled into the room carrying a pot of bean stew, smiling at them both. "I think it's wonderful that Junior found something he enjoys," she cooed, placing the pot on the table. "Now, I won't have you two fighting tonight, not when Junior just came home. Sit down and eat, and Junior can tell us all about his new hobby."

"A hobby?" The dragon choked, covering his snout to muffle his laughter. Sir Roger glared at him.

"If thou finds my tale this funny, perhaps I should stop…"

"No, no." The dragon straightened, waving a claw for him to continue. "Go on, please. So, after your…er…talk with your folks, did things get any better?"

"Actually," Sir Roger sighed, looking mournfully at his teacup, "things only got worse from there."

"Mother!" Sir Roger called, stepping into the living room. No sign of either of his parents, though he knew his father was out in the fields. Puzzled, he gazed around, and saw his mother's plump frame outside, chopping wood. Small she might be, but she did not shirk honest work. A bit guiltily, Sir Roger wandered outside to the chopping block.

"Mother, hast thou seen my sword? I left it beside my bed last night and now it has…" He trailed off in horror. "Mother, what art thou doing!"

His mother smiled at him cheerfully, then hefted his sword in both hands to bring it down on another log, splitting it with a crack. "Good morning, dear! This is quite the blade you have. It's much sharper then our old axe."

"Mother, that sword was used to slay yon Greater Demon of Hellfire! It cut down hundreds of evil minions and defeated yon dark evil warlock! Twas not meant to be used to split logs!"

"Pish, dear." His mother waved it off, still beaming. "What good is a blade if it cannot be used? You don't see any evil warlocks around here, do you?"

"But…"

"Junior!" His father glowered at him over the fence. "Get over here and hold your horse. Darned thing won't sit still to be harnessed!"

"Harnessed?" Sir Roger squeaked, gazing to where his horse stood in the field, half-hitched to a crude plow, looking annoyed. "Thunderclap is a registered war steed, not a common donkey!"

"Yeah, well, Penelope strained a fetlock the other day and can't pull heavy items. The harvest still needs planting, boy!"

"This is a nightmare," Sir Roger groaned, putting his head in his hands. His mother tapped his elbow.

"Junior, dear, since you're up, I've a few bags of sweet potatoes that need to be delivered to Alice and her family. Be a sweet and take them for me? They're rather heavy and you have all those nice muscles now." She winked at him and went back to chopping wood with his sword.

Gloomily, Sir Roger trudged down the narrow, winding paths to the cottage on the edge of the fields, where a hoard of screaming children romped and played in the dirt outside. As he set the bags down on the steps, one of them, a flaxen haired boy who looked about ten, stopped what he was doing and approached shyly.

"Are you...a knight?" he asked, a short stick clutched in one hand. The end had been wrapped in string, making a crude hilt. Sir Roger smiled down at him.

"I am indeed, lad. I am Sir Roger, hero of Avatonia."

"Wow." The boy gazed at him with starry eyes. "Have you slain any dragons? Or wizards? Or rescued any princesses?"

"James." Alice appeared in the door, frowning at the boy. "Don't pester the nice man with your questions. Go play with your sisters, now."

The boy cringed, but nodded. "Yes, Ma."

Sir Roger watched the boy run off wistfully. "Sorry about James," Alice said, picking up one of the bags. Sir Roger hurried to help her, taking them himself. "He spends all his time running around fighting imaginary dragons and dueling black knights."

"Tis not such a bad thing," Sir Roger said, following Alice into the tiny cottage, putting the sacks in the corner as directed. "I remember a young lad doing nearly that a few years ago."

"That's the problem," Alice sighed. "James is a simple boy. Our lives here are simple. We don't dream of going to far away places, we don't wish for excitement and adventure. I don't want James getting wild ideas into his head." She sighed again. "I shudder to think what he would do if he knew about the dragon."

Sir Roger did a double take. "Dragon?"

"Oh yes. There's a big dragon living in the caves a few miles west of here. We don't think much about it, and it leaves us alone as well. We don't have much livestock for it to prey on, I guess. It's sort of our white elephant, the secret everyone knows about but doesn't discuss."

"That's it!" Sir Roger cried, making Alice blink. "If I slay this dragon and bring back its head, everyone will recognize me for what I am: a hero."

"I don't really think—" Alice began, but Sir Roger wasn't listening.

"Lady, I thank thee!" he cried, racing out the door. "I must away to battle! If I do not return by morning, then the beast has likely eaten me. My sword…I must retrieve my sword…and my horse!"

The dragon blinked as Sir Roger finished his tale and his tea, putting the cup down with a sigh. "So, now here you are."

"Here I am," Sir Roger agreed morosely. "Forsooth, beast, I have no desire to slay thee, but I fear I must to show the farmers of Beandale that I am truly a hero and a knight."

The dragon regarded him seriously. "And do you really think bringing back my head will change any of their minds?" he asked. "Do you think they will see you as anything more than an odd, humble farmer's boy playing knight?"

"Nay," Sir Roger said with a heavy sigh. "They never will."

The dragon thought a moment. "You know," he ventured at last, "far to the north, over the Mountains of Despair, is the kingdom of Grandonia. Rumors are, they're under the rule of an evil tyrant who eats small children and bathes in the blood of virgins every Tuesday."

Sir Roger perked up. "Truly?"

The dragon nodded. "What Grandonia needs right now is a hero of some kind, wouldn't you agree? Someone to free the masses from oppression?" He shrugged scaly shoulders. "Of course, it would be suicide to try to help them; the tyrant is supposedly immortal—"

"Huzzah!" Sir Roger cried, leaping off the stool. "If Grandonia needs a hero, then a hero is what they shall have! Thunderclap!" He whistled, and the stallion appeared at the mouth of the cave, snorting. "Fare thee well, dragon!" he called as he strode out of the cave. "I thank thee for the tea and the companionship, but I have heroic duties to attend, now!" Leaping into the saddle, he started to kick the steed into motion, then pulled him to a halt. "Oh, and one more thing!" he called, peering back into the cave. The dragon gazed back serenely.

"Wouldst thou be willing to do me a favor?"

Beandale slept. Exhausted after a hard, honest day's work, the farmers went to bed early and slept hard, planning to rise with the sun. Their dreams, when they dreamed, were simple: home, hearth, family, and beans.

Except for one resident of Beandale, a small boy with flaxen hair, who lay in bed surrounded by his siblings, dreaming of a heroic knight with a mighty sword, riding off to slay demons and challenge evil and rise above his lot in life.

A noise woke him, and he sat up, peering out the grubby window.

A dragon stood beside the old mill, huge and scaly in the moonlight, a monstrous beast of legend and nightmare. As the boy watched, openmouthed, it took a letter in two talons and delicately placed it on the step of the small shack. Tiptoeing away, it snaked its long neck around, and somehow caught sight of the small face, peering at it from the window of the neighbor's cottage.

The dragon winked. Opening its wings, it rose soundlessly into the night, leaving Beandale and its villagers far behind, unaware of the creature's visit.

Except for one. A small boy watched the dragon disappear behind a cloud, then turned and fished a makeshift sword out from under his pillow. Staring at the crude weapon, he smiled.

Dear Maggy —
Best wishes and
enjoy!

July '15

OATHBREAKER: A TALE OF THE WORLD OF RUIN

Erik Scott de Bie

The Border Kingdom of Echvar—Winter 966, Sorcerus Annis

ARMIES CLASHED LIKE ROLLING thunder upon the blackened field of battle. The blades of Winter and of Summer strove against the barbaric Children of Ruin for control over this ground, and death was the only victor that terrible day.

Opposing blades sang the ballads of pain and blood as serpents of flame swept hungrily through the battlefield. The unstoppable warmachines of House Ravalis that birthed those fires rolled over fallen friend and foe alike, grinding them into the blighted ground. Where they faltered, pulled down into the mud and blood by their own massive weight, hatches opened atop them and swordsmen of House Denerre boiled forth against the barbarians of Echvar. Men swarmed over the clanking engines, hewing armor with their blades and tearing flesh with their teeth. Rain like acid fell in burning patches, searing leather and flesh alike.

Everywhere, men wept and died.

And yet, for all the power arrayed in that place, the battle was decided not upon the field, but rather in the mildewed and weather-scarred tent of Zvina, war-chieftain of the Children in Echvar. Victory fell, as it so often did, to a single man with a single blade, one that slipped unseen between would-be shields and saved a thousand lives by taking one.

Regel Winter. The blade in the darkness, he who bore the coldest steel.

Regel saw her from the shadows, gazing out over the battlefield: a goddess of a woman, tall and broad as any man, her blonde hair pulled back and secured with a bone clasp. He felt as much as heard her sigh. "There is no purpose in fighting, is there?" she asked.

"No." Regel released the second of her bodyguards to slump beside the first, his throat oozing bright blood.

Zvina the war-chief looked over her shoulder, and Regel was startled to see her visage: both pained and proud. Her deep blue eyes seemed almost purple.

"That is the great Frostburn?" She gestured with her chin at the sickle-curved sword held naked in his hand. "Look not so surprised that I would know it. We tell stories among my people, Winter's Shadow—we are not the barbarians you think us."

"No." Regel raised the shining blue steel to beckon her. "You are worse."

At that, she smiled.

Her attack came faster than he could have expected. She brought up a concealed warcaster and fired, but he batted the bolt out of the air scant inches from his chest. Only the Frostburn cut so fast.

She'd meant the casterbolt as a distraction: her true strike came in the form of a great axe that came chopping down at him. It angled perfectly for his neck, aimed so as to split him in two. She gave him no time to block and no chance to dodge.

He did not need to.

Frostburn cut coldly through the air, leaving a faint mist as it passed through the haft of her axe. Her weathered blade—old but honed to a fine edge—sailed harmlessly over Regel's shoulder. Zvina staggered and gasped. They stood separated only by Frostburn—and the three inches of frozen steel sunk into her belly.

"Exquisite," she said. "Steel of the ancient sorcerer-kings...of the world before. You honor me." She withdrew from the blade and caught at her wound. "Kill me now."

The urge to kill rose in him—the sword murmuring in its own terrible hunger—but Regel resisted its call. He would fulfill his primary task first. "Tell your forces to stand down," he said.

"Coward." Zvina fell back, clutching her midsection and breathing hard. "Kill me!"

"Why bother?" came a voice from the entrance to the tent.

Out of the boiling rain came the striking figure of Paeter Ravalis, general of the forces arrayed outside. The Blood of Summer made him bright in all the ways the Blood of Winter made Regel dark: a fiery mane compared to Regel's short black hair, a bright hazel gaze against the assassin's almost black eyes. Outside, the battle was ending, the barbarians of Ruin routed before the warmachines and soldiers of their allied noble houses: the Summer House Ravalis and the Winter House Denerre.

Or was it *only* the Summer House fighting this war? Precious few of the troops on that field owed loyalty to his Winter King Orbrin Denerre, and none of the war machines came from his Northern city of Tar Vangr. The Summer House Ravalis was a guest in the Winter City, he thought, and Paeter was a prince and consort-heir by marriage. That did not bode well for Denerre, the House of Winter.

By his triumphant sneer, it seemed Paeter was thinking the same thoughts. "The day belongs to the Ravalis." His gaze passed over Regel to Zvina, who had fallen to one knee, bleeding from her middle. His lip curled hungrily. "I'll have my spoils now."

He lurched for her, but she slapped aside his reaching hands and he fell back with a pained cry. He looked down at the line of blood seeping through the leather gauntlet on his forearm. Zvina drew back, brandishing a curved razor she'd secreted in her sleeve.

"I like it when they fight," Paeter said with a sneer.

Zvina caught them both by surprise when she looked not at her foe but at Regel. Her eyes held pride, but also a plea. The dying sun blazed through the tent and glowed in her hair. Regel thought she looked like—but no, that wasn't possible. His princess was hundreds of miles away, safe in Tar Vangr. Safe, and far from her Ravalis husband.

The vision made him hesitate, and it was over before he could move. Zvina lunged at him. Perhaps it was reflex, or perhaps it was Frostburn's own hunger, but either way, the blade rose and cut the distance between them. It plunged through Zvina's breast, slit her spine, and burst out her back as she smashed into him.

Paeter murmured something, but Regel could not hear him.

Zvina's legs crumpled and she sagged in his arms, her lips by his ear. "Ruin's kiss," she murmured, and coughed blood onto his neck. "You kill all you hold—may it ever be so."

Then she slumped, leaving a bloody trail down his front, and was dead before she touched the floor. She died a warrior's death.

"What a waste." Paeter clicked his tongue. "I've not had a woman like that in years."

Regel stared down at Zvina on the floor. The blood seeping through her pale blonde hair and her agonized face made her seem a fallen angel, her wings become a bloody stain on the ground. Her face...

"Stupid barbarians," Paeter said. "Come away, Syr Shadow. If we sweep up this war today, we may just get back in time for Ruin's Night."

Regel stared at the life-blood on his hands, and down at the corpse. Though he couldn't say why, he trembled.

In all its glory and squalor, Tar Vangr, the last mage-city of the Old Calatan Empire, embodied the chief reason its father nation had fallen. It was a city divided: poised spectacularly on a thick web of mage-glass above, the wealthy and powerful made residence and held court in high-city, while the impoverished made do in the dusty slums at the city's base. The sharp division between rich and poor allowed discontent to fester, and the forces of Ruin without the city grew stronger every year. Such had befallen Echvar, after all, and now that city lay in waste.

Today, many had paid the fare to climb to high-city to welcome the returning heroes—if only for some relief from the harshness of life in the lower City of Winter.

Regel met it all with a sigh.

Despite its pomp and fury, Regel's homecoming proved a somber affair.

Oh, for a surety, the horns struck up a rousing chorus as Tar Vangr's flagship—the *Avenger*—clanked into the high dock of the two-tiered city. Folk cheered while the rusty pincers ground shut, securing the airship in place. Then, as the hold opened and the victorious procession came forth, cloudbursts of flower pedals cascaded from every window and rooftop. Joviality met them on every street leading to the palace, where a feast awaited.

House Ravalis would suffer no less a spectacle for their conquering prince.

For Regel, however—the king's assassin, unknown and uncelebrated—the manufactured gaiety held no solace. Indeed, its shameless deception crossed past uselessness into offense. The joy was false.

What had happened in the tent of the Echvar warlord had been terrible, but also real. Why had he hesitated? He, for whom killing came as easily as breathing?

Even with the crowds, the familiar streets of Tar Vangr proved no great obstacle. He cut gracefully through alleys, around corners, and over rooftops. The snow drifted thick this winter, and a fall could prove deadly. From a building in high-city, he could plunge a thousand paces to a shattering death among the rocks and shanties of the low-city slums.

No one stopped him—no one knew his face, after all. He would hardly make an effective shadow of the Winter King if they did.

He moved without thinking, distracted. He could not push a vision from his mind: a blonde woman sprawled on the ground, blood in her hair, eyes staring...

A white-gloved hand fell on his arm. "Regel?"

The terrible image must have seized more of his attention than he thought—that, or he needed more sleep. Regel shook himself and scanned his surroundings.

Somehow, he had arrived at the great palace, where he now stood outside the king's private audience chamber. He must have traveled countless blocks and scaled the palace walls without realizing it. Had he gone all that way in a dream?

The crimson-haired woman at his side, however, was no dream, and for that, he was infinitely grateful. "Ovelia," he said. "My apologies. I was...far away."

"Does it pass well with you?" She pursed her red lips into an uncertain heart.

"Fine, just—" He shook his head. "It is nothing."

Ovelia Dracaris did not look convinced, as Regel expected from her. The King's Shield was sharp as steel and hard as cold iron, and her eyes saw much. Her face was not that of the refined beauties of a royal court, but it held a certain frankness that welcomed trust.

He could tell her anything, but he chose silence.

Not this, *Tall-Sister*, he thought. Not this time.

"As you say," she said. Ultimately, she accepted his deflection—at least for the time being. Her hand on his wrist itched at his skin, where only days before he'd worn a sheen of barbarian's blood.

The doors opened, and a herald with the pale skin of winter blood leaned into the sitting room and announced them. Then he turned back out into the hall. "His Majesty and Their Highnesses, Blood of Winter, will hear you now."

"Highnesses?" Regel's heart leaped.

"You've been away a long time," Ovelia murmured.

They made it only two paces inside before an imposing figure met them.

The Winter King Orbrin Denerre stood tall and regal in the silver and white armor of his house. Even as a young man, his silver-blond hair had made him seem old, and only now, in his forty-fifth winter, had the wrinkles in his face caught up to this seeming age. Regel knew the war had reached the home-front as well.

They greeted each other as they always had.

"Lad," the king said with a nod.

"Old man." Regel returned the nod in a desultory fashion.

"And this, Semana"—Orbrin beckoned, drawing someone

out from where she had hidden behind his robe—"this is your Uncle Shadow."

"Uncle—" Regel's eyes widened.

Semana Denerre nô Ravalis looked up at Regel with hazel eyes, watery with sleep, and the fire of curiosity kindled in her gaze. "Shadow," she said sleepily. "Uncle Shadow!"

Regel did not know what to say to the tiny princess, so stunned was he by the curves of her face, the shoulder-length mop of silvery-blonde hair, and her bright hazel eyes. Of course he knew of the princess, but when he'd gone to war, Semana had been a warm swell in her mother's belly. Now, she was a tiny person and shared her mother's beauty.

"They grow fast," said a voice from behind the king.

Of course. She'd heard his thoughts, as ever.

The woman in the chair by the window put them all to shame, with her visage like sunlight sparkling on fresh snow. Her vivid purple eyes held a softness he couldn't help but explore, and the intricate braiding of her waist-length silver hair invited hours of contemplation. Her beauty and her meticulous bearing gave him no excuse to look away.

She was Lenalin Denerre, Orbrin's daughter, heir of Tar Vangr, mother to Semana and wife to Crown Prince Paeter Ravalis. She was the woman Regel loved more than anything, and the one he could never have.

"Highness." He bowed at the waist to her. He extended this courtesy to none but her.

Lenalin sat facing away from them, seemingly interested in her own visage in a mirror. Regel could see the sparkling outer curves of the intricate serpentine tattoo that soared up the full of her back. But for that hint of daring beneath her radiant visage, she seemed every inch a princess of Winter, and might have been chiseled of ice.

"The war passed well, I hear," Orbrin said. "You seem to have survived."

"So it seems." He looked again at the wonder that was Semana, words trailing off.

"Darak could not join us, I fear," Orbrin said. "He was too excited to greet his father."

Regel grimaced. Yes—Paeter and Lenalin's first-born son, more a Ravalis than a Denerre. The folk gathered in this chamber owed their loyalty and love only to Orbrin. Had Darak fallen so far from the Blood of Winter? Much had changed in three years.

Regel thought of Paeter and grimaced. "Will you not meet your conquering hero?"

"I have done so—but if I must also bid welcome to my son-by-marriage, so be it." Orbrin nodded to the anxious herald waiting at the door. "I'll take my leave."

"I'll accompany you," Regel said.

"No, no—take rest while you can. I'll have need of you on the morrow." Orbrin scooped up Semana, who giggled. "Coming, Ovelia?"

Ovelia looked to the king, then to Lenalin. "My lady? Will you not join us?"

"The princess feels unwell this eve," said Orbrin. "I trust my best sword can attend her."

Regel's stomach roiled. What was Orbrin saying? "But...your Majesty—"

But Orbrin was already sweeping out of the room, Semana in his arms. Ovelia looked back at Regel briefly, as confused as he was, then followed the king. The doors closed, leaving the two of them—assassin and princess—alone in the windowless chamber.

They basked in the silence a long moment. He realized, after a time, that she was looking at him in the mirror, but when he met her reflected gaze, she looked away.

"You seem older than when I saw you last," Lenalin said. "Practically an old man."

"Three years of war, Princess," Regel said. "You are just the same." He detected a slight flush in her cheek.

"Princess," he said, taking a step forward. "I—"

"Were there women in Echvar?" Lenalin asked, still looking away.

"What?" Regel had not expected that. What was she asking him?

"Women," Lenalin said. "Whores? Camp followers? Battle captives?"

"No," Regel replied. "Never."

"Good." She met his gaze in the mirror. "But something happened when you were away."

Before his eyes, he saw again a warrior woman lunge upon his sword—saw her pale hair matted with blood. *"You kill all you hold,"* she had said. *"May it ever be so."*

"No—" He trailed off. He could tell her. He wanted to tell her. "Only...no."

"Regel." Lenalin eased down from her stool and took his face in her hands. "What is it?"

He could not keep silent, not when she looked upon him as she did now, her eyes so soft and welcoming—her hands so warm upon his cheeks.

He told her all—unfolded all that had befallen in Zvina's tent at the final battle of Echvar. He told her haltingly of Paeter's assault on the barbarian queen—a story Lenalin heard with cool dispassion—then finally Zvina's last words to him.

"I began to doubt myself. I was meant to slay her—to end the war then and there—but..."

"You didn't want to kill her." Lenalin pressed her forehead against his. "Regel, sometimes...sometimes there's no easy answer, or no answer at all. Once we have chosen a path, we are trapped upon it. We cannot escape and cannot be rescued."

"No. I refuse to accept—" Regel touched her wrist and she winced. "Lena, are you hurt?"

Before she could pull away, he saw a purple bruise on her wrist where her silver lace sleeve had ridden high. He knew, without words. "Old Gods," he said. "Paeter did this."

Paeter Ravalis had been with him at the front, of course, but he'd retired to Tar Vangr more than once. He came only to take the glory, and fled back to the Winter City when things looked bleak.

She drew away and rose, rounding on him. The regal ice fled her eyes, replaced by surging flame. "And what do you know of it?" she demanded. "Nothing!"

"Only that it's still going on," Regel said. "After I killed three of his guards to still him."

"Six guards," Lenalin said, "and whatever fear you put in his heart turned quickly to anger. That was three years ago—do you think a man like that stays afraid for so long?"

"I will stop him." Regel turned to go. "I swear to you, I—"

Lenalin laughed at him. "Did you hear nothing I have said?" She took his hand, staying him. "You cannot solve this. I have chosen my path, and I will walk it for the good of us all."

"I will tell the king," Regel said. "He will ward Paeter off—at least another year."

"No." Lenalin pulled closer to him and pressed her face into his chest. Every inch of him lit with expectant fire. "You can't tell anyone. On your oath to me."

"I swore to Orbrin to protect you," he said. "I cannot stand by and let that monster—"

"You swore another oath to me." Lenalin's fingers curled into his back and shoulders. There was desperation in her touch. "You swore to be mine in all things, and I abjure you to do nothing."

"If you would command me," Regel said, "then why won't you meet my eyes?"

Lenalin shook her head. He could feel dampness through his tunic—she was weeping.

He cupped her face between his hands and raised it. Lenalin looked upon him, her lip trembling. There was fear in her purple eyes—fear and an aching need that sent Regel spinning. She was strong, Regel's princess of ice, but she was terrified too. She shook her head and mouthed a plea, but he saw clearly what she wanted in her heart.

"Lena," he said. "Princess, I—"

Her gaze slid past him, over his shoulder. "Paeter," she said, looking away.

The crown prince stood in the door to the chamber, wearing an unreadable smirk. "Lenalin," he said. "My beautiful, obedient, loyal wife."

Regel stepped away from the princess and looked upon Paeter levelly. "Prince."

"Syr Shadow," Paeter said. "Don't you have somewhere to be? Hunting down and murdering some foe of the crown, perhaps?"

Regel thought about the steel at his belt—about how easily he could draw Frostburn. In that moment, slaying a foe to the crown was *exactly* what he felt like doing.

"Come, my Lady." Paeter turned to Lenalin and firmly put up his arm. "Your father said you were ill, but to me you seem well enough to greet your adoring subjects."

It was not a question or a request. Lenalin could not decline, and like the queen she would one day be, she did not hesitate. She swept gracefully past Regel, letting her hand trail across his arm.

He felt her touch like the brush of a fiery lash: a plea and a promise.

When Paeter smirked and walked away, it was all Regel could do not to draw steel.

The rippling crimson dragon danced in the candlelight, undulating in time with the flesh beneath. Its roar was silent. Regel put his hand upon the sweat-gleaming scales, and the heat within nearly singed his fingers. The woman who was mistress of the tattoo shivered at his touch. She consumed him as he coursed in her.

"Princess," he said.

"Yes," she moaned, grinding hard into him. "Old Gods—"

Beyond them, out the window, fire danced through the sky to welcome Ruin's Night.

He sat up to cradle her in his arms, and she pressed herself back against him, throwing her arms wide. He seized her hard, wrestling her to his will, and she surrendered to him. She panted for more, and he rose to her challenge with a fury.

"Princess," he gasped. "Lena—"

She cried out, heedless in her desire and pleasure.

A vision came to him unbidden—blood running through her tangled hair—and he lost himself in a moment of terror. Spent in that heartbeat, he collapsed to the sweaty blankets, desire fled. He covered his face with his hands.

She sat a moment, the object of his affection, her beautiful nakedness silhouetted against the light of the fireworks outside. Then she shook herself to awareness and climbed into the bed. "Regel," she said. "Regel, what passes wrong? Are you...are you *weeping*?"

"No." In the mostly-darkness, he wiped his damp eyes.

She reached across him and brightened the oil lamp, spoiling the illusion they had built together. Her eyes were not the purple he had half-expected, but rather yellow-brown that gleamed red in the moon and firelight. "Talk to me, Regel," Ovelia said.

He sighed. How could he tell her what he had seen? What had come to pass?

"Nothing," he said. "Three years, it—it has been so long."

The red-haired swordswoman crawled back atop him, her hard muscles grinding into his, but he pulled away from her kiss. "Very long," she observed coolly. "Was it something I did?"

"No." Regel glanced out the window, taking in the last of the fireworks that summoned the new year. "Ruin's Night," he said. "This was my thirtieth winter."

"And my twenty-fourth," Ovelia replied.

"We do grow older, do we not? And yet we find no answers."

"Older, yes," Ovelia said. "But wiser?"

He smiled.

"Very well then," she said, straddling him anew and giving him a full showing of her excellent body. "I will please myself while you watch, but only if you call me *Princess* again."

That kindled warmth in his belly, and he reached up to catch her face between his hands. He brushed a strand of blood-red hair out of her eyes.

"What?" she asked.

Regel smiled sadly. "It need not always pass this way between us," he said.

"No?" she whispered. "You would make love to me, and not *her* through me?"

"Would you have it so?" he asked. "Do *you* prefer I share your bed, or hers?"

She gave no answer, for a discreet knock came at the door,

interrupting their moment. "My lady, the king calls."

Ovelia sighed. "And I answer," she replied. "Duty, it seems, must spoil our mummery."

Regel smiled with mirth he did not feel. When he pulled Ovelia into his arms and kissed her, however, that was genuine. She tried to wriggle free, but he held tight.

"Am I to keep the king waiting?" she asked.

"For this," Regel said, adjusting her legs around his waist. "A man can wait years."

The servant tapped on the door to Ovelia's chambers more insistently. "My Lady!"

"Alas." Ovelia leaned down to kiss Regel's brow, her hair hanging like a curtain to hide their faces. "Rest, Syr Shadow. Years of war have made you old and weary, but I expect a second bout when I return in an hour or so."

Regel nodded. Already, sleep bid him shut his eyes, and he could only watch dimly as Ovelia pulled her breeches around her shapely legs. Again, he thought her Lenalin, but with hair of blood and not of silvery snow.

Lenalin...

When he woke, Regel knew in his bones something was wrong. His fingers closed around the hilt of the blade under his pillow, and his eyes snapped open.

Dawn broke cold outside the murky windows, and the wind drummed like knucklebones on the glass. The room stood empty, the lamps barely flickering. It did not surprise him that Ovelia had not returned—they rarely spent the night together—but he felt an emptiness in the chamber that shook him to the core. The room seemed a tomb, the palace a graveyard.

Blonde hair, smeared red with blood...

An agonized cry reverberated down the hall, and the sound crawled across his skin like a thousand spiders. He recognized the voice with a certainty that made his heart race.

Following the sound, Regel arrived in the antechamber of Lenalin's personal chambers within ten breaths, pulling on his clothes as he went. He carried his sword Frostburn in both hands, clenched so hard it hurt his fingers.

He found a somber gathering indeed. Orbrin stood in his sleeping gown, face as pale as snow, staring down at his hands. Ovelia, her face streaked with wet lines, held a languid Semana in her arms. Even the young prince Darak stood half-hidden in the shadowed corner. Regel thought the boy must have seen his seventh winter by now, and he was becoming a man—becoming his father. His orange-red eyes gleamed in the candlelight, watching all with deadly interest.

Regel steadied himself and eased his hand away from his sword. His heart beat between his ears. Though he knew the answer, he asked the question anyway. "What passes?"

None spoke. Orbrin made no acknowledgement of his presence, and Ovelia could only shake her head, ashamed. Darak ran a hand through his crimson hair—so like his father's that Regel reached for his steel anew.

Then Semana roused herself—indeed, it seemed Regel's arrival had stirred her—and she climbed down from Ovelia's arms. Once on her own feet, she walked—none-too-steadily—over to Regel and put her tiny arms around his knee.

"Don't cry, Uncle Shadow," she said.

Then the inner door clicked open and a low moan escaped— one of surpassing pain. A gray robed chiurgeon stepped across the threshold, blocking with her body a humid room of candles and dust. The reek of blood swirled into the antechamber, punctuated by incoherent sobs and soothing voices of more attendants.

The chiurgeon looked up at the royal assemblage, then looked away, her face pained. The towels in her hands dripped dark blood onto the floor. She did not have to speak to make her message clear.

Blood running through pale hair. Blood on Regel's hands.

Regel extricated himself from Semana and strode forward. The chiurgeon's face turned white and she tried to pull away, but he shot out his hands and caught her. "Tell me!" he said.

The woman's eyes grew wide as twin moons. "S-syr, I—"

"Regel, stop." Ovelia stepped between him and Lenalin's door.

Regel thrust the chiurgeon away and dropped his hand to his sword. "Stand aside."

"Regel, please—" She put her hand on the hilt of her sword.

"Stand"—Regel drew Frostburn in a flash, putting the blade up between them—"aside."

He knew Ovelia understood, but she could not back down.

"There is nothing you can do," King Orbrin said behind him. His voice trembled, spoken by a man in terrible shock. "It was an accident. She—"

"Paeter said so." Regel kept his eyes on Ovelia, speaking as much to her as to Orbrin. "You believe that god-burned rutter of a man." He leaned toward Ovelia. "*You* believe him."

The King's Shield stared at him, her lip trembling. Angry but fearful. Weak.

"Hold." Orbrin had regained himself, and spoke with royal authority. He pushed Semana into Darak's arms and indicated the outer corridor. The children left, but Semana's reddish eyes lingered on Regel until Darak closed the door behind them.

Regel stared at Lenalin's door—gazing right through Ovelia— another moment, then turned to Orbrin. "How dare you," he said.

The king looked startled. "Careful, lad."

Regel crossed the three paces between them in a split second and had the king by the collar, sword at his throat. "How *dare* you!"

Ovelia drew steel in an instant, but Orbrin stayed her with a gaze. "Speak, Regel," he said.

"You didn't wake me. You didn't *tell* me."

"Should I have?" Orbrin looked down at Regel's hand on his collar. "And let you act rashly, as you're doing now? No."

Regel could feel his blood thundering in his veins. His head pounded. "Your own—your own *daughter*, burn it all!" he said. "You let that monster do this to her."

"It was an accident," Orbrin repeated. "Paeter—"

"Paeter." Regel spat the name. He started toward the outer door, back into the palace.

"You swore an oath to serve us," Orbrin said. "Vengeance serves no one."

Regel stopped, and the glare he gave the king was treason itself. "It serves *her*," he said, "and if I am the only one who will do this for her, then so be it."

"If you love her, then you will not do this," Orbrin said. "If she dies, then Paeter becomes the heir to the throne. Would you kill him and start a civil war?"

"If I must," Regel said. "I'll kill anyone. *Everyone.*"

Truer words, he had never spoken.

"*Semana.*" Ovelia's hand fell on his arm, and he turned to face her. "What of Semana, and Darak? What will be their fate, should harm befall Paeter?"

Regel glared at Ovelia, and he saw her brace for a strike. He hated her. They were lovers, yes, but in that moment, he hated her.

"Pray then," Regel said, "that she does not die."

He wrenched his arm from her grasp and left the chamber.

Out in the corridor, Regel stared at his hands, and the world faded. It must have happened when he'd grasped the chiurgeon, but he thought it had happened long before—years and years before.

His hands were slick with fresh, red blood.

Lenalin's blood.

The funeral bells for Princess Lenalin Denerre nô Ravalis tolled in the early morning darkness, and Regel swore they would ring again within the hour.

Ovelia came searching for him, of course, and half a hundred Ravalis soldiers. They sealed off the palace gates with slabs of stone, posted guards at every corridor, and even delved into the secret passages that riddled the palace. As Paeter Ravalis sat smoking his pipe disconsolately, Ravalis guards checked every corner of his chamber. They locked the castle tighter than a mage-hewn lock and scoured every thumb's breadth of the ancient stone edifice for a ghost.

But he wasn't there.

As the sixth toll rang, a shadow moved on the wall outside Paeter's window, dislodging a thick coat of snow to float down a thousand feet to low-city. It drifted on the chill winds that danced about the high palace on the mountain.

On the seventh toll, a blue-steel sword emerged from beneath the shadow's cloak—a sword, blessed of winter, that absorbed the night's awful cold. In time with the funeral bells, the blade tapped the window pane three times, cutting three small flaws in the glass.

It was the only warning the monster within received—and far more than he deserved.

A dark shape swung out from the palace wall and back, feet-first, into the window, which shattered inward in a rough triangle. Paeter Ravalis—who had found sleep again in the early hours—stumbled screaming from his bed, away from the dark shape.

Heedless, Regel strode to the door and slammed his shoulder into it, knocking back the guard who'd tried to open it. He slid the metal bar in place, and the door bent inward but did not give way. Regel stood over the naked crown prince as the last of twelve funeral tolls faded in the wintry dawn.

Eyes focusing, Paeter Ravalis blinked up at Regel and grinned. "King's Shadow—"

Regel brought his fist down with all the force of his arm and sent the smiling prince to the floor. Blood spattered the rich silken rug.

"Well," the prince said, touching his split lip. He pulled the blanket around himself. "Even if I couldn't hear the bells as well as the next man, *striking me* tells me why you're here."

Regel grasped Paeter by the hair and drew him up, sword raised.

"That first I'll give you," Paeter said. "You're upset, I understand. But think—"

Regel brought the pommel of his sword down on Paeter's brow, and his words shattered in a dizzy moan. Paeter fell squirming to the ground, and Regel stalked around him.

The prince chortled through his bloody lips. "That second, as well. The fact that I'm alive, however, says much." He coughed. "Orbrin told you no, did he not?"

Regel stopped his pacing and glared down at him.

"Of course he did," Paeter supplied. "What love he bears his slut of a daughter. And you obey, like a good little shadow." He grinned, teeth streaked with blood. "Oh yes, I know what you are, just as I know what she is—or rather, *was*."

He was goading Regel, but was it the spite of a vicious man about to die, or did he have a plan? Did he mean to inflict even more harm upon Regel?

Regel put the point of his blade to Paeter's throat.

The prince seemed not the least bit fearful. "Go on, do it," he said. "Orbrin was right, you know. Ravalis will not suffer this, and Denerre is weak. There will be war, and you will not win. You will bring Tar Vangr to its knees, and Ruin will hold sway over all."

"That—" Regel hadn't meant to speak but couldn't stop himself. "That won't happen."

"Then why do you stay your blade?" He sat up straighter, tracing his soft throat along Frostburn's edge. "Do it, King's Shadow. Spill my blood, and thus the blood of your precious king, of your whore the King's Shield, and all the House of Winter. Keep whatever vow you swore to my wife and kill me—then watch as the kingdom and all you love crumbles to nothing."

Regel's hand trembled, and though he drew away the sword, he kept it poised to open Paeter's throat in a heartbeat. Guards pounded on the door, crying out for Paeter.

"You saw Ruin, did you not? In the border kingdoms? I remember it." Paeter's eyes gleamed. "Folk who kill without honor or humanity, who live only to hate. How long would Tar Vangr last in their hands, with no heir to sit upon the Winter throne?"

"We have Semana," Regel said. "The Ravalis would not kill their own scion."

"A half-breed sliver of a wench," Paeter said, "and not my daughter anyway, unless I claim her as such. Already, there are rumors that my lamented wife took lovers outside my bed. How long do you think Semana would last without me?" He smiled to accentuate the point. "*You* do not have Semana—I have Semana. Or will you take her from me?"

Regel knew Paeter was right. The winter throne was melting in the heat of summer: penned on all sides by Ravalis swordsmen, meant to be inherited by Ravalis stock, and drowned in Ravalis blood. If he did this—murdered Crown Prince Paeter Ravalis in his own chamber—how much longer would Denerre last? How could Semana—that beautiful child, innocent of their many sins—long survive her father?

And yet, how could he not do it?

He had sworn two oaths—to obey Lenalin and to honor her—and they warred within him. If he did this, he betrayed Lenalin, and yet if he did not...

They clashed, the two men. They fought for all the things one man loved, which were all the other hated.

Regel saw blood in Lenalin's hair—blood on his hands.

We are trapped, Lenalin had said. *Trapped upon the path we choose to walk.*

"No," Regel said.

Frostburn moved. The glittering blue steel flashed across the space between them. The air hissed in its wake, and the sword cut too fast for Paeter to flinch. A red slit appeared across the left side of Paeter's throat. Blood welled and trickled down Paeter's skin.

Paeter's eyes widened instantly. "You dare?" he asked. "I am as good as the king of Tar Vangr, while you are a common-born thug. You are as *nothing* to me!"

Regel knelt before Paeter, sword held wide and dripping Ravalis blood onto the floor. "I am death to you, Prince Ravalis," he said. "If you raise your hand against Orbrin or any of his scions, I will fulfill the pact we have made this day. This oath, I'll not break. Do you hear me? Do you understand?"

Paeter's eyes narrowed. "You think you'll walk away from this. You really think—"

"Send what blades you wish," Regel said. "I will serve them all, and every drop of their blood will be as this—" he pressed the bloody edge of his sword to Paeter's face—"your blood."

The door was splintering, the bar nearly knocked off its perch.

Regel rose, crossed to the window, and paused. "I am sorry," he said.

"You aren't forgiven," Paeter said. "I will hurt you for this, even if—"

"I wasn't talking to you," Regel said. "You should beg her forgiveness as well, for what she has done for you."

"That whore?" Paeter asked. "What? What has she done for me?"

"Saved your life."

Then the door broke open, and he was out the window.

∾

About The Authors

MARIE BILODEAU began sharing stories as a professional storyteller, telling in theatres, tea shops, bars and under disco balls. She is the author of the Heirs of a Broken Land fantasy series (*Princess of Light*, *Warrior of Darkness* and *Sorceress of Shadows*) and the space fantasy adventure, *Destiny's Blood*. Her stories have also appeared in multiple anthologies and magazines. Check out www.mariebilodeau.com for more information and ramblings.

STEVE BORNSTEIN has been in the military, travelled to distant lands, and held the sorts of jobs you watch shows about on the Discovery Channel. His heroes include MacGyver and the Stormtrooper who whacked his head on the blast door. He lives in central Texas with his wife and four insane pets, and likes to roleplay dead sexy villains. This is his first professional fiction sale.

XANDER BRIGGS is a writer of eclectic speculative fiction with credits in several online and print publications, some of which are better not mentioned in polite company. Currently, he lives at the edge of the Arizona desert with far too many cats and fictional characters. Rumors that he disappears around the full moon are thus far unsubstantiated.

ERIK BUCHANAN grew up on the Canadian Prairies where he spent his spare time acting, writing, studying martial arts and reading everything he could get his hands on. He moved to Toronto, Canada, and combined his love for history, mythology, weaponry and theatre into a 13-year career as an actor and fight director. Erik left the business after the birth of his daughter and now makes his living as a writer and communications professional. Erik is the author of *Small Magics* (2007) and *Cold Magics* (2010), both published by Dragon Moon Press.

BRIAN CORTIJO is a college administrator for a public university in New York City, who spends his spare time as a freelance designer for tabletop role-playing games. Although he lives in New York, he maintains summer homes in the worlds of Faerûn and Golarion, and visits these places as frequently as possible, hoping to meet far-flung friends that have happened to stop by while he was away.

ERIK SCOTT DE BIE has long had a fascination with fantasy which he credits/blames on all that D&D he played starting back in grade school. He is the author of four novels in the Forgotten Realms universe, the latest of which—*Shadowbane*—tells of one man's quest for redemption in a city of sin. His work has also appeared in numerous anthologies, including *Close Encounters of the Urban Kind*, *Cobalt City Timeslip*, and *Beauty Has Her Way*. His tragic tale "Oathbreaker" continues in his forthcoming fantasy epic, *Shadow of the Winter King*.

J.M. FREY holds a BA in Dramatic Literature, where she studied playwriting and traditional Japanese theatre forms, and a Masters of Communications and Culture, where she focused on fanthropology. She is an active in the Toronto geek community, presenting at awards ceremonies, appearing on TV, radio, podcasts, live panels and documentaries to discuss all things fandom through the lens of Academia. She loves to travel (disguising it as research), and has visited nearly every continent. She also has addictions to scarves, *Doctor Who*, and tea, all of which may or may not be related. *Triptych* (April 2011, Dragon Moon Press) is her first full-length novel. She has previously published poems, academic articles, and short stories.

JIM C. HINES introduced the world to Jig in *Goblin Quest*, the first of three books about the hapless goblin and his pet fire-spider. He recently finished a four-book series about butt-kicking fairy tale heroines (because Sleeping Beauty was always meant to be a ninja, and Snow White makes a bad-ass witch). He's published more than forty short stories in markets such as *Realms of Fantasy*, *Sword & Sorceress*, and *Turn the Other Chick*. He lives in Michigan with his wife, two children, and a medium-sized menagerie of pets. For more about Jig and Jim, visit www.jimchines.com.

CHRIS A. JACKSON Born in a land-locked small town in southern Oregon, Chris A. Jackson fell in love with the sea the first time he set eyes on those majestic rolling waves. After college, graduate school and a lengthy career in biomedicine, he and his wife decided to change their lives forever; the sea was calling their names, and the call could not be ignored. The couple have lived on a sailboat for years, and are now cruising full time. They are sailing the east coast and Bahamas; follow their journey at www.sailmrmac.blogspot.com. *Scimitar Moon* (2009, Dragon Moon Press) was ForeWord Magazine's Book of the Year gold medal winner in Science Fiction and Fantasy.

ROSEMARY JONES wrote two fantasy novels set in the Forgotten Realms, *Crypt of the Moaning Diamond* and *City of the Dead,* which introduced her to a lively crew of writers and artists. Her short stories have appeared in numerous anthologies including *Realms of the Dead.* She happily hangs out in Seattle's coffeeshops, plotting superhero adventures, magical mayhem, and other dire doings with similar souls. Check her website at www.rosemaryjones.com to find out more.

JULIE KAGAWA was born in Sacramento, California. But nothing exciting really happened to her there. So, at the age of nine she and her family moved to Hawaii, which she soon discovered was inhabited by large carnivorous insects, colonies of house geckos, sharks, and frequent hurricanes. Her love of reading led her to pen some very dark and gruesome stories, complete with colored illustrations, to shock her hapless teachers. The gory tales faded with time, but the passion for writing remained, long after she graduated and was supposed to get a real job. Julie now lives in Louisville, Kentucky, where the frequency of shark attacks are at an all time low. She lives with her husband, two obnoxious cats, one Australian Shepherd who is too smart for his own good, and the latest addition, a hyper-active Papillon.

JAY LAKE lives in Portland, Oregon, where he works on numerous writing and editing projects. His 2011 books are *Endurance* from Tor Books, and *Love in the Time of Metal and Flesh* from Prime Books, along with paperback releases of two of his other titles. His short fiction appears regularly in literary and genre markets worldwide. Jay is a past winner of the John W. Campbell Award for Best New Writer, and a multiple nominee for the Hugo and World Fantasy Awards.

TODD JOHNSON MCCAFFREY wrote his first science fiction story when he was twelve and has been writing on and off ever since. Including the New York Times Bestselling *Dragon's Fire*, he has written eight books in the Pern universe, both solo and in collaboration with his mother, Anne McCaffrey. His shorter works have appeared in many anthologies, most recently, "The Dragons of Prague" in *Dr. Who - Short Trips: Destination Prague* (2008). He is currently working on several non-Pern projects. Visit his website at www.toddmccaffrey.us.

J. P. MOORE writes in southern New Jersey--a long way from the settings of his novels and stories. He has fond memories of a childhood in the Jersey Pine Barrens, where endless tracks of mossy wilderness informed the spirit behind his fiction. In 2009, J. P. Moore's *Toothless* gathered legions of fans across the globe as a podcasted audiobook. Praised by critics and fans alike for its original spin on the zombie apocalypse tale, Toothless is now available as a trade paperback and ebook from Dragon Moon

Press. Publishers Weekly hails *Toothless* as "moving, intriguing, and highly entertaining."

PEADAR Ó GUILÍN In September 2007, Peadar Ó Guilín published his first novel, *The Inferior*, which the Times Educational Supplement called "a stark, dark tale, written with great energy and confidence and some arresting reflections on human nature." Foreign editors liked it too, and soon the publishing rights had been sold in a dozen countries. A sequel, *The Deserter*, was released in Ireland and the UK in May 2011, with other territories to follow. Peadar has sold a lot of short stories to markets such as *Black Gate* and *Weird Tales* and has had his work broadcast by Pseudopod.org. For more information and free reading, check out his web site at www.frozenstories.org.

SHANNON PAGE was born on Halloween night and spent her early years on a commune in northern California's backwoods. A childhood without television gave her a great love of books and the worlds she found in them. She wrote her first book, an adventure story starring her cat, at the age of seven. Sadly, that work is currently out of print, but her short fiction has appeared in *Clarkesworld*, *Interzone*, and *Fantasy* (with Jay Lake), *Black Static*, *Tor.com*, and several independent press anthologies. Shannon is a longtime practitioner of Ashtanga yoga, has no tattoos, and lives in Portland, Oregon, with seventeen orchids and an awful lot of books. Visit her at www.shannonpage.net.

TONY PI was born in Taiwan but came to Canada at age eight. He holds a doctorate in linguistics but has turned his attention to writing in recent years, first appearing professionally in Writers of the Future XXIII. Since then, he has been a finalist for the John W. Campbell Award for Best New Writer in 2009, and for the Best Short Form Work in English category of the Prix Aurora Awards in 2008. His work appears in many venues such as *Clarkesworld*, *Fantasy Magazine*, *Orson Scott Card's Intergalactic Medicine Show*, and *The Dragon and the Stars*.

PHIL ROSSI—writer, a musician, and an embracer of new media—has a passion for story-telling matched only by the pleasure he derives from keeping his fans awake at night. *Crescent*, Rossi's debut novel, was originally released as a podcast in 2007 and has since lured tens of thousands of listeners and readers into a dark, twisted world of nightmares and things that go bump in the night. Phil Rossi's writing has been paralleled to Stephen King, Philip K. Dick, and HP Lovecraft. Phil lives in Virginia with his wife, daughters, and menagerie of rescued animals. He believes the need for sleep is a myth.

About The Editors

ED GREENWOOD is a busy and award-winning Toronto-born fantasy and science fiction writer and game designer whose writings have sold tens of millions of copies worldwide in more than two dozen languages. Best known as the creator of The Forgotten Realms® (arguably the largest and most detailed fantasy world-setting ever), Ed has been hailed (by award-winning fantasy author J. Robert King) as "the Canadian author of the great American novel" and "another of Canada's stealthy, pleasant surprises" (by sf great Roger Zelazny). He has been nominated for science fiction's Nebula Award, and has served as a judge for the World Fantasy Awards and the Sunburst Awards.

Ed's published fiction includes over twenty-five novels, including the New York Times bestsellers *Spellfire* and *Elminster: The Making Of A Mage*, more than forty short stories, literally thousands of magazine and web articles, and several bestselling collaborative novels.

GABRIELLE HARBOWY (www.gabrielle-edits.com) is a San Francisco-based editor and award-nominated writer. As a third generation reader of fantasy and science fiction, a passion for books is in her blood. She edits fantasy and science fiction for publishers including Pyr and Seven Realms, is a staff proofreader for Lambda Literary, and is currently editor and Associate Publisher at Dragon Moon Press, where the horrors of the slushpile and the thrill of bringing new and talented writers to print only reinforce her love of the genre. Books she has worked with have gone on to become finalists and winners of literary awards including the Aurora Award, Sir Julius Vogel Award, ForeWord Book of the Year, and the Bram Stoker Award. She lives with two cats who are named after chocolate, and a spouse who is not.

Other books from
authors featured in

*WHEN THE HERO
COMES HOME*

PUBLISHED BY DRAGON MOON PRESS

DESTINY'S BLOOD
Marie Bilodeau

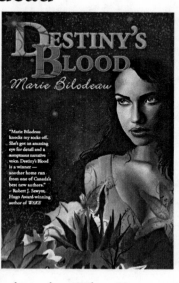

Marie Bilodeau knocks my socks off. She's got an amazing eye for detail and a sumptuous narrative voice. Destiny's Blood is a winner—another home run from one of Canada's best new authors.
--Robert J. Sawyer, Hugo Award-winning author of WAKE

Layela Delamores wants nothing more than to settle into a quiet, peaceful life, running a small flower shop with her twin sister, Yoma. But Layela is tormented each night by terrifying visions that she cannot remember when she wakes. When Yoma vanishes, Layela is certain that her nightly visions hold the key - but only her sister's thieving friend, one of the last survivors of the ether races, can unlock them. Layela suspects that her friend isn't telling her the whole truth, instead sheltering her from her own visions.

Ripped from the safety of her flower shop into a universe of smugglers and assassins, Layela must pursue her sister across space in a desperate bid to overcome the destiny of destruction foretold in her dreams. But without full knowledge of her visions, Layela has no way to prevent them from coming to pass. And the fate of a whole world is on the line: the mythical First Star is on a path to self-destruction and the annihilation of all life.

Unless Layela finds a way to stop it. But to stop it would mean sacrificing her sister.

ISBN: 978-1-897492-11-6

SMALL MAGICS
Erik Buchanan

Small magics is a great read, and is a brilliant first novel from author Erik Buchanan. The characters are very interesting and well developed and the world Buchanan creates in the novel is vivid and imaginative. This author knows his knives and rapiers, as well as how to write riveting chase sequences and fist fights. Definitely worth purchasing! A very exciting book. ~Mary Garden

In a world where no one really believes in magic, one man is stealing all that's left... Erik Buchanan's first novel introduces Thomas Flarety, whose first visit home from school in four years brings him face to face with a juggler who can create a ball of light from air, a Bishop who can control men with his voice, and a plot to steal what magic is left in the world. Before long, Thomas is thrust into a nightmare of betrayal and murder, where all that he has is threatened by a power he does not understand, and where learning to master a power he did not know he had may be the only way he can survive.

ISBN: 978-1-896944-48-7

COLD MAGICS
Erik Buchanan

Award-nominated novelist Erik Buchanan returns with the sequel to Small Magics.

Cold Magics

A NOVEL BY
ERIK BUCHANAN

"...a stunning coming of age tale... The snow and adventure will sweep you up and carry you away!"

PHILIPPA BALLANTINE
award-winning author of
Chasing the Bard

Thomas Flarety has magic. He used it to destroy a corrupt bishop who tried to steal all the world's magic for himself. And so far, Thomas has managed to keep it a secret. Then raiders attack the northern Duchy of Frostmire with fire and magic. Henry, son of the duke and Thomas's friend, convinces Thomas to leave his studies and go help. But the church is also investigating the rumours of "witchcraft" in the north, and the Archbishop's Envoy is as interested in Thomas as he is in the raiders. Now Thomas must use all his wits, his skills and his magic to figure out who the raiders are and how to stop them. He must protect Eileen, the girl he loves, from the intrigues of the duke's court. He must find a way to keep the duke from turning him over to the Archbishop's Envoy. And he must do it before the raiders destroy them all.

ISBN: 978-1-897492-06-2

CRESCENT
Phil Rossi

Crescent is the ultimate sci-fi / horror mashup. It's a wicked blend of the claustrophobia seen in Ridley Scott's Alien, *and the viral demonology of Carpenter's* Prince Of Darkness *with the hard-drinkin' bad attitude of* Battlestar Galactica *added for good measure. The future has never been so frightening. Phil Rossi brings it. --J.C. Hutchins, author of Personal Effects: Dark Art and 7th Son: Descent*

Darkness has inspired fear since mankind first watched the sun go down. Bad things hide in the dark feral beasts with mouths full of razors waiting for a taste of flesh. But now, the darkness is stirring with a life of its own. Crescent Station is the last bastion of civilization, floating in the cold, outer systems where colonized space gives way to the sparser settlements of the Frontier. Like the boom towns of distant Earth s Old American West, Crescent Station is a gateway to power, wealth, and opportunity for anyone who isn t afraid to get his or her hands dirty. But deep within the station s bowels, in Crescent s darkest and most secret places, an ancient evil is awakening and hungry, and it threatens the very fabric of space and time. Will the residents of Crescent Station find a way to stop it before the terror drives them insane? Or is it already too late?

ISBN: 978-1-896944-52-4

TOOTHLESS
J.P. Moore

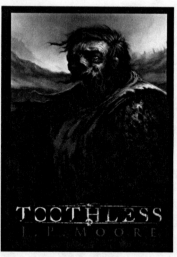

*Despite the title, this gritty
supernatural historical has plenty of
bite. In 12th-century France, corpses
are being animated by a force called
the Black Yew. Resurrected Templar
Martin, now called Toothless, breaks
free of the Yew's domination to fight
against its depredations. Compelling
and well told with only occasional
lapses into cliché, this is an unusual
mapping of familiar fantasy territory.
Moore explores the troubled unlife
of a reformed zombie in detail, both
from Toothless's perspective and through the eyes of the skeptical
living. Toothless himself is an introspective, complex protagonist,
and his quest to recover what he can of his past is by turns moving,
intriguing, and highly entertaining. ~Publishers Weekly*

An ancient evil leads a rampaging army of demons and undead
warriors across the countryside. Martin, a failed Templar, is slain
on the field of battle only to be reanimated in service to the
very evil he hoped to destroy. The Black Yew, the dark force that
controls the undead army, considers him a gifted minion. But life
is not done with him yet.

ISBN: 978-1-89749-218-5

TRIPTYCH
J.M. Frey

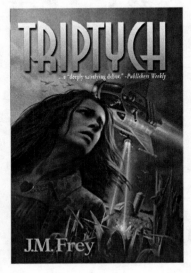

Time travel, aliens, and the politics of sexuality combine with tragic violence in Frey's deeply satisfying debut [...] imagining a world at once completely alien and utterly human. - Publishers Weekly Starred Review

"A stirring adventure, as well as a tender love story. ...A refreshing twist on the genre!" - Lambda Literary

In the near future, humankind has mastered the arts of peace, tolerance, and acceptance. So we claim.

But then they arrive. Aliens—the last of a dead race. Suffering culture shock of the worst kind, they must take refuge on a world they cannot understand; one which cannot comprehend the scope of their loss.

Taciturn Gwen Pierson and super-geek Basil Grey are Specialists for the Institute—an organization set up to help alien integration into our societies. They take in Kalp, a widower who escaped his dying world with nothing but his own life and the unfinished toy he was making for a child that will never be born.

But on the aliens' world, family units come in threes, and when Kalp turns to them for comfort, they unintentionally, but happily, find themselves Kalp's lovers.

And then, aliens—and the Specialists who have been most accepting of them—start dying, picked off by assassins. The people of Earth, it seems, are not quite as tolerant as they proclaim.

ISBN: 978 -1-897492-13-0

SCIMITAR SUN
Chris A. Jackson

2009 Gold Winner of the
Foreword Magazine's Book of
the Year Award, Fantasy

The pirates of the Shattered Isles live and die by on simple oath: By blood, by wind, by water and wave, loyal as one, or a watery grave... With that oath, their lord, Captain Bloodwind, would build a nation of pirates. He doesn't want much, after all... just everything. And what he cannot have, he will destroy. The only man to ever stand against him, the legendary seamage Orin Flaxal, paid that price. But his orphaned daughter, Cynthia, has plans of her own, and revenge is top on her list. She is no warrior, and thanks to Bloodwind's murder of her parents, she will never be a seamage. But she has one family trait that nobody can destroy: she can build ships, like her grandfather did. She will build ships that no corsair can match, and use them to starve the pirate nation to death. And with the help of a bedraggled seasprite, a crippled old sailor and a retired ship's cook, who could stand against her? But Bloodwind has spies and assassins in every port, and Cynthia's new ships would make fine additions to his pirate fleet. Meanwhile, Odea, goddess of the sea, has her own plans for Cynthia Flaxal. So when Cynthia's ships finally set sail, both Captain Bloodwind and Odea are ready.

ISBN: 978-1-896944-54-8

SCIMITAR SUN
Chris A. Jackson

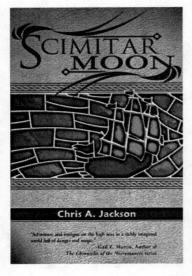

"Adventure and intrigue on the high seas in a richly imagined world full of danger and magic."
- Gail Z. Martin, Author of The Chronicles of the Necromancer series

The Shattered Isles are at peace. Or so it seems. The vile pirate lord, Bloodwind, has been vanquished, and Cynthia Flaxal has everything she always dreamed of: the mystical powers of a seamage, a successful shipyard, the love of a great man, and a child on the way. But trouble roils both above and below the waves. A school of vengeful merfolk harbors a secret and terrible agenda. An empire perceives Cynthia's growing fleet as a threat. A small band of surviving pirates hatches a devious plot to regain supremacy in the Shattered Isles. A favor to an old friend leaves Cynthia with a powerful but undisciplined young pyromage on her hands. And as all these forces converge, the Seamage of the Shattered Isles finds herself and her unborn child caught right in the middle.

ISBN: 978-1-897492-17-8

SCIMITAR HEIR
Chris A. Jackson

The sea hath no wrath like a seamage betrayed.

Cynthia Flaxal and Feldrin Brelak desperately pursue the mer who have stolen their son. They seek the floating city of Akrotia, forsaken a thousand years ago, which the mer aspire to restore to enchanted glory with the life of their child. And along the way Cynthia must persuade the powerful young pyromage, Edan, to help, not hinder, their quest.

But while the Seamage of the Shattered Isles is absent, vengeful eyes turn toward Plume Isle. Sam seeks revenge against her for killing the infamous pirate Bloodwind. Parek and his pirates seek to recoup Bloodwind's horde of treasure. The emperor seeks to bring the upstart seamage to justice for her crimes. And the cannibals seek prisoners... Camilla alone can save her loved ones from this assault, but does she possess the will to make the ultimate sacrifice?

Perils near and far threaten to destroy all that Cynthia has achieved. But little does she suspect that the greatest evil of all lurks deep in the heart of her home.

Watch for SCIMITAR HEIR - Fall 2011